You Should Have Died on Monday

Frankie Y. Bailey

This book is a work of fiction. All names, characters, places, and events are either the product of the author's imagination or are used fictitiously. Any resemblance to actual events or persons, living or dead, is entirely coincidental and beyond the intent of either the author or the publisher.

ISBN 13: 978-1-57072-319-3
ISBN 10: 1-57072-319-2
Copyright 2007 by Frankie Y. Bailey
Printed in the United States of America
All Rights Reserved

1 2 3 4 5 6 7 8 9 0

To my mother, Bessie Fitzgerald Bailey,
who, I am happy to say, was not the model for Becca.
And to the other magnificent women in my family, past and present,
including my own grandmother, Carrie Price Fitzgerald,
a woman of strength and determination,
and Catherine Fitzgerald Holt,
special aunt and beautician extraordinaire.

Acknowledgments

I would like to thank the people who have helped make this book possible:

Robert W. Smith, Chicago attorney and fellow mystery writer, who came to my rescue during my trip to Chicago to do research by taking the time from his busy schedule to drive me about and answer my questions, both then and later.

Colleen McSweeney Moore, Circuit Court Judge, Cook County, who was both cordial and gracious, making time for lunch with an inquisitive writer and following it up with an e-mail reference.

Joanne Barker and Joycelyn Pollock, two good friends, who took turns keeping me company during my week-long research trip to New Orleans, who listened as I pondered plot issues, and who offered useful and logical suggestions.

David W. Neubauer, my own criminal justice colleague in New Orleans, who provided me with clippings and information and who, with his wife, Carole, invited two visitors to their city to join them for dinner and a walk through the French Quarter.

The staffs at the Chicago Historical Society and at the Main Branch and Northeast Regional Branch of the New Hanover County Public Library in Wilmington, North Carolina, who confirmed my faith in librarians with their helpful suggestions as I worked my way through Lizzie's research.

To the members of the Wolf Road Irregulars: Joanne Barker, Audrey Friend, Ellen Higgins, Angie Hogencamp, Caroline Young Petrequin, and our newest member, Beth Anderson, who are always my first readers.

To Alice Green, who again created a terrific recipe that reflects the theme of the book and that can be eaten while reading.

To my publisher, The Overmountain Press—in particular, Karin O'Brien, tireless and creative marketing director, and Sherry Lewis, the tough editor with a sense of humor whom every writer should have.

I am deeply grateful for the support I have received from all of these people. Any errors in this book are completely my own. My thanks as well to:

The organizers and attendees of Love is Murder, for giving me a reason to come to chilly, but wonderful, Chicago in February to attend a great conference.

The organizers and attendees of the Cape Fear Crime Festival, who each year provide me with the best of reasons to spend Halloween weekend in Wilmington, North Carolina.

The people of New Orleans, who are struggling to rebuild their city. In this case, Lizzie's somewhat tart opinions do not reflect my own. New Orleans is one of my favorite cities.

The readers who have taken the time both to read my books and to tell me they enjoy them. Especially to fellow author Lonnie Cruse and to Shelia Clark, organizer of VDAY Bethesda, both of whom kept asking when the next book was going to be done.

I hope you all enjoy this book.

C H A P T E R · 1

When the dog began to howl, did Becca want to howl too? Kneeling there on that Chicago sidewalk with Reuben's blood on her hands, did she want to howl out her rage and grief and disbelief to the heavens? Were her sobs and screams too paltry, insufficient for pain so primeval? Did she want to reach up with her bloody hands and yank down the sky and send the moon and the stars and the planets tumbling and crashing in white-hot fury around her?

I have tried to imagine what it was like for her on that night . . . but only from a safe distance. I refuse to put myself in her place and imagine Quinn dead.

The year was 1969, and I was not there. I was four years old and lived with my grandparents in Drucilla, Kentucky. Becca, my mother, was in Chicago because she had fled there when she left Drucilla. On the night Reuben James died, she was a few months short of her twenty-second birthday.

According to the newspaper I read on microfilm, New Year's Day, 1969, dawned cold enough to break records. Frigid air stretched from the Midwest to the Deep South.

By the next day, the temperatures in Chicago and vicinity had climbed back into the twenties, but the mercury dropped again that night. Anyone who didn't have a good reason to be outside stayed in.

It was after 11:00 P.M. when the summit meeting ended with promises of cooperation all around. The street was empty when Reuben, Becca, and TJ came out of the house. I can't swear to every detail of what happened next, but here is how I have imagined it, based on the article in the newspaper and what I learned later. . . .

"Damn, it's colder than a—" TJ stopped and glanced up and down the shadowed street. "Where the hell's Wesley with the car?"

"He'll be back," Becca said. "I sent him over to the Shack to get us some fried fish."

TJ wheeled on her. "You what?"

"He was just sitting out here doing nothing, and I'm hungry."

"You're hungry?"

"That's what I said. So I sent Wesley to—"

"Who do you think you are, girl? You don't give orders to—"

"Hold it, you two," Reuben said, holding up his hand. "TJ, it's cool. Wesley'll be back in a minute."

Becca said, "So there's no reason for you to get your drawers in a knot about it, TJ."

TJ glared at her. "It wasn't your place to tell Wesley to go nowhere. Reuben may be keeping you busy on your back, but that don't mean the rest of us care what you—"

Becca sprang at him. TJ threw his arms up to protect himself from the blows that she rained on his upper body.

Laughing, Reuben caught her around the waist and hauled her away. He kissed the top of her head. "My woman's got fire," he said.

"Your woman?" TJ said. "Ain't you forgetting about—"

Reuben cut him off. "Don't go there, man,"

"I'm Reuben's woman," Becca said. "All his." She twisted around and slid her hands inside Reuben's jacket as she cuddled up against him. "As soon as JoJo comes back to town, I'm going to take care of everything."

TJ scowled at her. "What you getting JoJo into now?"

"None of your business. She's just gonna help me with something."

Reuben held her away from him. "Help you with what, Becca?"

"It's all right, baby. I'll tell you all about it later." She pulled his head down to hers and whispered in his ear.

Reuben laughed and drew her closer.

TJ clapped his bare hands together and stamped his feet. "Damn, Wesley. Where are you, man?" He turned to Reuben again. "I'm getting some bad vibes about this."

Reuben smiled. "You get bad vibes about getting up in the morning."

"Ain't you the one always telling us about staying alert?"

"We just shook hands with our enemies. We made peace."

"And now we're freezing our damn asses off."

"Prime Chicago weather, man. Just chill."

"I ain't no damn Eskimo."

Reuben had stopped listening; Becca was whispering in his ear again.

Snowflakes danced in the wind that whipped around them. Up the street, a mangy-looking dog paused beside the lamppost, its hind leg raised.

TJ cursed. "This ain't making it. I say we go back inside and wait for—"

Tires squealed, and a car barreled around the corner, its lights on high beam. TJ plunged his cold-numbed hand into his jacket, fumbling for the gun in his shoulder holster. He yelled out Reuben's name and leaped toward him. Reuben shoved Becca to the ground as he went for his own gun.

The bullets ricocheted off the concrete wall behind them. Becca screamed as Reuben fell. TJ fired back, but he was down too.

The car roared off into the night. The silence hung there for a moment, and then the mangy dog howled.

Becca crawled to Reuben, sobbing, calling his name.

TJ struggled to sit up. "Reuben?" He toppled sideways.

Becca screamed.

The dog echoed her distress, but no one rushed to Becca's aid. . . .

Maybe she did love Reuben James.

Maybe my mother loved Reuben as much as she was capable of loving anyone.

C H A P T E R · 2

GALLAGHER, VIRGINIA, SATURDAY, JUNE 5 (SEVERAL DECADES LATER)

When I woke up, it was raining, but I felt pretty good for 8:45 on a soggy Saturday morning.

I didn't see it coming. No goose walked over my grave.

I was in the shower when the telephone rang. Certain it was Quinn, I turned off the water and grabbed a towel.

"Hi! Hold on. I've got water running down my back."

"Professor Stuart?"

It wasn't Quinn. The last time his voice had been that high-pitched, he would have been going through puberty. "Yes, who is this, please?"

"This is Ray Nathan, your renter."

Calling from Kentucky when I didn't have time to talk to him.

"Oh, Mr. Nathan, I'm sorry. I have an appointment at ten, and I'm rushing. Could I call you back this afternoon?"

"My wife told me to call you. We've got a shutter loose on one of the bedroom windows, and it keeps banging."

"I'm sorry about that. I'll ask Mr. Womack to come over and fix it."

"My wife says you need to tell him to check the roof too. When it rained yesterday, it was leaking in two places in the upstairs hall."

Just what my bank account needed, a new roof and ceiling repairs. "Thank you for telling me. I'll ask Mr. Womack to climb up there and have a look."

"Another thing about the house, it creaks and groans at night."

"There's not much I can do about that, Mr. Nathan. The house is almost a hundred years old. At night it needs to settle its old bones."

"My wife says with all that creaking and groaning, maybe you got a ghost."

I bit down hard on my lip to keep from laughing. Ray Nathan was heart over head in love with his flighty little bride. What she said was his gospel.

"Please tell your wife that if there is a ghost, it's either Hester Rose, my grandmother, or Walter Lee, my grandfather, and they're both friendly."

Well, Walter Lee would be anyway. Hester Rose as a ghost might be more difficult to live with.

"My wife thinks you might have mice up in the attic. She's been hearing scurrying around and gnawing coming from up there when she's trying to have her nap."

She was on safer ground there. At various times, squirrels, even a pair of raccoon, had found their way into that attic.

"I'll ask Mr. Womack to add the attic to his list. If he can't deal with the problem, he'll call in a professional."

"My wife wants me to go up there and put down some traps and rat poison."

"No, please don't do that. We don't want anything to die up there and begin to smell. Mr. Womack will handle it." I hitched my slipping towel. "I really do have to run, Mr. Nathan. I'll get all of this taken care of, I promise."

"The weatherman's forecasting rain today. What do you want us to do if the roof starts leaking again before your handyman gets over here?"

"I'll ask Mr. Womack to get there as soon as he can. But if you should have another leak, there ought to be two or three big plastic buckets out on the back porch."

"I had to use those when I was digging up the flowers."

"Pardon me? You were doing what?"

"Digging up the flowers. I hated to dig up the peonies and the day lilies. My mama used to grow those. But those red ones—my wife said they call them 'bleeding hearts.' That didn't sound too good to have a flower with a name like that growing by the house. I got the blue ones that looked like little bells, too, and the . . . what do you call it? The . . . crepe myrtle?"

It took me a moment to find my tongue. "Are you telling me that you dug up all of the flowers growing in back and around the sides of the house?"

"I had to. My wife likes to open the windows in the morning to let the house air out. She said all those flower smells coming in on the breeze were bothering her sinuses."

"So you dug up—?"

"Those tulips alongside the front walk had to go too. And the rose bushes."

"The rose bushes? You—"

"I chopped those down. Then I dug out the roots. Too many bees were coming around. My wife got stung once when she was a child, and she's afraid of bees."

I had to squeeze my words out of my tight throat. "Mr. Nathan, henceforth, before you remove or change anything in my yard or in my house, you are to ask my permission. That is in your lease. You would know that if you had bothered to read it."

"The lease? We didn't think you'd mind if we—"

"Not mind if you dug up all my flowers? You didn't think I would mind that?"

"I had to do it. My wife's sinuses—"

"Yes, her sinuses. And she might've been attacked by a marauding bee." I closed my eyes, took a deep breath, and told myself, *Please let me be calm, when I want to throttle this man.* "It's not me you have to worry about, Mr. Nathan. It's my grandmother."

"Your grandmother? You mean the one that's dead?"

"That's the only one I have. It was her house, and those were her flowers."

"You don't really think she. . . . There's no such thing as ghosts."

"Well, you'd better ask your wife about that. Meanwhile, I'll ask Mr. Womack to come over and see to the other problems." I hung up the telephone, careful not to slam it down.

I did not have time to stop and cry over dug-up rose bushes. I had to get dressed for my optometrist's appointment. But first I needed to call Mr. Womack and get him over there to check the roof before the Nathans dealt with the leak by burning down the house.

It was 10:08 when I rushed through the doors of the eyeglass superstore. My tardiness turned out not to matter. I spent the next half hour cooling my heels in the reception area.

The optometrist to whom I'd been assigned seemed competent, but she made me feel every one of my thirty-nine years. If I had seen her on campus, I would have sworn she was a senior—or a master's student, at most. She wore a short denim skirt and pink tee shirt under her white coat. Her dark brown hair hung in a thick braid down her back. She had dimples and a toothy smile. She told me her name was Trish Bauer.

She leaned over me, peering into my eyes with her light. She went back to the right one and said, "Ummm."

"Is something wrong?" I had made this appointment because I had a faculty insurance voucher for an eye exam and new reading glasses. I did not want to leave with bifocals.

She stepped back and looked down at me. "Did your former optometrist ever mention that your pupils are asymmetrical? The opening of one of your pupils is wider than the other."

"What? I mean, no. Wider?"

She reached for a piece of paper and began to draw. "They look like this," she said, holding it out to me. Her drawing showed a significant difference in the size of the two holes. "What that means is that more light is passing through one pupil than the other."

"He—Dr. Prentice—never mentioned that. I went to him all my life from the time I was twelve when I got my first pair of reading glasses."

But Dr. Prentice was a small-town "eye doctor." I had continued to go to him as an adult because I didn't want to hurt his feelings. Maybe both he and his equipment had been past their prime. With his death and my move to Gallagher, over two years had passed since my last exam.

"It could be a fairly recent development," Dr. Bauer said, echoing my thought.

"I haven't noticed any change in my vision."

She stood back and surveyed my eyes. "It's not obvious when I look at you. Nothing's evident to the naked eye. But sometimes a problem can sneak up." She smiled and touched my arm. "I'd like to have one of my colleagues have a look-see. Sit tight."

When she came back into the room, she was accompanied by her gray-haired colleague. He introduced himself as Dr. Nielsen.

"I agree," he told her when he'd finished his own peering.

"You agree about what?" I said.

Dr. Bauer, my young optometrist, touched my arm again. Obviously in school they had taught her that touch soothed nervous patients. She said, "We both think you should come in for some additional testing."

Dr. Nielsen nodded at me. "You're in good hands. I need to get back to my own patient."

"Thanks," she called after him. She smiled at me. "I'm new at this, so sometimes I like a second opinion."

"What do you think it might be?"

She sat down on her stool. "Let's wait and see what the test shows. We want to check your visual field." She made a notation on my chart. "How about we get you back in here this coming week to get that taken care of?"

"Is it that urgent?" I asked.

"Well, we want to find out what's going on. No point in waiting, right?"

"Right," I said around the lump of panic forming in my throat.

CHAPTER · 3

I was almost calm by the time I got home. I had even stopped at the supermarket. Quinn's black Bronco was parked at the curb. I pulled around his car and into the driveway of the glossy white, three-bedroom, ranch-style house that I had been leasing since last August. If it had been my house, this spring I would have planted flowers to soften the lines of the boxy front lawn.

I pulled the collar of my jacket higher and reached for my umbrella.

"Hi, sweetie!" Mrs. Cavendish, my neighbor across the street, waved from her front yard. Her yellow rain slicker and hat matched her sunshine yellow house.

She pointed to the side of her house, where Quinn—wearing an identical yellow slicker but no hat—stood on a ladder propped beside the trellis of scarlet roses that climbed toward the second-story windows.

"Got a clogged rainspout," Mrs. Cavendish called out, sharing that bit of information with me and the rest of the neighborhood.

I nodded, waved again, and gathered up my plastic bags from the backseat.

My landlords confined their flowers to the abstract explosion of red poppies on the fabric that covered the living room sofa. Given their traveling ways, I had been puzzled by the wide-screen television opposite the sofa until I discovered their alphabetized collection of documentaries about exotic locales. At the moment, they were in Helsinki. Their attorney had sent me a lease for another year. If they intended to work their way down the list to Zanzibar, I could probably stay even longer.

But, as I had been reminded this morning, life is unpredictable.

Out in the kitchen, I took the cellophane off the daffodils I had bought at the supermarket and put them in a vase. Then I put my groceries in the refrigerator. Fifteen or twenty minutes later, I heard the front door close. By then I was sitting at the table, cradling a warm mug of peppermint tea in my hands.

"Hi," Quinn said as he came in.

He had discarded his rain slicker, but his damp hair still clung to his head. Dry, it would be thick and full, burnished auburn with gray at the temples. Brows of that same auburn arched over eyes that glistened silver like a mountain stream dappled with sunlight. High cheekbones stood out against fair skin that was not prone to tan, even during our Southern summers. When it came to coloring, the one-eighth Comanche had been upstaged by the Irish and Scot.

"Hi, yourself," I said. "Want a towel?"

"These will do." He tore a handful of paper towels from the roll on the counter and walked toward me as he rubbed at his hair and around the collar of his blue sweatshirt.

"Sorry I wasn't here when you arrived," I said. "I had an appointment with the optometrist."

He leaned over me. "I have a key now, Lizabeth. I can let myself in."

"Yes, you can." I breathed in the scent of rain and a hint of aftershave as his lips brushed mine.

His fingers caressed my nape. "You got a haircut."

"A trim yesterday."

"It feels like baby's fuzz."

The image of a half-bald baby sprang into my mind. I pushed his hand away and felt the whorls of hair on my scalp. "I cut off too much this time, didn't I?"

He laughed. "I said it *felt* like baby fuzz, Lizabeth, not that it looked that way. Fuzz on babies doesn't do a thing for me." He kissed the side of my mouth. "But on you, half an inch of hair is damn sexy. You taste good too."

He tasted like cinnamon. Mrs. Cavendish must have rewarded him for his rainspout duty with his favorite pastry.

I moved closer, deepening the kiss.

He raised his head. "Is the movie marathon still on? Or would you rather—"

"Yes, I would. But the movies are research for that chapter that was due two weeks ago. I promised the editor of the anthology that it would be in her e-mail on Monday."

"Then I guess we'd better make some popcorn."

"I've already made coffee."

He ran a finger down my cheek. "Thank you, Lizabeth. I appreciate the thought."

"The *thought*, Quinn? I think my coffee-making has improved significantly in the past few months."

"Absolutely. You make better coffee than any tea drinker that I know."

"Faint praise." I pressed my hands against his chest. "Out of my way, sir. I'm going to commune with Spike Lee."

We sat on my landlord's sofa and watched *Do the Right Thing*, about the hottest day of the summer in a Brooklyn neighborhood. Racial tensions simmered in a series of encounters between the owners of an Italian pizzeria, their black employee, the Korean grocery store owner, and the assorted black residents of the neighborhood. The day ended with a riot triggered by a brutal arrest by the police.

Quinn had been silent through most of the film. I had been silent too, because half my mind was on what the optometrist had said and the fact that I hadn't told Quinn yet.

I would tell him later. I wanted one more afternoon when we were thinking only of romance.

I almost laughed at that thought. If I wanted romance, we should have been watching *An Affair to Remember*, not *Do the Right Thing*.

I put my coding sheet down on the coffee table. On the screen, quotes from Martin Luther King, Jr. and Malcolm X about violence appeared before the closing credits.

I glanced over at Quinn, who had slouched down on the sofa. But I suspected it wasn't from boredom. "So, what did you think of this movie the first time you saw it?" I asked.

"I've only seen it once before. I was one of the cops assigned to attend a screening to see what kind of trouble we could anticipate. Some higher-ups had heard the movie was going to set off race riots in New York, and they wanted Philly to be prepared."

"Quinn, I know that the media and even some black intellectuals were predicting that the movie was going to cause trouble. But are you saying you were actually assigned to watch it and make an assessment?"

"Back in 1989, having people on the screen rattling off a litany of racial slurs seemed pretty explosive. The way the cops were portrayed in the movie worried us too."

"After you watched it, what did you do?"

"Nothing. Nobody rioted."

"I know that, but what would—"

"I'd rather talk about what's going on here, Lizabeth." He reached for my hand. "What's up?"

"You sound like Bugs Bunny."

"I'm trying to decide if I need to retreat to my hole. The past couple of hours have felt a little strained, and I don't think it was the effect of Spike Lee's racial commentary. Are you upset with me about something?"

I shook my head. "It was just a really bad morning."

"Want to tell me about it?"

"First, Ray Nathan called. He had a list of repairs that need to be done on my house in Drucilla, from a leaking roof to mice in the attic."

"A new roof could be expensive."

"I know that, but it was the flowers that upset me. He dug up all the flowers, Quinn. All of Hester Rose's flowers."

"Why the devil did he do that?"

"Because his wife has sinus problems and she's afraid of bees."

Quinn's response was succinct and obscene.

I nodded. "That's exactly what I wanted to say."

"I'm sorry about the flowers, babe. I'll help you plant some more when you take me to Drucilla."

"Thank you." I sniffed and straightened. "It was just that he made me so mad and there was nothing I could do about it."

"You could have told him to get the hell out of your house. I don't suppose that occurred to you."

"Yes, of course, it occurred to me. I almost did. But I need to have someone in the house, and they haven't been bad tenants . . . except for the flowers."

"The flowers are a big 'except,' Lizabeth. Sometimes, sweetheart, you're too damn nice."

"I'm not nice," I said. "I mean I am nice. But that doesn't mean I'm incapable of being assertive."

"You're perfectly capable of being assertive. You just have a hard time being nasty to people, even when they deserve it."

"I told him Hester Rose would get them."

Quinn laughed. "From what you've told me about your grandmother, she just might."

I smiled. Our gazes held, and the expression in his eyes changed from amusement to something more intense. He said, "If we've finished with our Saturday afternoon at the movies—"

"I do need to watch *Fury* again."

"Later?"

"Later," I agreed.

He started to reach for me, then stopped. "You said, 'First, Ray Nathan called.' What else happened?"

"There was—"

The cell phone that he had unclipped from his belt and put on the coffee table began to ring. He glanced at the phone, then back at me.

"It's all right," I said. "It can wait."

He picked up his phone. "Chief Quinn."

As the university police chief of Piedmont State University—a campus with 26,000 full- and part-time students, plus faculty, staff, and visitors—Quinn was prone to receive calls even when he was off duty. Monday would be the beginning of the first six-week summer session. The undergrads were flocking back to the dorms. The grad students had never left. Something was always going on.

Unless he had a good reason not to, Quinn answered his cell phone whenever it rang. I, on the other hand, was still inclined to turn off the one he had given me and shove it to the bottom of my shoulder bag.

That would have to change come fall semester when the Institute for the Study of Southern Crime and Culture opened its doors. As the executive director, I would have to be accessible. But I intended to have one last cell-phone-free summer.

Quinn listened as the person on the other end talked. I picked up our empty mugs from the coffee table and headed for the kitchen.

I had my head in the refrigerator, surveying my ingredients and debating the merits of making a big pot of vegetable beef soup, when he spoke from the doorway.

"Lizzie?"

"I know," I said, pasting a smile on my face. "That was your office. Something's come up on campus and you have to go in."

"No, that was Wade."

Although he was Quinn's good friend, Wade Garner was holding two shoes that could rock my world. Either one of them might be about to drop.

I tried the best-case scenario. "Was he calling to thank you for the birthday gift you sent to Josh?"

"They haven't opened it yet. Bree wants to wait until the party tomorrow and let Josh open his gifts."

"He may need some help with yours. Those were pretty big boxes for a three-year-old to open on his own."

Quinn, the three-year-old's godfather, did not rise to my teasing about the railroad set that I had seen and he had insisted on buying. "Lizzie, there's something we need to talk about."

Was it Becca? Or was he about to tell me that he had decided to take Wade up on his offer of a partnership in his international security firm? Either way, I really didn't need any more unsettling news today.

I closed the refrigerator door. "I'm listening."

He gestured toward the table. "Let's sit down."

"I don't want to sit. Just tell me."

Quinn took my arm. "We are not going to have this conversation standing in the middle of the floor. Sit down."

I sat down in the chair that he pulled out for me. "Is it about Becca? Is she dead?"

CHAPTER · 4

Quinn squatted down in front of me. "There's no reason to think Becca is dead. But Kyle Sheppard, the investigator Wade put on the case, has filed his initial report. It's not good."

"How bad is 'not good'?"

"In 1969, in Chicago, a mobster named Nick Mancini was stabbed to death in the office of the supper club he owned. Becca was working at that club as a singer. She seems to have been the motive for the murder."

"I see . . . well, that would explain why you wanted me to sit down. Go on."

"There was a young black man named Robert Montgomery working as a piano player at the club. He and Mancini got into an argument about Becca—"

"And the piano player killed the mobster? What did Becca do?"

Quinn hesitated. "She wasn't there when it happened. She had done her show and left for the evening."

"But what did she do when she found out about it?"

"She seems to have left town on the night of the murder. Wade's investigator is trying to get a lead on where she might have gone."

"Gone on her own steam? Men shedding blood over her, but she didn't even bother to hang around?"

"She might have preferred to avoid the police, Lizabeth. Not to mention Nick Mancini's associates."

"So we certainly can't blame Becca for hightailing it out of Chicago when her other boyfriend knocked Mancini off. Move, please. I need to get up."

Quinn shot to his feet, looking alarmed.

I heard him let out his breath when, instead of throwing up in the sink, I reached for the kettle and started to fill it.

His hands closed on my shoulders. "Lizzie, I can tell Wade to call off the investigation."

"No, it's too late for that now. I decided to open this particular box. Whatever flies out, I'll have to deal with it."

"No, you don't. We can stop this now. You can stop trying to find her."

"No, I can't do that."

"Why?"

I turned to look at him. "She's my mother. I can't pretend she doesn't exist."

"You don't have to pretend. You can decide to leave it alone."

"If it involved your mother, would you decide to leave it alone? If you didn't even know your father's name—whether he's alive or dead—would you decide to leave it alone?"

He shoved his fingers through his hair. "Dammit, Lizzie, I understand that you want to know about your father. But this isn't starting out well."

"I have noticed that, Quinn. But after thirty-nine years of not knowing, I finally have information about my mother. I can't just leave it alone."

"I hate how Becca affects you."

"Given the fact that she took a bus out of town and out of my life five days after I was born, I think I handle the matter of my mother reasonably well."

He sighed. "Reasonably well might not be good enough if you get any deeper into this."

"Then I'll do better. I'll get tough, Quinn. You haven't finished the story. What happened to Robert Montgomery?"

"He was arrested and charged with Mancini's murder."

"Charged? Was he convicted?"

"There was no trial. He confessed."

The kettle began to whistle. I moved it off the burner. "How long was Montgomery in prison?"

"He was paroled five years ago."

"Why was he in so long?" I asked. "He should've come up for parole long before that."

"He had another sentence added on for a manslaughter conviction while he was in prison. He killed another inmate during a fight."

"So there went a big chunk of his life."

"He killed a man, two men—"

"Yes, but the first one was over Becca. I'd rather not talk any more about this right now. Could we change the subject?"

"What would you like to talk about?"

I linked my arms around his neck. "I'd rather not talk."

His silver gaze held mine. "You're right. We've talked enough."

I felt his kiss all the way to my toes.

When he carried me into my bedroom to make love, there was no laughter—only his concentration on the task at hand . . . on making sure that my attention was focused on the two of us and nothing else. He managed that quite well. Even Bond couldn't have done it better.

Later, I leaned up on my elbow, watching him sleep. He was snoring. He did that when he slept on his back. I nudged his shoulder and then slid down in the bed and turned on my side. I wiggled back against him. He rolled over and wrapped his arm around me. The snoring stopped. Amazing how well that worked. I threaded my fingers through his, listening to the rhythm of his breathing.

According to all those books on relationships that I had read, "children" was one of the topics that a couple should discuss early on. *Do you want children? Yes? No? Maybe?* It was one of the few topics that Quinn and I had not tackled. Even when we were having our frank discussions about interracial relationships, neither one of us had said, "And suppose this does work out between us? What about children?"

If Quinn had given the matter even passing thought, he knew that we didn't have years to ponder this one. I would be forty on my next birthday. If he wanted children and wanted them with me, he would have to bring the matter up soon. If he did, and if I reminded him of my own uncertain paternity, he would tell me that was irrelevant. He would say it decisively and confidently, and it would be reassuring to hear.

The problem was that it wouldn't be true.

"Becca, get on your knees and pray . . . pray for you and that child growing inside you." Those had been Hester Rose's dying words when in her delirium she believed she was speaking to her pregnant teenage daughter—my mother—Becca.

My father had been someone my dying grandmother called "that man." Someone about whom she had told the absent Becca, *"It would kill your daddy if he knew. We can't never let him find out. We can't never let nobody find out."*

And she hadn't. Not my grandfather, not me. Until she was on her deathbed, I had believed her when she told me she didn't know who my father was.

Now only Becca knew the truth about my paternity.

Three months ago, I had been given a lead in the form of two ancient postcards from Chicago that she had sent to a high school classmate. I decided then to look for her.

Now there was too much at stake for me to retreat.

I had told Quinn about Hester Rose's dying words. What I couldn't bring myself to do was ask if he might want me to be the mother of his children. That smacked a bit too much of backing him into a corner and demanding a commitment.

But if I couldn't ask him that question, then I couldn't explain that one of the reasons I needed to find Becca was because our own relationship was going so well.

It was going so well that now I had no choice but to risk screwing it up.

But, of course, if I was losing my sight, then finding Becca might not matter a heck of a lot.

"Lizzie?" He was awake and leaning over me, his hand on my upper arm. "Are you all right? You were shivering."

I rolled over on my back. "You were hogging all the covers."

"Was I? Then I should make up for that."

"Yes, you should."

CHAPTER · 5

Quinn might have arrived in Gallagher by way of Philadelphia, but he had developed a Southerner's appreciation for authentic barbecue and settled on one particular practitioner of the art. After we shared a shower, he kissed me on the shoulder that he was patting dry and said, "How about driving to Greensboro for an early dinner?"

Translated, that meant, "How about driving for over an hour in the rain to eat braised pork, fried okra, hush puppies, and cole slaw in a barbecue joint called Short Ribs, run by a huge man named Jim-Bob, who sweats a lot and wears a stained apron?"

I nodded an affirmative because I knew Quinn was doing his best to distract me from brooding about Becca. Undoubtedly he thought that worrying about getting food poisoning from Jim-Bob's cuisine would be more effective than a romantic dinner in a restaurant that provided printed menus and clean tablecloths.

The odd thing was that he was right. I was not in the mood to get dressed up and pretend I was enjoying myself.

"Do you mind if we swing by campus on our way out?" I said. "I need to pick up an article I want to cite in the chapter that I'm working on."

It was after three-thirty when we left for campus, almost four when we walked into Brewster Hall, the massive, gray, stone-with-gargoyles academic building in which the School of Criminal Justice is housed. As usual, the equally Gothic elevator creaked and groaned in protest at being required to make the trip up to the fifth floor.

I led the way down the corridor to my office. No one poked a head out. In spite of the chilly weather outside, summer vacation had begun two weeks ago. Not much was happening during this intersession between the end of regular classes and the beginning of first summer session on Monday. Besides, it was Saturday.

In my office, I dropped my umbrella beside the chair and plopped my shoulder bag down on the desk. I was riffling through the files in the bottom desk drawer for the article I wanted, when Quinn reached around me. His hand came back holding the framed photo that I had forgotten was sitting beside my computer.

I hadn't told him that I had finally worked up the nerve to put his picture there on my desk for everyone to see. It wasn't that I had been worried about what people would say. It was just that I was bashful about public proclamations.

Quinn looked amused as he stared down at the image of himself in a dark gray suit and tie and a crisp white shirt. "Where did you get this?"

"I found it in one of your photo albums. I had it enlarged."

"Kind of formal, isn't it?"

"Yes, but I didn't want all the women in the building stopping by to drool over you in blue jeans."

He laughed. "That's something you really don't have to worry about, Lizabeth." He put the silver frame back in its place. "Now, with you, on the other hand, I did have to consider the drool factor. I like my cops to be able to keep their minds on the job. If I'd brought in that picture that I have on my desk at home—"

"Thank you for not doing that," I said, my mind flashing to that photo of me eating cotton candy that he had taken at a winter carnival. I picked up my shoulder bag and umbrella. "Let's go get that barbecue."

"We don't have to go to Greensboro. We can pick up a steak and go back to my place. George has been wanting to see you."

"It's probably that doggie treat I brought him when I came by on Thursday." I shook my head. "Let's go to Greensboro. Then we can come back and spend the evening with George."

"Lizzie, you—"

"I'm all right, Quinn. It isn't as if the news about Becca caught me completely off guard. I wasn't expecting glad tidings."

"There may be something else we need to talk about," he said.

"What?"

"Let's wait until Wade calls back. I asked him to have Sheppard follow up with one of his sources, but it might not work out." He gestured toward the door. "In the meantime, Professor Stuart, let's get out of here."

We crossed the expanse of the uptown bridge, passing over the Dan River, where broken tree branches bobbed in the frothing water. Two years had passed since the river last flooded, but it often looked as if it longed to escape its banks. Heading up the hill, we drove past the city park, where workers in rain slickers were out in force. Tomorrow was the kickoff of the sixth annual "Every Sunday in June" music festival. Since the new riverfront pavilion that was planned as a part of the downtown Project Renaissance was still on the drawing board, the city's largest park was again hosting the festival. The banner announcing the event, sponsored by the Gallagher Merchants Association, flapped in the wind and rain, but if the Channel 13 weatherman was right, the sun would be out tomorrow.

We were passing the uptown facilities of the Mercantile Cotton Mills when Quinn's cell phone rang.

"That was fast," he said to the caller. "Hold on a moment, I'm driving. I'd better pull over." He turned in to the Food Lion shopping plaza and turned off the ignition. "Wade? What do you have?"

Quinn's ability to keep his expression neutral no matter what he was hearing or seeing was a product of all of his years of discipline and training, from West Point to major in the military police, and after that as a Philadelphia homicide detective. On occasion, I found his "cop face" more than a little irritating.

"Yeah," he said into the phone. "I know. Thank Sheppard for me. We'll get back to you." He put his cell phone down on the console and started the car.

I waited until we were under way again before I said, "What are we going to get back to Wade about?"

"Robert Montgomery . . . the piano player—"

"Yes, I remember who he is. What about him?"

"He was uncooperative the first time Sheppard contacted him. He told Sheppard to get out, that he had nothing to say to him."

"But something has changed?"

"I asked Wade to have him try again. This time Sheppard told Montgomery that his client is Becca's daughter and that she wants very much to find her mother."

"What did Montgomery say?"

"He said that he'll talk to you. Only you."

"Thank you, Quinn. I know that you—"

"There's something else. Montgomery has emphysema. He's dying."

"Dying? Then I have to go there right away."

"How did I know you were going to say that?"

"You know me well?" I said.

"Yeah, I do. That's why I'm going with you."

"Can you get away right now? You said the president was really concerned about the vandalism in the parking lot and—"

"I have detectives working that case. You're not going to Chicago alone."

"I'm not arguing. I'd just as soon not go alone."

The light in front of us turned yellow, and Quinn brought the car to a stop. "After you've talked to Montgomery, will you think about letting this drop?"

"How can you ask me to do that? If he tells me something that might help me find Becca—"

"Whatever he tells you, it isn't going to be something you want to hear. Finding Becca could end up being worse than—"

"We seem to have come full circle in this discussion."

"That's because I'm trying to make you see—"

"What? See things your way?" I tugged at the collar of my blouse. "My grand-mother lied to me, Quinn. She lied to me all my life. Aside from anything else, I'd really like to know what it was about my conception that was bad enough to make a church-going, God-fearing woman like Hester Rose lie."

The driver behind us honked to point out that the light was now green. Quinn waved in apology and turned his attention back to the traffic.

After a moment, he said, "All right, I've already agreed to this trip to Chicago. But there's one thing I want you to be absolutely clear about, Lizabeth."

"What?"

"I love you. And I have way too much time and effort invested in courting you to get dropped because you're upset about what you find out about your long-lost mother. You are not getting rid of me."

From any other man, I might have found the announcement that I was not getting rid of him a threat. From Quinn, I only hoped he intended to keep that promise.

"I love you too," I said. "I don't want to get rid of you. And I'm sorry that I gave you such a hard time in the beginning."

"You're still giving me a hard time. But sometimes that isn't a bad thing."

He winked, but I certainly didn't blush. Even if I had, with my tawny brown skin, he wouldn't have been able to tell. I had explained that to him before.

Still, he must have found it fascinating that Becca's daughter was sometimes shy.

CHAPTER · 6

With my eyes still closed, I fumbled for the ringing telephone. Quinn's arm was already there to keep me from rolling out of bed, and I realized I was in his bed not mine.

I settled back against the pillow. It was still dark outside. No one would call in the middle of the night except Quinn's office.

It was probably more vandalism. A few nights ago, someone had spray-painted graffiti on the cars parked in one of the dormitory lots. The worrisome part was that the graffiti had included gang tags.

Gangs were a new phenomenon in Gallagher. But now the Gallagher PD and the local newspaper were talking about them. Talking in foreboding terms about gangs and drugs invading a city that was more prone to think of itself in terms of the Civil War museum and the historic Victorian houses on Main Street, than of crack and turf wars.

I was inclined to think they were overreacting. I had put it down to "white panic" over an alleged invasion by black and brown gangbangers from the urban hood.

In a hard, detached voice, Quinn said, "Where is she now?"

This wasn't vandalism. I pushed myself up in the bed to listen.

"Tell Degrassi to stay at the hospital until the parents arrive," he said. "Tell her I'm on my way to campus."

The caller said something else, and Quinn replied, "No statements until I arrive." He looked at me as he shut his cell phone. "A student's been raped."

"Is she all right? I mean—"

"They had to sedate her when she arrived at the hospital. But no physical injuries she won't recover from. Not stabbed or strangled."

"That's good at least."

"We aren't going to be able to make our flight, Lizabeth. Channel 13 already has the story. Before this morning's over, I'm going to be up to my eyeballs in calls from concerned parents and frightened female students and faculty. I need to be here."

I nodded. "I understand that you can't leave when something like this is going on. I can go alone."

"You're not going to Chicago alone. In a few days—"

"In a few days, Robert Montgomery could be dead."

"I'm not letting you go up there alone."

"You're not letting me go? In case you haven't noticed, Quinn, I'm an adult. I'm fully capable of—"

"Capable of getting yourself into more trouble than you've ever been in before." He scowled at me. "Dammit, Lizzie, we're talking about the mob."

"The mob in 1969, over thirty-five years ago. Mancini's associates have probably all retired and moved to Florida. Kyle Sheppard has been asking questions, and he's still alive and well." I shoved back the comforter and reached for my robe. "I'm going to Chicago today, Quinn. I need to talk to Robert Montgomery before he dies."

He caught up with me halfway across the floor to the bathroom. He stepped in front of me, blocking my way. His silver eyes glistened. His mouth was tight.

But he kept his hands clenched at his side. The one thing I had learned during our occasional disagreements was that he avoided touching me when he was angry. He would neither hit nor attempt to subdue with a kiss.

We stared at each other. I waited for him to break the silence that was filled by our breathing.

"All right," he said. "You're going. When you go see Montgomery, I want Sheppard to go with you."

"That works for me. No problem."

He reached out, tracing his finger along my jawline. "Why do you have to be so stubborn?"

"I'm not being stubborn. I'm doing something I have to do."

"Then there's something I have to do. Stay there."

I watched as he strode, buck naked, over to the dresser. He yanked open the top drawer. When he started back toward me, he looked less confident. A flush of pink washed across his cheekbones and downward toward his chest. John Quinn blushing?

"Quinn, what on earth—"

"I hadn't intended to do this now."

"Do what?"

"This." He held out a small black velvet box. "I . . . uh . . . I thought of you when I saw this."

He opened the lid and I stared down at a ruby with fire at its heart. It was flanked on each side by a small diamond. The gems were clasped in a woven antique setting.

"It's beautiful," I said when I could speak. "Is it an early birthday present?"

He held the box out for me to take. "We'll talk about that when you get back from Chicago."

"When I. . . . What should I do with it in the meantime?"

"You might try it on to see if it fits."

"I. . . . Which hand?"

"That's up to you." He drew me into his arms. "You're going, and I can't stop you. Just start thinking about which finger you're going to wear the ring on."

I pressed my nose against the smooth, musky skin of his shoulder. "It's up to me, huh?"

"Entirely up to you."

I closed my eyes and held on tight. I still needed to tell him about my eye exam. I hadn't done that yet because he was not going to be happy when he heard I had canceled my Tuesday appointment with the optometrist.

We would get into an argument about my priorities, about my search for Becca. We were already having that argument. I didn't want to add kindling to that fire.

But before I allowed him to propose, I would have to tell him if there was any possibility that I might need a seeing-eye dog. If I did, would he offer to have George, his yellow Lab, trained for the task?

Or maybe I would be noble and send him off to find a woman with two good eyes.

CHAPTER · 7

I drove to Greensboro to catch the flight to Chicago. Since Quinn wasn't there, I took the aisle seat and left the middle one empty. The man occupying the window seat was making me nervous. It was not because he looked like a suspicious character; when he claimed his seat, his accent—whatever it was—had been quite charming. He was attractive, with olive skin, dark eyes and hair. But the man couldn't sit still. Since the moment he sat down, he had been in perpetual motion. He wagged his well-shod foot and jiggled his legs in his pressed khaki slacks. He flipped rapid-fire through the in-flight magazine in his lap.

I closed my eyes to block out his twitching, but I wanted to stay awake. If I fell asleep, I would feel even more sluggish when I woke up than I already did. I needed to hit the ground running when I arrived in Chicago. I had booked a Wednesday afternoon flight home, because I was scheduled to meet with some university administrators on Thursday morning to brief them about the opening conference at the Institute. That gave me two days to see Robert Montgomery, the ex-con piano player, and to learn what I could about Nick Mancini's murder and Becca's time in Chicago.

My head jerked on my neck. I pushed myself upright in my seat and reached for the novel I'd bought at an airport newsstand. I'd seen the author on a television interview show. By the time I'd finished the first three pages—in which a serial killer pursued his terrified victim through a deserted building, shot her in the groin, and then carved his initials into her dying body—I was wondering if the witty, erudite man I'd seen on the talk show could have written this book.

Criminal justice professor I might be, but some things make me squeamish. Graphic violence perpetrated with knives and guns is high on the list.

In spite of my dislike of guns, Quinn had persuaded me to go to with him to the firing range. He wanted me to be more comfortable with the presence of his gun. That had come about after my startled cry when I opened my dresser drawer and discovered that he'd stored his holstered weapon there.

He said he had been trying to get it out of my sight when he was undressing the night before. I said depositing it among my panties and bras wasn't the way to do that. We had ended up at the firing range.

I fired until I had gotten past what Quinn described as my "liberal objection" to touching a weapon and started to hit the target. I assured him my objection to weapons had nothing to do with firing at inanimate objects. It was not the first time I had handled a gun.

My grandfather, Walter Lee, was a hunter. He also considered the shotgun he kept in his bedroom closet protection in case we ever needed it from rabid animals, snakes in the backyard, or two-legged human predators. When I was thirteen, he announced that my grandmother, Hester Rose, knew how to use his shotgun, and now it was time I learned how to use it too. We went out into the backyard and I fired at tin cans.

The same principle was at work in Quinn's mind when he asked me to come with him to the range. If his gun was in the house, I should know how to shoot it.

I understood his reasoning, and I was less concerned abut the physical presence of his gun than what it symbolized. Of late, violence seemed to be a part of my life. I had paid a psychologist good money to listen to me ramble on about how in the past two years since my grandmother's death and my departure from the safe haven of Drucilla, Kentucky, I had found myself getting involved in more than my share of situations involving someone's death.

However, it seemed that compared to both Hester Rose, who had witnessed a lynching at twelve, and Becca, who was almost twenty-two when her mobster lover was killed, I was a late bloomer. Was it something in our genes? I had almost said that to Quinn when we were discussing Becca, but he would have dismissed it as superstition. Some version of the "bad seed" theory that we both knew was ridiculous.

What he should realize by now was that he was involved with a superstitious woman. That much Hester Rose had definitely passed on to her grandchild. I knocked on wood, and in spite of being a social scientist who knew better, I worried about whether the Stuart women carried a taint of violence.

If we did, it was just as well I was involved with a cop who understood violence. Except he didn't think I was tough enough to cope.

I had the feeling we were about to find out.

Quinn's ring hung on the chain that I had tucked inside the collar of my blouse. I touched it for luck. Then I reached for my book and flipped to the last page.

"That's cheating." My seatmate grinned at me.

"I know," I said, "but sometimes it helps to know how it all turns out."

He nodded and plucked the airline merchandise catalog from the pocket of the seat between us. He hunched over it, tearing out the pages of the items he found interesting. I was tempted to ask why he didn't just take the catalog with him, but I assumed he wanted to avoid the bulk. The good news was that he had stopped twitching.

I skimmed through the first chapter and then settled down with my novel. It got better after the burnt-out, suicidal cop replaced the serial killer as the narrator. I could handle a character's angst better than his bloodlust.

C H A P T E R · 8

CHICAGO, ILLINOIS

Tugging my carry-on luggage behind me, I weaved my way over to the man in the chauffeur's uniform who was holding up a sign that had my name on it, complete with title, "Professor Lizabeth Stuart."

"Excuse me. I'm Lizzie Stuart, but I wasn't expecting to be met."

"Courtesy of Mr. Wade Garner," he said in an accent that was blue-collar Chicago with the edges smoothed and polished. "Mr. Garner ordered a limo to take you to your hotel."

I digested that. "How thoughtful of Mr. Garner."

"He faxed this note to our office and asked that your driver give it to you."

I accepted the envelope he held out to me. He reached for my suitcase handle.

Wade had written, "Welcome to Chicago, Lizzie. John called. Kyle Sheppard will be at your service while you're in town." He had followed that information with what was presumably Sheppard's telephone number.

"Did Mr. Garner call from Arlington to order the limo?"

"Bright and early this morning," my driver said. "Do you have luggage at baggage claim?"

"No, this is all I have."

"Then are we ready to go?"

"Yes, thank you."

As chauffeurs went, this one had pizzazz. In his late thirties, he was of medium height with dark wavy hair and a bad-boy handsome face. A chauffeur-driven limo into the city was certainly a step above an airport shuttle bus.

It was probably unfair of me to be suspicious of Wade's generous gesture, but just how big was that favor he owed Quinn? Quinn said that was why we were getting the services of one of Wade's investigators for free. I couldn't help wondering if Wade hoped that if what I found out about Becca was bad enough, it might drive a convenient wedge between Quinn and me. That would give Quinn a good reason to leave Gallagher.

With that in mind, Wade had everything to gain by being helpful.

Or maybe, given the limo driver walking in front of me, Wade was hoping that if he couldn't get rid of me, he could co-opt me, win me over to his side with a taste of what the money would be like if Quinn became his partner.

That assumed that Wade was as Machiavellian as I was making him out to be. The only problem with that assumption was that Quinn was an excellent judge of character, and he trusted Wade. It was possible that Wade was being thoughtful because Quinn was his friend and I was important to Quinn.

And there was another aspect of Wade's job offer that I should consider. If Quinn would be happier as Wade's partner but stayed in Gallagher because my career was there, the situation might affect the longevity of our relationship.

Wasn't that known as a Pyrrhic victory? You won but you still lost?

The limo driver looked back and apparently noticed something in my expression. "Everything all right?"

"Fine," I said. "I'm a little tired."

"I'll have you at your hotel in time for a nap before lunch."

I can't deny that I could have curled up on the limo's plush leather seat and taken that nap. But I resisted the temptation. I also ignored the elegant box of gold foil-wrapped chocolates, the minibar, and the media system. I stared out the tinted window at the bustle of a big city in the middle of a workday.

In spite of Carl Sandburg's description, I had never thought of Chicago in terms of its brawn. I was sentimental about Chicago because I had come to this city for the first time with my grandfather, Walter Lee. We had come by train from Kentucky the year after he retired from almost thirty years as a sleeping-car porter. I could still remember arriving in Union Station. I could still remember riding on the el and trying to see everything at once.

We had stayed with Walter Lee's old friend Calvin. Calvin's family had been among the migrants who had left the South and made the trip north at the urging of the legendary black newspaper, the *Chicago Defender*. Arriving in 1918, they found not "the Promised Land," but a black ghetto. Still, it had been better than what they'd left behind in Mississippi. During those four days we spent with him, Calvin had regaled Walter Lee and me with stories about "Bronzeville," black South Side Chicago in its glory days.

I had been to Chicago any number of times in the years since that first visit; it was one of my favorite cities. These days I came to attend conferences, and I spent much of my time in one of the hotels in the downtown area. Chicago was not a city that I knew intimately, but it felt knowable. The skyscrapers were friendlier and less overpowering than those of New York City. In Chicago, you could see daylight and space.

This morning the city sparkled in the June sunlight.

I reached for a foil-wrapped chocolate and curled my legs up on the seat. I might as well enjoy the ride. Who knew when I'd ever be in a limousine again?

To quote the ever-resilient Doris, *"Qué será, será.* What will be, will be."

That bit of Spanish wisdom reminded me that I needed to call Tess and let her know I had arrived. Tess Alvarez had been my own best friend since college. Or, at least, she had been until a summer vacation in Cornwall, when I had met Quinn and lost Tess. *Lost* is not completely accurate. We had maintained the structure of our friendship with cards and letters and occasional chats on the phone. But since that summer, a barrier had gone up between us that I kept trying to get around or over.

That barrier was labeled "Michael," for Tess's ex-husband. He had been in Cornwall; he was still our bone of contention.

Until now, she had vetoed any suggestion that we get together. She was always too busy with her new job as a travel show producer or with her baby daughter, Elena. But when I announced I was coming to Chicago, she sounded almost relieved. After a moment's hesitation, she even suggested that I stay at her place.

I hadn't been up to dealing with that hesitation and the hunt for my missing mother both at the same time. I told her that I needed to stay at a hotel so I could be in contact with Wade's investigator. That excuse hadn't made sense, but she accepted it readily enough. Still, the fact that she wanted to see me suggested that we might at least be able to talk about what was wrong.

First I needed to call Kyle Sheppard. Then I'd know when I would have time to see Tess.

My stomach growled a reminder of how little I had eaten of the toast, juice, and cereal that Quinn had gotten on the table while I was dressing. Another piece of chocolate would tide me over until I could get that lunch the limo driver had mentioned.

We turned away from Lake Shore Drive, where joggers chugged along the path and small craft bobbed in the blue water. On Balboa, a fountain in the park shot water up toward the sky. A few minutes later trees gave way to buildings. We were headed into the heart of downtown Chicago.

I straightened in my seat and began to think about whether I was supposed to tip a driver hired by someone else. And, if so, how much? Small-town girls from Kentucky, even the ones who had made it through grad school, were not bred to have that kind of knowledge at their fingertips.

The driver stopped at the light opposite the hotel I'd found on the Chicago tourism Web site. We were on North Michigan Avenue, the section between the Chicago River and Lake Shore Drive known as "The Magnificent Mile." I had once seen this wide boulevard described as Chicago's version of the *Champs-Elysées*. Never having been to Paris, I couldn't testify to the accuracy of that comparison, but the boulevard was an out-of-towner's mecca with restaurants, businesses, and upscale stores ranging from Crate and Barrel and Disney Store to Bloomingdale's and Saks Fifth Avenue.

No problem identifying the out-of-towners. We were always torn between looking in the store windows and gaping upward at the skyscrapers. I loved walking past the *Chicago Mirror-Examiner* building at night when the lighted upper stories stood out like a beacon, but my favorite building on North Michigan was at the opposite end of the Magnificent Mile. Resembling a rich kid's miniature castle, the Old Water Tower was an anachronism on this bustling street. It was one of the few buildings that had survived the Great Chicago Fire in 1871. Historic preservationists had managed to save it from demolition during the building boom back in the 1920s and 1930s.

The hotel I had found on the Internet dated back to that building boom. I had never stayed there, but the Web site had described it as "one of Chicago's stately older hotels, newly renovated." Quinn had been impressed when I told him that I'd gotten our room at a "summer deal" price. Too bad he wasn't going to be here to share it.

The limo door opened. I remembered in the nick of time not to clamber out head-first. Instead, I swung my legs out, then accepted the strong hand the chauffeur offered me. Of course, the effect was spoiled by the fact that I was wearing slacks and flats rather than silky hose and drop-dead high heels. But I was tall at 5'7" and slender at 128, even if I wasn't city chic.

I thought I carried off the leg swing rather well. Next stop: the Oscar night red carpet with applauding fans.

"Thank you," I said to my driver and slipped a ten-dollar bill into his hand.

"Thank you, Professor Stuart," he said, discarding his professional smile for a grin.

Was he amused by my graceful exit, or should the tip have been more?

Oh, to heck with it. He was probably amused because I shouldn't have tipped him at all. Wade had probably already taken care of that.

"Enjoy your stay," he said, touching an invisible cap.

"Thank you," I said.

He gave me another salute as he left me.

I turned toward the bellman, who had come to escort me into the hotel. At least, I knew how much to tip him. I didn't fight him for the privilege when he reached for my one piece of pull-along luggage. There is something about riding in a limousine that enhances one's willingness to let other people do all life's minor tasks. We entered a vestibule occupied by the bell captain's desk across from a seating area formed by a large chintz-covered sofa and two matching armchairs.

"The main lobby's on the first floor," the bellman said. He held out a slip of paper. "If you'll give this to the desk clerk when you check in upstairs, I'll see that your luggage is delivered to your room."

I tipped him and offered my thanks. He pushed the elevator button and held the door when it slid open.

I was about to step inside, when someone called out, "Professor Stuart." It was the limo driver.

"Did I forget something?"

"I just received a telephone message for you. Mr. Kyle Sheppard would like you to meet him. I have the address. He wants me to bring you there."

"Right now?"

"That's what I was told."

I looked at the bellman, who asked, "Would you like me to store your luggage, ma'am?"

"Yes, please, if you would."

I followed the driver back out to the car. He held the door. This time, I wasn't quite as graceful as I slid across the seat. I tapped on the glass when he had gotten in behind the wheel. He slid it back.

"Did Mr. Sheppard's message say what's at this address we're going to?"

"Sorry, all I have is the address. But it's not far. Sit back and relax. I'll have you there in nothing flat."

I sat back, puzzled and a little uneasy.

CHAPTER · 9

The address was only a few streets over, on N. Wells, within walking distance of my hotel. We pulled up to the curb in front of a three-story brown brick building sharing chocolate brown columns with the building next door. According to the lettering on the purple awning that extended out over the sidewalk, the ground-floor shop in the building next door was called the Sahara. Colorful Middle Eastern handicrafts and exotic jewelry were showcased in the window.

The window of Club Floridian, my destination, featured a lush display of green foliage. The club gave every appearance of being closed.

My driver got out and held the limo door for me. We were parked beside one of the shade trees planted at intervals along the street.

Neither the woman walking a fox terrier nor the young man in red shorts, chest bare, who loped around her, showed any interest in the limo. They and the other people passing by on either side of the street must be accustomed to limos pulling up outside the club in the middle of the afternoon. Or maybe they were too Chicago-sophisticated to be impressed.

"Thank you," I said to the driver as he helped me out of the car. "Could you wait for a moment, please? Until I make sure Mr. Sheppard is here."

"No problem," he said.

Last night, I'd asked Quinn the name of Nick Mancini's club when I was searching without success for anything on the Internet about the Mancini case. He said Wade hadn't mentioned it; we would find out from Kyle Sheppard when we arrived.

This was a situation I hadn't anticipated.

I gave myself a moment to think by pausing to study the mural set in the recess between the columns of the two buildings. It seemed to be a representation of beige desert sand with patterned scarves of green and blue scattered across the expanse.

The street number was displayed boldly on the top panel of the Club Floridian's door, which was painted an enameled forest green and sported a sleek, modern, silver door handle. Pressing my face to the window, I pushed the buzzer. Beyond the palm trees and other foliage, white-clothed tables rose on three levels. Up front was a small stage with a red velvet curtain. A brass bar with bottles and a mirror occupied the adjacent space.

No one was moving around inside. I pushed the buzzer again. Then I reached out and pulled on the door handle. The door opened.

Behind me, my chauffeur said, "I'd go on in. They're expecting you."

"Yes," I said. I couldn't keep him standing there while I dillydallied.

I stepped into the foyer, leaving the door ajar. If they were expecting me, it was awfully quiet. For all I knew, Sheppard had wanted me to join him in "casing the joint."

But I was inside now. "Hello? Is anyone here? Hello?"

A door in back slammed. Footsteps came down the hallway.

"Professor Stuart?" The man coming toward me had thinning gray-blond hair that he had slicked back. He had a bony nose and a scruffy gray mustache. His torso and limbs were skinny, but he had a round little belly. His belly would have been a beer gut on a heftier man. It made a mound under his black silk shirt and distorted the drape of his narrow-legged black slacks. He had left the shirt open a few buttons to display a chunky gold chain dangling among his scanty gray chest hairs.

"Hello," I said as he reached me, his hand outstretched, a smile on his face. "I'm afraid I don't know who you are. Kyle Sheppard sent a message asking me to meet him here, but he didn't explain who we would be seeing."

"Now, Professor, should I be insulted that you didn't even think that I might be your private eye?" He clasped my hand. His smile displayed crooked but bleached white teeth. "Sonny Germano. I run this place. Thanks for coming."

His grip was strong for a skinny man, and I eased my hand from his. "I didn't realize you had invited me, Mr. Germano. Is Mr. Sheppard here?"

"He's in back. We're having some lunch in my office." He gestured for me to precede him.

"I'm sorry. But I need to ask . . . was this Nick Mancini's club?"

"It was. I'm his widow's cousin. I took over running the place for her after Nick's unfortunate demise." He gestured again. "Please, Professor, come join us."

"Excuse me for just one second." I went back to the door.

My driver was still leaning against the limo. "Something I can help you with, Professor?"

"Yes. Could you wait for me until I'm ready to leave? I won't be long."

"No problem."

Germano shook his head when I rejoined him. "Now, Professor, tell me you weren't just making sure of your backup? You aren't imagining that I'm planning something underhanded?" He pressed his hand to his heart, displaying a gold, monogrammed pinky ring. "I swear to you, your gumshoe is back there in my office enjoying the lunch we ordered in." He looked genuinely hurt, his hound dog eyes long and sad.

"I'm sorry," I said. "I didn't mean to offend you. But this has caught me by surprise, and I'm finding it a little awkward."

"And a woman can't be too careful, right? A man either, for that matter." He guided me toward the back hallway, walking beside me. "You look like your mother. Did anyone ever tell you that? They must have."

I swallowed hard before I could speak. "Did you know my mother?"

"I caught her show now and then. I saw her perform the night Nick died. She was wearing this black gown, and she looked like a million bucks. She had the crowd eating out of her hand."

"You thought she was good, then?"

"Even as young as she was, she already had it. That magic, that way of grabbing an audience and holding them." He shook his head. "Of course, after the tragedy here with Nick. . . . But I've always hoped your mother went on with her career somewhere else."

We had come to two doors in the shadowed hallway. The one marked "Emergency Exit" had an alarm that would sound if opened. To the side was another door showing a blank face. Germano turned the knob.

An executive-size desk faced the door. It was bare except for a flat-screen computer and what looked like an account book, open on the leather blotter. A visitor's chair was adjacent to the desk. A burgundy crushed-velvet sofa and matching chair and a coffee table formed a conversation area.

The man who, I assumed, was my PI sat by the window at the glass-topped dining table. Big, bald, and dark brown, he was using chopsticks to help himself from one of the white cartons on the table. He looked up when we walked in, then he put down the chopsticks and lumbered to his feet.

Something brushed against my ankle, and I jumped back, almost colliding with Germano.

"Precious," Germano said as he reached down and scooped up a large white Persian cat. "Have you no manners? You startled our guest."

Precious turned her blue gaze in my direction. Then she made a sound of protest, and Germano put her down on the floor. She lifted her tail flag-like, arched her back in a stretch, and then strolled away, disappearing beneath the desk.

I turned my attention back to the other man in the room. He was walking toward us with a kind of splayfooted limp that must be the result of arthritis rather than his allegiance to the hip-hop generation. Was this Wade Garner's investigator? This man must be in his early sixties, around the same age as Germano. The belly under his vest and suit jacket was more than a small mound.

His hand engulfed mine. "I'm Kyle Sheppard, Professor Stuart." His voice was a pleasant rumble. "Welcome to Chicago."

I looked into intelligent eyes that sized me up with a thoughtful glance.

"Thank you," I said. "It's a pleasure to meet you, Mr. Sheppard."

The large hand that had closed over mine had knuckles several shades darker brown than the rest of his hand. They looked as if he had punched something too hard and permanently bruised them.

"Now, isn't this pleasant, getting together like this?" Germano said. "Some unfortunate history, of course. But I wanted to meet so we could put the past behind us, clear the air. Let's sit down and break bread—or rather egg rolls—while we talk."

He gestured us back toward the table. Sheppard motioned for me to go first, and when we got to the table, he held my chair and saw me seated. Germano nodded in approval and sat down.

I was hungry. The chocolates I had nibbled in the limo seemed a long time ago.

Germano indicated the Chinese food take-out boxes and said, "Please, help yourself."

"Thank you," I said. Not as proficient as Sheppard or Germano with chopsticks, I opted for a plastic fork. Germano asked what I'd like to drink and got up and brought me bottled water from the fridge behind the bar. He brought back two more bottles of beer for himself and Sheppard.

When we had been eating for a few minutes, I said, "What is it that you want to talk about, Mr. Germano?"

"Sonny, please. We should all be on first names here. And what I want to say to you is that if I can help you in any way, all you have to do is ask. I mean that sincerely. We all want the same thing for you."

"We do?" I said.

"We do absolutely." He bit into an egg roll. He chewed and patted his mouth with a paper napkin. "We want you to find your mother and be reunited with her."

"Why do you want that for me, Mr. Germano?"

"Sonny, call me Sonny. Actually, it's Lorenzo, but I've never cared for that name. Which brings me to my point."

"It does?"

"My father gave me that name. He chose it. My mother didn't like it. But she died when I was born, so he gave me the name he liked. That was the way it was my whole life." His droopy eyes held my gaze. "And I could never please him. Now, my mother I might have. My aunt, the wife of my mother's brother . . . her brother was the one of who set up the marriage . . . my aunt always told me that I was like my mother." He gestured with his hand. "You know why I ended up embarrassing myself trying to be a stand-up comedian here in this club on the night Nick was killed?"

He had lost me somewhere in that tale. Rather than try to unravel it, I shook my head. "No, I don't."

"Of course you don't. That was a rhetorical question." He smiled. "You're an educated woman. You wouldn't expect a man like me to know words like that, right? I know them because I read. I read because I wanted to be an actor from the moment I saw my first movie. But my father laughed his head off. His son, an actor? No son of his was going to do a fag—forgive me, *unmanly*—thing like acting."

"What did he think of tough-guy actors like Bogart and Cagney?"

"He loved them. Especially Cagney. But he informed me that I was no Cagney."

"I'm sorry about your difficult relationship with your father," I said. "But I don't quite see—"

"Excuse me. Of course, you don't," he said. "I got it from my mother. That woman was where I got my love of words, of theater and acting. If she had lived, she would have believed in me, encouraged me."

"Yes," I said. I glanced at Sheppard, who was concentrating on his food. "Yes, I'm sure she would have."

"Now, your mother," he said, gesturing with his chopsticks. "She was young when you were born. She wanted the bright lights." He carried a shrimp to his mouth, chewed, and swallowed before he spoke. "You have to remember that and forgive her. She's probably thought of you often. But it's hard to take that step, you know, to try to go back and fix things."

"Yes," I said.

"So that's why I want you to find her, Lizabeth. You don't mind if I call you Lizabeth? I'm sentimental about mothers. And I want you to find yours. Who knows? You might even have brothers and sisters."

I had thought of possible siblings before, but I really didn't want to discuss it with Sonny Germano over Chinese food.

"Actually, I prefer Lizzie." I said. Only Quinn called me Lizabeth. "And doesn't it bother you at all that my mother was supposed to have been involved with your cousin-in-law? That she was the motive for his murder?"

Sonny touched his paper napkin to his mouth. "That she was the cause of an argument between two men that proved fatal to one of them?" he said. "That sometimes happens with beautiful women."

"That's generous of you."

"Now, you see, Lizzie, here I have to be honest. You have to understand where I'm coming from on this. You see, I love my cousin Angela. She's a wonderful woman. But I'm afraid Nick was never faithful to her. He was a good provider, even in some ways a good husband and father. But to put it bluntly—and forgive me for saying it this way to a lady like yourself —Nick couldn't keep his pants zipped."

"So you don't blame my mother at all for what happened between them?"

Sonny shrugged. "She was young. Nick had lots of charm, and he kept his women in style."

I was trying to come up with a response to that when the office door opened. Sheppard made a half movement in his chair as he saw the man in the doorway.

"It's all right," I said. "He's the driver of the limo." I stood up as my driver strolled into the room. "Have I been too long? Do you have to leave? I can ask Mr. Sheppard to—"

I broke off as he kept walking toward us, silent, smiling, ignoring what I was saying. When he got to the table, he reached for one of the egg rolls.

"If you're going to eat, sit down," Sonny said to him as if he wasn't at all surprised to have someone's chauffeur walk in and make himself at home.

My limo driver pulled out the empty chair and sat down. He reached for a paper plate. As he picked up one of the cartons of food, he glanced at me. "You don't mind if I have some lunch, do you?"

"No," I said. "But I'm afraid we're having a private conversation. If you wouldn't mind taking your plate and eating somewhere else—"

He laughed and leaned back in his chair. "Did you hear that, Cousin Sonny? The lady doesn't think a chauffeur is good enough to eat at your table."

"Cousin?" I said.

My erstwhile chauffeur smiled at me, his gaze mocking. "Sorry about that. I didn't get around to introducing myself, did I? Nick Mancini Jr., at your service."

CHAPTER · 1 0

My mouth dropped open. I swerved toward Kyle Sheppard.

He looked exactly the way he should have. Embarrassed. Like he had screwed up big-time and knew it.

But before Sheppard could offer more than an apologetic shrug of his big shoulders, Sonny Germano said, "Now, Lizzie, no need to be distressed. Nico knows the owner of the limo company that was hired to pick you up. He offered to fill in for the driver they were going to send. Of course, I can see you might not appreciate his little joke, that he didn't introduce himself. Believe me, I did scold him when he called to tell me what he was up to." He gestured toward my chair. "Sit down, please. Everything's still good between us."

"Everything's dandy between us," I said. "But I've had enough of this meeting." My face felt hot, burning with my mortification and outrage. I glared at Sheppard. "Are you coming, or do I have to flag down a taxi and hope it isn't being driven by a relative of Robert Montgomery's?"

Sheppard rose from his chair.

Sonny came to his feet too. "Speaking of Mr. Montgomery," he said. "I advise you to exercise some caution in that quarter. He lives in a bad neighborhood. Gangs, drugs, not a healthy environment even for a dying man. If you go there, be careful."

"Thank you for that advice," I said. "But we do have gangs and drugs back in Gallagher. And I suspect I might be safer in a bad neighborhood than sitting down to lunch."

I wanted to be out of there. I marched toward the door.

"It was a pleasure meeting you," Sonny said. "Nico, your manners. Say good-bye."

"Good-bye, Professor Stuart," Nico said. "Thanks for the tip . . . and for satisfying my curiosity."

I turned to look at him. "Your curiosity about what?"

"About what my old man saw in your mother. A little more makeup and a hot dress, and you—"

I used an expression that I didn't realize was in my vocabulary. But it popped right out of my mouth.

He laughed. He was still laughing when I slammed the door.

Out on the sidewalk, I stopped. I stared at the black limo gleaming there in the afternoon sunlight, occupying two parking spaces as if by right. Would Tess come and bail me out of jail if I threw a brick through one of its windows?

But there were no bricks in sight, and even if there had been, childish behavior would accomplish nothing. The limo didn't belong to those two in the club. They had borrowed it for their little gag. The limo was not responsible for the fact that I had let Nico bring me down to his level with my parting suggestion about what he could do.

I heard the door of the club open and click shut. I turned, and Sheppard held up his hands. "Professor Stuart—"

"How could you let that happen? How could you sit there having lunch with Sonny Germano while the son of the man my mother was involved with was driving me around?"

"Professor Stuart, I know you're upset. But calm down and—"

"Don't tell me to calm down. Wade Garner said I could count on you, and you let Nick Mancini Jr. pick me up at the airport."

"I got outfoxed on that one, and that doesn't happen too often." He held up his hands again as I started to speak. "Let me explain what happened. I dropped by here last night to see Sonny again for a follow-up on our first conversation. He was busy. He said he didn't have time to talk to me, but why didn't I come back by this morning. Just before I called him this morning to get a firm time, Wade Garner called to tell me that you would be coming in alone but that he'd arranged a limo to pick you up. I mentioned that to Sonny because I was explaining that I wanted to see him before you arrived. In fact, he asked if I needed to pick you up at the airport, and I told him a car had been arranged. I didn't tell him which limo service. They must have checked around and found—"

"You should have anticipated that. And what about that message you sent telling me to come here?" I gestured at the club. "You might have considered the fact that when I got here I wouldn't know what to do. Instead of being out here to meet me, you were sitting back there having lunch."

I turned away from him and took a deep breath. I was standing out on the sidewalk, in full view of passersby, having an argument with a man I didn't even know. Blaming him for what had happened did nothing at all to change the fact that I had been an idiot. If I had ended up in a landfill somewhere, it would have served me right. *Great going, Lizabeth,* I told myself. *Hop right into a shiny limo with anyone who shows up wearing a chauffeur's uniform and holding a sign with your name on it.*

Quinn would love this.

Quinn was never going to hear about this if I could help it.

Behind me, Sheppard said, "It wasn't the food that kept me back there in Sonny's office. I wanted to have a quick look around while he was getting the door."

I turned around to face him. "Did you find anything?"

He shook his head. "I should have known that if there was anything I could get a glimpse of, he wouldn't have left me in there alone. But I was hoping he was careless."

"He may not be careless, but he is peculiar."

"He is that. But he's in his element running the club. Customers like him. He knows how to make sure they have a good time. In fact, you might describe it as a real lucky break for Sonny when his cousin Angela's husband got himself bumped off."

"Do you think Sonny had anything to do with the bumping?"

"There's nothing to connect him to it. Robert Montgomery confessed." Sheppard rubbed at his chin with the back of his hand. "Still it's the kind of situation that makes you wonder."

"Yes." I glanced back at the green door of the club.

Sheppard said, "My car's just down the street. Will you let me give you a ride back to your hotel?"

"May I see your picture ID, Mr. Sheppard?"

He chuckled. "You learn fast."

"I mean it about the ID," I said.

He reached into his jacket for his wallet. "Fake identification can be made or purchased."

"I know. But having been a gullible idiot once, I don't intend to accept anything else at face value."

"Exactly the way you need to think."

He handed me a business card, his driver's license, and a private investigator's license. They all identified him as Kyle C. Sheppard.

"Okay?" he said when I handed them back.

"Okay," I said.

He gestured toward the club. "Just for your information—not that you're likely to be inclined to come back—they have pretty good music here. Live every night with two supper shows. Blues, jazz, a little soul. Not the crowd you would expect either."

"No gangsters and their molls."

"No, just ordinary citizens. Some natives. Some tourists." He started down the sidewalk, half limping. "About Nico, he's kind of interesting. Come on, I'll tell you about him in the car."

CHAPTER · 11

Sheppard started talking as he maneuvered his midnight blue Caddie out of its space.

"A licensed bush pilot?" I said. "You're kidding."

"Nico started taking flying lessons after he finished high school. Kept on taking them while he was getting a business degree at Northwestern. Then he spent some time up in Alaska. Eight years. The last three, he and another bush pilot—a woman—had their own operation. When she was killed in a crash, he came back to Chicago. He bought into a charter company that flies hunters and fishermen around the Midwest and out as far as Colorado and Wyoming."

"So he's not involved at all in running his father's club?"

"The club's all Sonny's. Nico's mother, Angela, lives in Florida. Nico has an older sister too. She married and moved to Portland, Maine. Nico himself was a babe in his mother's arms when his father was killed. He never knew him, and he never seems to have had much interest in the family business."

"The club or the mob?" I grabbed for the dashboard as we accelerated.

"Either," Sheppard said. "But come to that, Sonny doesn't seem to have kept up with the old gang either. Of course, he was never a full-fledged gangster, according to what I'm told. Mancini threw him a bone now and then because he was his wife's cousin. But Sonny had to pay his rent with legit gigs—waiter, security guard. Shoe salesman was his last. This was while he was trying to break in as a stand-up comic."

"Didn't he just tell us that he was rotten at that?"

"From what I've heard, he was," Sheppard said. "But that didn't stop him from getting up on stage whenever anyone would give him the chance."

"Then Mancini was killed, and Sonny took over as manager of the club and has been for all these years. Are you telling me that both he and Nico are legitimate businessmen?"

Sheppard maneuvered around a delivery truck. "As to that, I can't say. All kinds of stuff might be going on beneath the surface." He threw me a lopsided grin. "You gotta remember, Professor, this is Chicago."

"Yes," I said. "Tell me again how we ended up having lunch with Sonny."

"He wanted to meet you. I thought it might be useful. I didn't know that

Nico was your chauffeur when I called the limo company and asked the driver to bring you to the club. I don't think Sonny did either. He got a call from Nico right after I called the limo service. He seemed more than a little put out about whatever he was hearing."

Sheppard slammed his foot on the brake and his big hand down on the horn. I grabbed for the dashboard again.

"Some people shouldn't have a driver's license," he said without rancor.

"So you think that Nico came up with the limo prank on his own?"

"Of course, Sonny might have been annoyed that he wasn't informed first." Sheppard glanced in his rearview mirror and swerved into the far right lane. "I want to take you by the courthouse. Criminal Court over on 26th and Cal. There's someone we need to see."

"Who?"

"Robert Montgomery's lawyer."

"Oh." I would have liked to stop at my hotel long enough to unpack before plunging right in. But I had only two days. "Does he know you're bringing me by?"

"She," Montgomery said. "I called her this morning. She said she could give us a few minutes if we can catch her between arraignments."

I braced my feet against the floor as we gained speed. I was beginning to suspect Sheppard had once been a New York City cab driver.

"Why do we need to see her?" I asked.

"Because Montgomery has changed his mind about talking to you. I'm hoping we can persuade his lawyer to speak to him and try to change it back again."

"When did you learn he'd changed his mind?" I said, keeping my tone level.

"Now, don't get upset again, Professor. I didn't know about this before you got on the plane. I called this morning to try to set up a time for you to see Montgomery. That's when Mrs. Duncan told me that he had changed his mind about talking to you."

"Who is Mrs. Duncan? His lawyer?"

"No, the lady whose house he's been living in for the past month or so."

"In the neighborhood that Sonny warned me about?"

"Sonny got that one wrong. Montgomery was living in the projects, but then after his last trip to the hospital, Mrs. Duncan brought him home with her."

"Is she related to him?"

"No, she's a church lady. She and some members of the congregation used to visit in prison, and she took on Montgomery as her special project. She's been watching over him since he got out. Like I said, after his last visit to the emergency room, she brought him to live with her and her son. A real nice lady. Owns a beauty shop."

"Did she say why Montgomery doesn't want to talk to me now?"

"She says he's been in a lot of pain and his doctor increased his medication.

The meds are making him even more cantankerous than usual. But I guess if you're dying, you're within your rights to be hard to get along with. That's why I didn't push it too hard when I went to see him."

"But when you talked to him again, when you told him that I was Becca's daughter, he said he would see me."

"We talked on the phone, not in person. But I am kind of surprised he's changed his mind about seeing you."

"Why?" We zigzagged out of our lane, around a car, and back in again, narrowly missing the bumper of a Jetta.

"Because when I told him you were Becca's daughter, he sounded eager to see you. Or as eager as a man who's having trouble breathing can be."

"Obviously, he had second thoughts."

"And that's why we're going to see his lawyer. She might have better luck with him than Mrs. Duncan did. Gwendolyn Parker is the lady's name, and she's one tough defense attorney. She sharpens her teeth on baby assistant DAs." Sheppard threw me another glance. "There's something else you need to know about Gwen. She thinks Montgomery was railroaded."

"She thinks his confession was coerced?"

"She thinks the police helped him along with it. When she came on the case, she tried to get him to make that claim."

"And he refused?"

"Yeah, and that's why we may have a bit of trouble persuading her to help. To be blunt, she thinks he took the rap for your mama."

"She thinks Becca killed Mancini?"

"She's convinced her client didn't, and your mama's at the top of her list of other suspects."

"Why—"

Sheppard's cell phone chose that moment to ring.

"Hold on a minute," he said to me. He picked it up from the console.

I turned to look out the window while he talked to someone who sounded like a client wanting to know how his case was going. Something about a missing wife.

CHAPTER · 12

Sheppard was chuckling when he put down his cell phone. "Got to give the woman credit. She told a good lie."

I didn't ask who or what lie. He told me anyway. "Husband calls her from work that afternoon. She says she's in the kitchen making a cake for his birthday party that night. So that evening, he comes home from work and the decorations are up, food's ready in the fridge, cake on the counter. A note says she had to run out and get some candles to go on the cake. So the guests start arriving, and the party gets under way. And people are wondering what's taking so long with that trip to the store for the candles. Except she's long gone by then. Must have baked that cake the day before, because the neighbors saw her leaving the house that morning right after he did. Wherever she was when he called her, it wasn't at home in the kitchen."

"Why did she leave him?" I said.

"He claims he doesn't know. Says he gave her everything she could want." Sheppard rubbed at his chin. "That could be true. Sometimes people just get tired of their lives. She could have gotten tired of being married."

"Then why would you help him track her down?"

"He's paying."

"And that's sufficient? You—"

"I do what I'm paid to do. I'll find her if I can. Whether I tell him that I've found her depends on what she tells me about the situation."

"So if she has a good reason for not wanting him to know where she is?"

"Then I give him his money back and forget where I saw her." He glanced in my direction. "Not much different from your situation, Professor Stuart. I'm being paid to help you find your mama, who might not want to be found."

"Are you saying that if you find her and she doesn't want to see me—"

"She may not. But then you're a daughter, not a husband. So I don't have to worry that I'm going to have it on my conscience because I found her and you beat her up or shot her."

We were out on the expressway now, and Sheppard was free to pass slower moving cars. He did. I held on.

"Getting back to what you were saying before your phone rang, Mr. Sheppard.

You said Montgomery's lawyer believes Becca killed Mancini. Why would she have done that?"

"Lover's quarrel is Gwen's theory."

"How did she—Becca—even end up working at Mancini's club? What was she doing between the time she arrived in Chicago and when Mancini was killed?"

"That's a four-year period," Sheppard said. "There are still some gaps, but I do know where she was living from March 1968, a few weeks after she started working at the club, to April of '69 when Mancini was killed. He was paying her rent on a real nice apartment."

"Where was she before that? What she was doing?"

"For at least the last two years before she met Mancini, she was working at a place called the Shack, owned by a former blues singer named Mama Lovejoy, now deceased. The Shack did down-home, soul-food cooking. Whites and blacks went there for the food and the blues. That was where Nick Mancini met your mama. She was waitressing, singing now and then."

"And he heard her and hired her?"

"That's the story I got," Sheppard said. He checked his rearview mirror in preparation for another lane change. "The Shack's been closed almost twenty years now. The current occupant of the building is a check-cashing operation. Before that it was a storefront church. I tried to track down a couple of other waitresses who were there when Becca was. One's dead. The other got married and left town. The cook's dead too. He was having some health problems and died that year, in '69."

"What about the people in the neighborhood? The people who went there?"

"Mama Lovejoy is who they remember. Her waitresses came and went. It didn't help to jog their memory to say Becca was pretty. Mama liked to surround herself with pretty young gals."

"Because they brought in male customers?"

"And because she was fond of a pretty woman herself."

"She . . . are you saying she was gay?"

"Some of the old-time blues women were—or swung both ways. Not to say that Mama made any special demands on her girls. From what I hear, she didn't fire them if they weren't willing to do more than be her eye candy. And she made sure none of her male customers abused them."

"But Becca left her to go to work for Nick Mancini."

Sheppard hit his horn twice at the car that had cut in front of us. "He probably paid a whole lot better. And he was willing to let her sing more than an occasional song." He slanted me a glance. "Sonny showed me one of the posters that Mancini had made up. You look like her."

"It would have been helpful if he had shown it to me too. I've never seen a picture of Becca."

"Never?" Sheppard said.

"Not of her as an adult. When she left, she took our family photo albums with her. The only pictures of herself that she left behind were two framed photos that my grandparents kept on the dresser in their bedroom. She was a baby in one and about five years old in the other."

"Well, take my word for it. You grew up to look like your mama. On the poster, she looked older than she was with all that makeup and the black gown. She had an orchid in her hair."

"Like Billie Holiday? Do you know if Becca used drugs?"

"She might have now and then. It went with the lifestyle. But no one has mentioned that she had a problem. The bartender would have brought that up."

"What bartender?"

"The one working at the Club Floridian back then. I tracked him down. His name's Albert Carterra."

"Is there any chance I could talk to him?"

"You could if he wasn't out of town. When I called this morning to see if I could bring you over, his wife said that he and a buddy had gone up to Michigan to do some fishing."

"It's odd that he left as I arrived. Do you think someone told him to go?"

"It might just be a coincidence," Sheppard said. "He was willing enough to talk to me. And the guy is stone sure a fishing nut. Lures and nets and tackle boxes in their own little corner in his garage. His wife said it was a spur of the moment trip. When you're retired, you can do that."

"I wonder how he got up to Michigan?"

"How he got there?"

"Maybe Nico sent him on one of his bush planes."

"That's something to look into," Sheppard said.

"What did Carterra say when you talked to him?"

"I asked him about that quarrel your mama and Mancini were supposed to have had that night. Asked him about what the police report said he'd heard."

"What did he hear?"

"Just enough to be tantalizing. Your mama walks in that evening before the club opens. Mancini's talking to Carterra about some special customers who are coming in that night. Some guys he wants to make sure have a good time. He's giving the bartender instructions when Becca sashays in, and Mancini breaks off his conversation with the bartender and grabs her by the arm." Sheppard broke off his conversation with me to eye the red Corvette that had come alongside us. "I've always wanted one of those," he said. Then he glanced at me and grinned. "Sorry. What was I saying?"

"Becca sashayed in and Mancini grabbed her arm."

"He drags her into the hallway while she's laughing and teasing him about being in a hurry to get her alone. Mancini curses and tells her that he came by her place the night before and she wasn't home. He says he sat there in his car for two bleeping hours."

"But she didn't come home?"

"And Mancini gave up and went home. By the time Becca shows up at the club that evening, he's been brooding about it all day. He can't even wait to get into his office before he's yelling at her, demanding to know where she was and what she was doing. He tells her, 'I know you've been up to something. You think you can play me. I know you—' This is when Robert Montgomery gets heroic and tries to step in between them."

"This is the argument that Mancini and Montgomery are supposed to have had?"

"The start of it anyway. Montgomery tells Mancini to let Becca go. Mancini turns around and slugs him. He glares down at Montgomery there on the floor and tells him that he's fired. Then he grabs Becca again and hauls her into his office. But she's laughing while all this is going on."

"Laughing?"

"As Carterra put it, 'She was getting off on making Nick act like a maniac.'"

"Does he have any idea what happened in the office?"

"All he knows is that they were in there for a while. Maybe half an hour. Meanwhile, Montgomery is out front with Carterra, talking about how he ought to go in there. And Carterra's telling him he better be gone before Mancini comes out."

"But he stays?"

"He stays, and when Becca comes out, she's smiling like a sleek little cat who knows she's got nine lives. And she tells Montgomery that everything is cool. Tells him that Nick says he still has his job. And then she kisses Montgomery on his cheek 'for being so sweet' and tells Carterra to put some ice in a towel. She holds the towel on sweet Robert's nose herself."

"And Mancini?"

"Still in his office. He comes out when the customers he was expecting arrive. All smiles and good cheer."

"Umm, really?" I said.

"Yeah," Sheppard said.

"And that was it?"

"That was all the bartender witnessed. It was real busy that night. A couple was celebrating their anniversary with a bunch of their friends. Mancini's special customers were knocking back the booze and having a high old time. Then Becca does her show, and after that, Montgomery is up there on the stage alone, playing piano requests from the audience."

"And where was Becca? Did she stay after her show?"

"Carterra didn't see her after she left the stage. He says she usually went up to her dressing room on the second floor."

"The second floor? What else was up there? Did you ask?"

"I asked. He said a storage room and a studio apartment that Mancini used on the nights when he wanted to get away from both his women."

"What about Sonny? He told us he was there that night."

"According to Carterra, Mancini had given Sonny ten minutes to do his comedy routine. The audience was not impressed. Sonny drowned his sorrows at the bar while Becca was doing her show. Then he left."

We had exited from the expressway. At the red light, Sheppard braked. He sighed, and then he reached over and opened the console between us. He took out a cigar wrapped in cellophane. He contemplated it for a moment then put it back with another sigh. "Doctor doesn't like me smoking them."

"Your doctor's right," I said. "Getting back to the bartender, where was he when Mancini was killed?"

"Like I said, he was real busy until closing. Then he helps his last customer out the door and gets a big tip for pouring him into a taxi. He comes back inside and sees Montgomery sneaking out the back door. He goes into Mancini's office and finds him dead on the floor."

"What about Becca?"

The light changed, and Sheppard stepped on the accelerator. "He didn't see her leave. But he's pretty sure no one was in the club but him when he found Mancini. Nobody else was there when the cops came."

"So that exit in the hallway wasn't alarmed at the time?"

Sheppard shook his head. "A shipment of booze had been delivered through that door earlier that evening. It was warm that night, a balmy spring evening, and the door had been propped open with people stepping outside when they felt like a breath of fresh air."

We were driving through working-class neighborhoods now. I stared out the window at the people going about their business while I tried to put together what Sheppard had told me. He sat beside me, whistling under his breath, waiting for my next question.

I didn't have any more. His answers to the ones I had already asked had left me with too much to sort out.

We turned onto another street. A couple of blocks down, a massive, windowless, concrete block rose from the earth. The barbwire surrounding the structure gleamed in the sunlight.

"Division Eleven of Cook County Jail," Sheppard said. "High tech and maximum security. We're going to the courthouse here on your right."

He swerved toward a parked car. He threw his arm along the seat and looked back as he executed a perfect parallel park of the Caddie.

"Let's get inside and see if we can find Gwen," he said.

We were delayed at the security checkpoint when the guard found my disposable camera in my shoulder bag. She offered to let me take it back out to the car. Sheppard glanced at his watch, and I told her to keep it.

"Sorry about that," he said as we got in the elevator. "We don't want to miss Gwen."

"I can get another. I'd forgotten it was in my purse."

"Don't get your hopes up too much about this meeting. As I told you, she probably won't be sympathetic."

"I understand. All we can do is ask."

CHAPTER · 13

Gwendolyn Parker raised her gaze from the file in her hand when Sheppard called out, "Good afternoon, Ms. Parker."

She had her glasses balanced on the edge of her nose. She took them off and straightened her shoulders in her navy blue suit. The suit was no-nonsense, but she was wearing it with a softer navy and beige print silk blouse. She must have been 5'10", even without the three-inch heels on her navy pumps.

Sheppard performed the introductions. "Ms. Gwendolyn Parker," he said, nodding in my direction, "this is Professor Lizabeth Stuart."

Parker and I shook hands. She took her hand back and glanced at her diamond-studded watch. "I can give you five minutes. That's it."

"You know what we need, Gwen," Sheppard said. "Professor Stuart is Becca Hayes's daughter."

"Hayes?" I said. "What—"

"Sorry," he said. "That was the stage name your mama used."

"During the time she was entertaining at the Club Floridian," Parker said.

"Oh." I raised my chin and met her gaze. "Mr. Sheppard says you believe your client confessed to protect my mother."

"I think he confessed to a crime she committed, yes."

"Why would he do that?"

She looked down her nose at me. "Men—wet-behind-the-ears boys—in love can sometimes be damn fools. Your mother was the kind of young woman who played that for all it was worth."

"Did you ever meet my mother, Ms. Parker?"

"If I'd met her, *she* might have ended up in prison instead of that boy."

"Because you're convinced my mother killed Nick Mancini?"

"Someone did. It wasn't my client. And it was too amateurish for a mob hit."

"Amateurish how?"

"Mancini was killed with his own pruning shears."

"Pruning shears?" I said, startled.

"Nick Mancini grew flowering plants in his office. He kept the shears on a table beside the pots. Those shears were missing from his office, found in the alley outside. He was stabbed here." She clasped her left shoulder. "Here." She pressed her hand to the side of her neck. "Here." A hand to her chest. "And here." She pressed a hand against her stomach.

She shook her head. "Not a mob hit, Professor Stuart. Too haphazard. He lived long enough to get up from the floor and try to make it to his office door." She smiled, a twist of her lips. "He also had scratch marks on his face. The police weren't interested in those scratch marks. They had a confession."

"Some other woman . . . he had a wife. Maybe she—"

"His wife knew he was a dog. She was willing to look the other way as long as he provided for his family." Her eyes flashed with disdain. "Why should she kill him over *this* little mistress when she hadn't killed him over any of the others?"

"Maybe there was a third woman involved. Maybe he was cheating on his wife with someone besides Becca."

"We thought of that. We couldn't find that third woman."

"You really looked?" I said. "Public defenders rarely have the time to—"

Her eyes flashed again. "Robert Montgomery had a private attorney. His mother paid for one with her hard-earned money. I was that attorney's intern. We did everything we could to defend our client."

"Then you were involved from the beginning—"

"I knew Robert when he was still a college boy with a music degree from Fisk University. Before he was raped and beaten and abused and forced to kill to stay alive." Her lips curled. "Your mother did that to him."

I forced myself not to look away. "You seem very involved in this case, Ms. Parker."

"I hate losing," she said. "I hate seeing a good life wasted. A good black man's life wasted. And for your information, when I was a public defender, I worked my ass off for my clients then too."

"I'm sorry. I didn't mean to offend you," I said. "I would like to meet with Mr. Montgomery."

"Why?"

"He said he wanted to see me."

"I guess he changed his mind."

"But if you would speak to him, he might change it back. I want to ask him about my mother."

"There's nothing he can tell you about your mother."

"How do you know that?" I said. "I'm sorry he went to prison if he was innocent. But you still haven't told me why you think my mother killed Nick Mancini."

"She was sleeping with him. He was a bad-tempered, abusive bastard. I'm sure he gave her reason enough."

"Maybe he gave some other people reason enough too."

"That's entirely possible. But my client went to prison for your mother." She glanced at her watch. "Your time's up. I have an arraignment."

"Wait!" I reached out my hand to her. "Please—will you ask him to see me?"

"No, I won't. He's dying. He has the right to die in peace." She gave me one final glance and then strode away toward the open door of the courtroom.

I looked at Sheppard. "I didn't handle that very well, did I?"

"She had already made up her mind," he said. "Stubborn woman once she makes up her mind."

"I've heard that about myself. Do you think Becca did it, Mr. Sheppard?"

He whistled through his teeth. "Like Gwen said, Mancini probably gave your mama a reason or two. But, then again, it could have been his wife. Maybe she took all the stuff she was willing to take off him. Or maybe it was Sonny. Or somebody else we don't know about. The bartender said Mancini had been kind of jumpy for a couple of weeks, thought someone was watching his house and that he was being tailed."

"But Robert Montgomery confessed. If he did that because of Becca, because he thought she did it—"

"Or maybe he confessed because he did do it." Sheppard gestured back in the direction we'd come, and as we started walking, he added, "Either way, I don't hold your mama responsible for Montgomery. If he was innocent, she wasn't there when he opened his mouth and said he did it."

"But you said that Ms. Parker thought the police might have coerced his confession."

"They might have. If that's what happened, if the cops pressured him into confessing and left him too scared to take it back, then it's even less your mama's fault."

"That's comforting."

"This isn't one of those situations where there's a whole lot of comfort to be found."

"Not a whole lot," I said.

We waited for the elevator in silence until he said, "Did I tell you that I was born and spent the first fourteen years of my life in Memphis, Tennessee? I'm still a Southern boy at heart."

I tried to rally to his small talk. "I thought I detected a trace of an accent."

"I grew up loving the blues. I wish I could have heard your mama sing."

"I'm sure it would have been interesting," I said. "Do you think our church lady, Mrs. Duncan, might be persuaded to try again to get Montgomery to see me?"

"We can ask. But we don't want to bother her at her place of business. The last time I did that, she didn't appreciate it. I'll call her tonight and see if we can come over tomorrow."

"Okay." I had struck out with Gwendolyn Parker. I would let Sheppard negotiate with Mrs. Duncan.

CHAPTER · 14

Sheppard popped in a Wynton Marsalis CD for the ride back downtown.

I was thinking about how Nick Mancini had been killed with pruning shears. "What was that about Nick Mancini growing flowers in his office? Did he have some kind of Dion O'Bannion complex?"

Sheppard shot me a look. "So you know about Dion O'Bannion?"

"I'm a crime historian," I said. "O'Bannion was a gangster and also a florist. Al Capone had him killed in his own flower shop."

"Shot as he was shaking hands with the hit men. And you guessed right about Mancini."

"You mean he really did—"

"According to the bartender—the one who used to work at the club—Mancini was a spiffy dresser," Sheppard said. "He attended a meeting of the boys one day, wearing a flower in his lapel. One of his rivals makes a crack about Dion O'Bannion. Mancini takes it as a dare to prove he's not scared to flaunt the O'Bannion curse."

"So he starts growing flowers in his office."

"Better than that. He goes out and buys part interest in a flower shop."

"Just like O'Bannion."

"Of course, the flower shop also happened to be a nice legitimate place to funnel some of his ill-gotten gain."

I braked along with Sheppard as we came within inches of the bumper of the car that turned in front of us. Then I said, "Maybe Mancini should have taken the O'Bannion curse seriously."

Sheppard changed lanes, then he said, "Could be one of Mancini's associates decided to send a message about that curse."

"But Gwen Parker said it was too haphazard for a mob hit."

"Gwen's focused on those scratches on his face. The scratches and the stabbing aren't necessarily related."

"No, I suppose they don't have to be." I let go of the dashboard and tugged at the twisted strap of my shoulder bag. "What I really want to know is, what's up all of a sudden with flowers?"

"Flowers?" I felt his questioning glance. "What—?"

"Nothing . . . I was just thinking about that orchid you said Becca wore in her hair."

I didn't want to get into the story about Ray Nathan and his wife-inspired mayhem. But I really didn't like this murder-with-pruning-shears twist. Not after what Nathan had done to Hester Rose's flowers.

Flowers kept popping up. And that goose was walking over my grave.

Hester Rose wouldn't have approved of Mancini. She might have liked to do him in with his own pruning shears if she had known about what was going on between him and her daughter. But I couldn't imagine my grandmother getting on a train to come to Chicago and kill him.

It wasn't something I could imagine Walter Lee doing either.

Not that my four-year-old's memory could provide either one of them with an alibi. It was simply a matter of knowing what someone you loved was capable of doing.

What was probably bothering me was that it was all too Freudian. Becca had fled Drucilla and the flower-growing mother she couldn't get along with. She had come to Chicago, where she'd taken up with a flower-growing gangster with whom her relationship also had been tempestuous.

That gangster had ended up stabbed with pruning shears. And my long-lost mother had means, opportunity, and maybe a motive. She was Gwen Parker's prime suspect.

I pondered all of that while Sheppard drove. He left me alone with my thoughts.

When he pulled up to the curb in front of my hotel, I reached for my door handle. "Thank you for all your help today, Mr. Sheppard. I'll be waiting to hear from you about Mrs. Duncan."

"Hold on a minute." He rubbed at his chin. "Getting back to what happened this morning. You don't need to bother to call Wade. I'll call him myself and fill him in on what happened with Nico."

"No, please don't do that."

"What do you mean, 'don't do that'? The man's writing my check. And I screwed up."

"If you're on Wade Garner's payroll, he must consider you competent."

"I am competent. I've got over twenty-five years of experience in law enforcement and security. Had my PI's license going on fifteen years."

"Exactly. So obviously the mishap with Nico was not something even a competent investigator could have predicted. It wasn't your fault."

Sheppard stared back at me. "Woman, you've sure changed your tune since you were ripping me up one side and down the other out in front of the club."

"Did you learn that expression in Memphis, or do they use it up here too?"

He didn't return my smile. I tried again. "How long have you worked for Wade Garner, Mr. Sheppard?"

"I don't work for him. At least, not full-time for his company. Wade and I go back a long way. He gives me some freelance business now and then when he has an assignment that needs doing in the Chicago area."

"Then there's no problem. I'm your client, and I'm satisfied with how you're handling this particular assignment. What happened this morning is between us."

"Between us, is it? I think you'd better tell me why you don't want Wade to know about this morning."

"It's not Wade I'm concerned about. If you tell him, he'll tell John Quinn, the man I'm involved with. They're good friends."

"So that's why Wade told me to put extra effort into this one. This man of yours, why did he let you come up here alone?"

It was not the time to point out that Quinn didn't "let" me do anything. "He couldn't get away because of his job, and I don't want him to worry about me. I'll only be here until Wednesday afternoon. I think between the two of us, we can make sure that I avoid any more mishaps, don't you?"

"Couple of problems with that. First off, I like to keep things on the up-and-up. Second, related to the first, Wade gives me two or three assignments a year, and he pays me good money. If I screwed something up, he has the right to know."

"I respect your integrity, Mr. Sheppard. But couldn't you wait and put it in your report to him?"

"That won't pass muster if something else goes wrong. If something happens to you and I hadn't warned him about a potential problem—"

"Come on, you don't really think Nico and Sonny would do anything to me. You said they're legitimate businessmen."

"I said they *seem* to be legitimate businessmen."

"Well, even if they aren't—especially if they aren't—why would they risk attracting police attention over this?"

"Maybe they have their own reasons not to want you poking around in Mancini's murder."

I shook my head. "Didn't you hear Sonny assure me that he wants to help me find my mother?"

"Yeah, that soft spot he has about mamas." Sheppard tapped his fingers on the steering wheel and stared in front of him. "All right," he said. "I'll call Wade tomorrow around noon. That'll give you maybe until late tomorrow afternoon or evening before your man's on the phone to you about it. And since you'll be leaving the next day anyway—"

"If that's the best you can do—"

"That's the best. I'll give you a call after I speak to Mrs. Duncan."

"If I'm not in, please leave a message. I have a friend who lives here. We may get together for dinner."

"I guess that's okay. You might try to make it an early evening."

"I intend to. It's been a long day."

"Hold on a minute." He took out his wallet and handed me one of his business cards. "Keep it this time. You may need to reach me."

"Thank you," I said.

In the ground-floor lobby, the bellman from my first arrival greeted me and rang for the elevator. The old-world elegance of the main lobby extended to the desk clerk, who wore a blue blazer with a crest on the pocket. She checked me in and sent me on my way with a minimum of fuss.

My luggage arrived as I was staring out the window at the view of Chicago eleven floors below. I unpacked, washed my face, and brushed my teeth.

Then I tried calling Tess. She was away from her desk or on another line, according to her voice mail message. I waited for the tone.

"Hi, it's Lizzie. I'm here. I'm going out for a walk. I'm in serious need of fresh air, and there's an exhibit I want to see. I should be back here by around five. How about dinner tonight?" I left the hotel number and my extension.

I changed into a sundress and sandals and smeared sunscreen on the exposed skin. Then I found my sunglasses and headed for the door. Maybe fresh air would dull the throb that had settled in behind my left temple. The two aspirins I had swallowed weren't doing a thing.

Aspirin was not designed to deal with a stress headache caused by learning that your mother might have killed a man.

CHAPTER · 15

The sun warmed my face as I walked along North Michigan. Tiny droplets of water were in the air. Before I could figure out where they were coming from, I had walked out of it. I strode along, moving with the pedestrian traffic.

A young black woman standing on the corner held out a newspaper toward me. "*Urban Voice*. Get your *Urban Voice*."

I was about to shake my head when I heard a baby whimper. The woman turned to look behind her and made a shushing, comforting sound. The baby kicked and cooed in his carriage.

"How much is it?" I said, digging into my shoulder bag. "Give me two, please."

Farther down the street, a young man was selling the same newspaper. He had a catchy rap—"Doing this until I can do something better"—but I shook my head and held up my two copies.

When I got to the corner of E. Randolph, a brass band was playing. Five guys had their trumpets swinging. Another guy was peddling their CDs to the people who stopped to listen. I didn't stop. What I wanted to do was have a look at the blues exhibit that I had read about on the Chicago tourism Web site. As a destination for my walk, this one made sense. It was too late to go to the Chicago Historical Society today to search the archives for anything on Nick Mancini, so I might as well see what I could find about Chicago blues. Becca had been a blues singer.

In my research on crime and culture, I'd had occasion to examine the lyrics of old blues songs. I was interested in references to violence, particularly violence between men and women. And I had been looking at the link between blues music and prison. Actually, I had started with slave work songs and looked at how they had been transformed into music sung on the chain gang. I'd also spent some time looking at musicians like Lead Belly, who had spent time in prison.

But I had come late to an appreciation of blues as an art form. I had not heard that type of music in my grandparents' house when I was growing up. My grandfather, Walter Lee, had undoubtedly indulged his more liberal musical taste when his travels as a sleeping-car porter brought him to Chicago or took him south to Memphis or New Orleans. When I came with him on that first trip to Chicago, he and his friend Calvin stashed me with a neighbor lady that Saturday night while they went out to the clubs. When I pouted about not being allowed to come along, he told me clubs were for grown people, adding that my grandma would skin him alive if he let me get anywhere near one.

Hester Rose had been among those respectable black folk who believed the blues were "low down" and "the devil's music." She hadn't cared that much for jazz or Motown either. Music in our house tended to be Sunday morning gospel on the radio.

But Becca had worked for Mama Lovejoy, a former blues singer, before she went to work for Nick Mancini. Did Becca learn about the blues from Walter Lee? Did he ever bring her on a train to Chicago, as he had me?

There was so much I didn't know about their relationship. Walter Lee had rarely mentioned his daughter.

The exhibit had been set up across the street from the Cultural Center in two rooms laid out like honky-tonks. It took me about half an hour to make my way through. There were guitars, memorabilia, and other artifacts from the history of blues in Chicago. The exhibit featured a timeline of the migration of blues men and women from the South to the urban metropolis.

My luck was in. Among the photographs was one of Mama Lovejoy sitting at a table between two blues musicians who, according to the caption, had dropped by to enjoy her down-home cooking at the Shack. The black-and-white photo showed a smoky-looking room that conjured up the sounds and smells of a Southern honky-tonk—music and laughter and the spicy aroma of chicken or fish frying. Mama Lovejoy was wearing a fringed silk dress and sparkling headband. Her grin displayed the gap between her front teeth. The two blues musicians were grinning too. Glasses and a bottle sat on the table.

I leaned closer and noticed a young girl of eleven or twelve in the background. She was wearing a dress that drooped on her skinny body. She was standing there beside the bar, staring toward the viewer. Who was she and what was she doing there in the background?

If food was served at the Shack, children probably had been allowed. Maybe she was the daughter of one of the staff who worked there.

I studied the photograph a moment longer and then looked around, hoping for more of the Shack. But that was it. I finished my circuit through the exhibit and decided to go across the street to the Cultural Center and see what the gift store had on blues in Chicago.

I found several books on the blues, but only one of them made passing reference to the Shack and Mama Lovejoy. I made up for my disappointment by treating myself to a couple of CDs, classic blues from Bessie Smith and Alberta Hunter.

Back out on Michigan Avenue, I walked another block and then crossed the street because I wanted to see the river from the bridge. A young woman sat in a folding chair, offering passersby a brochure for a river cruise.

I turned away from the pleasant prospect of the river in sunshine. I was hungry and remembered the hamburger place I'd found the last time I was in Chicago. It was a couple more blocks down.

On the way, I stopped to look in the window of a sports and novelty store. Quinn was a devout baseball fan. I considered the black cap with "White Sox Est. 1901" in white letters. But for Quinn the significant date would be 1919, the year of the scandal when the White Sox were alleged to have thrown the World Series. Quinn had mentioned once in passing that his father had used the White Sox scandal to illustrate the consequences of unethical behavior and poor sportsmanship.

Quinn's father had ended his military career as a brigadier general, and from the little Quinn had said about him, the man had treated his son like one of his soldiers. But Quinn might still enjoy adding the cap to his collection. I went in and bought it and then went next door to Callahan's Burgers.

Callahan's was a classy hamburger joint. Duke Ellington's "Take the 'A' Train" provided background music for the tiny train moving on miniature el tracks suspended from the ceiling against a city mural. Chrome tables and chairs provided seating.

I ordered my hamburger medium-well with lettuce, tomato, and mayo and sat down at one of the tables to wait. The hamburger, when it came, was hot, moist, and delicious. It was the best thing that had happened since I stepped off the plane this morning. I didn't count the limo ride that Wade Garner had sprung for, since Nico Mancini had been behind the wheel.

I still wasn't sure what Nico had hoped to accomplish with his ruse. Had he been trying to see what I was like when I was off-guard and unaware, so that he could size me up? Or had it been a warning about how easy it was to get to me if he and his cousin Sonny wanted to? I couldn't believe that he would have gone to all that trouble simply to see the daughter of the woman with whom his father had been involved. All he had to do was come to the club and see me there.

When I had finished my burger and a large bottle of water, I asked where the restroom was. The waitress gave me a key on a piece of twisted wire. The restroom was beside a back door that stood open. The sign on the restroom door said, "Please understand our restroom is only for our customers." A polite "no" to tourists who weren't willing to spend money and to the homeless who had none.

Outside again, I turned back toward the hotel. The young woman handing out brochures for the river cruise was still sitting there. Two guys—one black, one white, both with shaved heads and wearing blue jeans and black leather vests over bare chests—had stopped to talk to her. The white guy, who also had a nose ring, was flirting with her.

"We'll have to do this tomorrow," he told her with a drawl that came from somewhere below the Mason-Dixon line.

Well, Southerners traveled too, and nose rings and black leather had made it down our way.

"Are you going to be here tomorrow?" he asked the young woman.

When she said no, he clutched his heart, pleading his dismay.

She handed me a brochure while the two of them continued their banter. The river cruise was ninety minutes long. I needed perspective, and being on water always gave me that. Quinn claimed it would work even better if I could swim. I didn't want to swim; I wanted the sensation of being on the water with the rocking of the boat and the spray in my face.

I had time to take the 3:30 cruise and make it back to the hotel not too long after five. If Tess called before I got back, she would leave a message.

I went down the steps to the dock and bought my ticket. People had already begun to queue up. I claimed my spot.

I had settled in my seat on board when the two guys in the leather vests arrived and took seats across the aisle from me. The white one looked over at me and grinned. "How ya doing?"

"Fine, thanks."

"I'm Earl," he said. "This here is Percy."

Percy glanced at him as if Earl's chattiness was beginning to irritate him. Then he looked over at me and nodded.

Earl grinned. "Percy's bashful around girls."

Percy scowled and turned to look at the scenery on his side of the boat. I did the same on mine.

The breeze was warm as we moved through the canyon created by steel and concrete. The engine throbbed, sending vibrations through the boat. Jason, our tour narrator, told us that we would be going through the locks to Lake Michigan, passing under the movable drawbridge. As we went by the Sheraton Hotel, he explained that with all new construction, builders were required to provide a river walk so that pedestrians could enjoy the view.

There was some shade under the boat's awning, but as we moved, the angle of the sun shifted. I considered getting out the cap I had bought for Quinn and putting it on to protect my head from the sun. But if I put it on, there was sure to be a gust of wind that would send it flying into the water.

As we slid down the river, Jason began to tell us about the high-priced real estate we were passing. Around me, cameras began to click. That was when I remembered the disposable camera that I had surrendered to the security guard at the courthouse. I made a mental note to pick up another one. I was not in Chicago to play tourist, but later I might want to snap a photo of something related to Becca or Nick Mancini.

I turned to look around me at my fellow sightseers. According to the sign, the boat had a 125-person capacity. About three-fourths of the seats under the awning were occupied, and more passengers sat out on the open deck up front. But from what I could see, the boat pilot, whom Jason had introduced as Andrew, and Percy and I were the only black people on board. That observation on my part was prompted by Jason's lapse into boosterism. He assured us that "Even the ghettos are clean here in Chicago."

As we moved out of the Chicago River into Lake Michigan, Jason asked those of us sitting by the railing to keep all body parts inside the boat to avoid being scraped by the concrete buoy. I removed my hand from the railing.

I half listened as he rambled on about the sewage system and about the fact that Chicago had more harbors than any other city in America. A water taxi passed us, and Jason pointed out the remnants of the naval air station where George Bush, the father, had done his military training during World War II. He told us about the lighthouses, the renovations on the marine police house, and the water filtration plant that gives Chicago "the best drinking water in the world." He either really loved his city or was a damn good actor.

Out on Lake Michigan, the aqua green water—"overspray" according to Jason—sloshed against the boat. I had one of those moments when I considered the foolhardiness of being out on a boat when I didn't know how to swim. I looked back for reassurance at the sign that announced that 125 adult life pre-servers were on board.

I thought of how vast this expanse of water must have seemed in the 1770s when Jean Du Sable, a black fur trader, had come up the Mississippi River and eventually founded the settlement that would one day become the city of Chicago. But he hadn't been alone. In the first marriage performed in the settlement, he had solemnized his union with Catherine, a Potawatomi Indian woman.

As fascinating as I found Chicago history, I had settled into a sun-induced trance by the time we started back. The sun was a blurred ball of golden-pink light. The sky was pale too, washed out by the sun. We passed Navy Pier, which Jason said received more than eight million visitors a year. The Ferris wheel stood out, tempting those who enjoyed being suspended in midair. I was not in that group.

But Gretchen, the twelve-year-old girl to whom Jason asked us to sing "Happy Birthday," might well enjoy it. She looked young and fearless, relishing, rather than being embarrassed by, the attention of her fellow passengers.

Actually, seen from the river, the Ferris wheel was rather striking. The red seats looked like jewels in a silver filigree setting.

I touched Quinn's ring on the chain around my neck. Maybe I should take it off and put it on my hand in case someone tried to snatch it. But I still didn't know which hand. If it was going to be the left, I should tell him first and give him the opportunity to change his mind, particularly if it turned out there was a problem with my eyes. When I got back to the hotel, I would ask to put the ring in a safety deposit box.

I glanced over at Earl and Percy. They looked bored. Obviously, flirting with the blonde handing out the brochures was more fun than sitting for ninety minutes while Jason rattled on about Chicago history, architecture, and harbor life.

Well, we were almost done. I would be glad to get back to shore too. The cruise hadn't been as soothing as I had hoped it would be. We chugged past the Wrigley Building, and Jason told us the story of how Wrigley had started out selling soap and baking soda and then switched to making chewing gum. He called our attention to the triangular shape of the Swissôtel Chicago. Percy yawned.

As we headed back through the canyon formed by skyscrapers, the river had a dank smell. But up above were buildings worth millions of dollars.

"Nooo!" A child uttered a high-pitched complaint.

"Stop whining! Stop it this instant."

Gretchen, the birthday girl, smiled as her mother yanked her little brother up from the deck and shoved him back in his seat. Her father looked on but didn't interfere. Across the aisle from me, Percy had leaned forward. He was scowling at the woman. A few minutes later, the boat docked, and Jason thanked us for sharing a "river adventure."

I was stepping across the ramp when I heard a woman cry out, "My camera!" It was Gretchen's mother. She was leaning over the railing. Apparently her camera had gone into the water.

"Sorry," Percy said. "I tripped."

"That camera cost me five hundred freaking dollars!"

"That much?" he said. "I sure hope it was insured."

She said something about his ancestry that should have blistered her children's ears. He shrugged and turned away.

Jason scrambled to get a hook to try to rescue her camera. She continued to rant, glaring at her husband, who stood there with a hand on each child's shoulder. Gretchen looked smug.

Percy's pal, Earl, was grinning when they came off the boat. Percy's expression didn't give anything away, but I suspected his stumble hadn't been an accident.

I climbed back up the steps to the street and headed in the direction of my hotel. I heard laughter behind me and glanced back to see the two of them. Earl waved, but I didn't wave back.

I was being paranoid. Just because they looked like they should be riding with a motorcycle gang instead of taking a river cruise was no reason to think they had taken the cruise because I did. The kind of wise guys that Nico or Sonny might send to watch me were not likely to be strolling around bare-chested in black leather vests or making themselves conspicuous by taking action against offensive mothers.

I resisted sneaking glances to see if they were still behind me during the fifteen-minute walk back to my hotel. When I looked back before going through the downstairs entrance, they were nowhere in sight.

CHAPTER · 16

"You're asleep, aren't you? Get up," Tess said in the tone she'd used to roust me out of bed for early morning classes back in college.

"Hi, I was just having a nap." I clutched the telephone receiver and leaned sideways to look at the clock. It was 6:18. "Are you still at work?"

"Just finishing up. We'll be by to pick you up."

"You and Elena?"

"No, Elena's with her sitter. We're going to be out past her bedtime."

I yawned. "Excuse me. So who is the 'we'?"

"Someone I want you to meet. His name's Luis. He's my guy."

"You have a guy?"

"Guess I didn't mention that, huh?"

"I think I would have remembered that."

"Well, I'm bringing him along. Can you be ready by seven?"

"Sure. See you then."

I rolled over and swung my feet to the floor. Suddenly, Michael, Tess's ex-husband and the cause of our strained relationship, was a nonissue. She might have mentioned she had a new man in her life.

Mumbling to myself, I stripped off my wrinkled sundress and headed for the bathroom. Of course, what I was really irritated about was that I wanted to call Quinn, the man in *my* life, and I couldn't. If I called, he would ask how things were going and I would have to be evasive. He always saw right through my attempts at evasion.

I had not liked Michael. I suppose that was why Tess looked as uncomfortable as a teenager bringing a boy home to meet her parents when she introduced me to Luis Mendoza. She said he was a photojournalist with the *Chicago Mirror-Examiner*. He was downright photogenic himself with golden skin, dark eyes, and a smile that should have come with a warning about dazzle power. His raven black hair winged back from a widow's peak. He had a small gold stud in one ear. In his tan jacket, beige tee shirt, and khakis, he looked *GQ* elegant but without the old-money arrogance that had been a part of Michael's style.

When Luis greeted me with a big bear hug, I knew he meant it. I didn't feel at all awkward about being swept up in the arms of a stranger.

That was just as well, since the man weighed at least 200 pounds and had to be two or three inches taller than Quinn's six-one.

When he released me, I looked over at Tess. She was wearing that same glow she had worn when she fell head over heels in love with Michael.

Her gaze met mine, and the glow dimmed. Well, heck, did she think I would just automatically disapprove of Luis because she was crazy about him.

I grinned at her and fanned my face with my hand. "You're lucky that I already have Quinn."

It wasn't what she expected me to say. She laughed. Maybe that wall between us was beginning to crumble.

We went to dinner on Division Street in the heart of the Puerto Rican community. I twisted around for another look at the abstract steel flag jutting out over the entry to the Paseo Boricua. According to my Chicago guidebook, it had a twin at the other end of the street.

Luis backed his Land Rover into a parking spot that had just been vacated. "It's too bad you missed the fiesta last weekend, Lizzie. That would have given you a real sense of the street."

"Elena loved the parade," Tess said.

We walked down the street, and Luis made a sweeping gesture with his hand, indicating the businesses we were passing. "The Paseo can provide for most of the needs of our community. From nail spas to law offices."

Tess pointed at another building. "That's the family center. And across the street are the offices of the state representatives and a county commissioner."

"I'm impressed," I said.

When we walked in, Luis was greeted with a hug and a handshake by the maitre d'. We were shown to a table with a view of the street and the bandstand, where Luis said merengue musicians would play later. The restaurant was upscale with salsa music, lanterns, and colorful tablecloths.

We looked over the menu and agreed to share several appetizers. Then we turned to the entrées. I decided to have the *pernil asado*, pork shoulder marinated in a blend of vinegar, garlic, oregano, and other spices and roasted. It sounded wonderful. Tess ordered *chicken mofongo*, chicken breast stuffed with plantain, and Luis chose the grilled tuna.

The appetizers came and we devoured them as if we hadn't ordered entrées and would probably want dessert. Or at least I would want dessert. I glanced around at the other customers, who also seemed to be enjoying the cuisine. The cross-section of people reminded me of the Orleans Café back in Gallagher. Food encouraged diversity.

When I made that observation out loud, Luis said, "The Paseo is definitely attracting interest from people outside the community. That's a good thing. We like being described as 'a cultural and economic phenomenon.'" He sighed, looking around. "But what we have to worry about now is gentrification. We don't want this area to become another Lincoln Park. We don't want to build it up and then have non-Hispanics move in and supplant us, because it's a good place to live."

Tess nodded in agreement. "We need our own place where our culture can be on display."

"The folks in Bronzeville seem to have some of the same issues," I said. "When I was on the Internet, I saw a couple of articles about the efforts they're making to bring back the black neighborhoods in South Chicago."

Luis glanced at Tess. She slid a glance back in his direction.

"What?" I said.

Luis smiled. "Not that we aren't enjoying this chat about community development, but—"

"But," Tess said, "I was telling Luis about how you're here to look for your mother. We hadn't quite agreed on whether we should bring it up over dinner if you didn't."

"If you'd rather not discuss it—" Luis said.

"But Luis knows lots of people, Lizzie. I thought there might be something he could do to help."

Luis said, "Tess says that you have a private investigator on the case, so I don't want to intrude."

"You aren't intruding. I appreciate the offer, and I would be grateful for any help. I just don't know what you can do."

"Why don't you tell us what information you have?" Luis said. "As much as you feel comfortable sharing."

Before I could speak, the waiter arrived with our entrées. Conversation lulled as we waited for him to leave.

After I had taken a bite of succulent pork, I said, "I can tell you what Kyle Sheppard, the PI, has found so far. But I'd better start from the time I arrived in Chicago." Between bites, I told them about my limo ride in from the airport, followed by the message that had brought me to the Club Floridian. I told them about Sonny and his invitation to lunch and described his office and Precious, the cat, and Sheppard.

Then I paused, knowing what I said next was bound to get a reaction from Tess. "And while we were eating lunch and chatting about Becca, the limo driver walked in and helped himself to an egg roll. That's when I found out he was Nick Mancini's son, and—"

Tess put down her fork with a click and stared at me. "Lizzie!"

"But as far as Sheppard can tell," I said, "Nico is a legitimate businessman."

"Legitimate businessmen don't pull those kinds of stunts," Tess said.

"I have to agree with Tess," Luis said. "He sounds like someone you need to watch."

"Watch?" Tess said. "She needs to stay away from him. This mobster threatened her."

I couldn't help it. I felt obliged to defend Nico on that one. "Tess, we don't know that he's involved with the mob just because his father was. It's not hereditary, you know. And he didn't actually threaten me. He just picked me up at the airport without telling me who he was."

"That was an implied threat," Tess said. "How do you get yourself into these situations, Lizzie?"

"Ladies," Luis said.

"Do you want to hear the rest of this or not?" I asked Tess.

Luis reached out and caught her hand. He carried it to his lips and gave her a smile. "Of course, we do, Lizzie. Please go on."

"Yes, go on," Tess said. "I know it's not your fault that these things happen."

"Thank you," I said. "After we left the Club Floridian, Sheppard took me over to the courthouse to meet with Robert Montgomery's lawyer."

"Robert Montgomery is the piano player, right?" Luis said. "The man you came to Chicago to see?"

I nodded. "Except he has changed his mind about seeing me."

"Changed his mind?" Tess said.

"That's what Mrs. Duncan, the woman who has been taking care of him, told Sheppard. That's why we went to see his lawyer, to see if she would help." I took a sip of my club soda. "She wouldn't."

"Why not?" Luis said.

I told them what Gwendolyn Parker had said about her client and my mother. When I was done, Tess and Luis sent each other sideways glances.

"You know," Tess said, "maybe it's better if you don't find out anything more. I mean, maybe there are things about Becca you'd be better off not knowing."

I looked back at her, thinking about how to reply. I knew she loved me and was thinking of my well-being. But she had never been able to understand what it was like not to be surrounded by loving kin. Hester Rose had been an only child, so had Walter Lee. They were my only family. Now they were both dead.

How could I explain that to Tess, who had three sisters and both parents? When you looked at an Alvarez family photo, you could see the big brown eyes and lush lashes, the dark, glossy hair echoed in each of the sisters. You could see what they would one day become in their mother's still-lovely face. You could see where they had gotten their determined chins and their laughing mouths when you looked at their tall, dignified father. It was all there in any photo of the six of them. It was there in the faces of the sisters' children and in the occasional baby pictures Tess had sent me of Elena.

As much as she loved me, Tess had never been able to understand what it was like not to be able to look into your parents' faces and see reflections of your own.

"You sound like Quinn," I said to Tess and smiled. "But I know too much now to go back to blissful ignorance."

Luis said, "So what's your next move?"

"I wait for Mr. Sheppard to call and tell me if Mrs. Duncan will try to persuade Robert Montgomery to see me."

"I suppose if the man's dying, you can't just barge in and demand to speak to him," Tess said.

Luis patted her hand. "I think Lizzie should save that as a last resort."

"Of course she should. I was only considering possibilities."

"If by Wednesday morning I still haven't gotten an invitation to stop by, I may just try that," I said. "Anyway, tomorrow I'm going to the Chicago Historical Society and see what, if anything, I can find there about Nick Mancini and mob activities here in Chicago back in the 1960s. There ought to be something in the newspaper files that— Dammit!"

"What?" Tess said.

"The police report on the Mancini murder investigation. Mr. Sheppard mentioned seeing it. I should have asked if I could get a copy."

Luis said, "And, if you'd like, I could mention the case to a few contacts and see if anyone has any thoughts."

"Thank you, I'd appreciate that. I'm sure Mr. Sheppard has been thorough, but maybe the people you know might have some other information."

"Consider it done."

I straightened in my seat. "Now, let's talk about something more pleasant. So, Tess, is being a travel show producer still better than living out of your suitcase?"

"Much. You know how I loved being a travel writer, but now I get to be involved in putting together features, and I still get to go home to my child every night."

"And your boyfriend," Luis said.

Tess smiled at him. "And my boyfriend." She shot me a glance. "Not that we actually live together. Luis is just around a lot."

"I'm trying to ease her into matrimony," he said.

"Oh," I said. "And are you going to be eased, Tess?"

She gave me a look. "I could ask you that same question."

"I haven't been asked."

"Really?" she said. "I've been wondering about that ring."

I looked down. Quinn's ring had slipped from beneath the summer scarf I had tied around my neck. It dangled there on its chain. I hadn't gotten around to putting it into the hotel safe.

"It's a ruby," I said.

"Yes, but why are you wearing it on a chain around your neck?" Tess asked.

"Because I haven't decided yet."

"Decided what?"

"Quinn said it was up to me to decide which hand I want to wear it on."

Tess said, "Don't do anything stupid."

"What would be stupid?" I said.

"Letting this whole Becca thing affect your decision," she said. "That would be stupid."

"Yes, ma'am." I turned to Luis. "Tess didn't answer my question, but I think you would be an excellent husband candidate."

He raised his glass to me. "Thank you, Lizzie. And I think John Quinn would be very lucky to have you."

"Now, if only we could all live happily ever after," I said.

The chill that brought gooseflesh to my bare arms must have been caused by a draft, a door being opened.

"What's wrong?" Tess said.

"Nothing." I picked up my glass. "Thank you both for a lovely evening, and may you have a long and happy life together."

When they dropped me off at the hotel, Luis got out of the car to open my door. He was about to walk me to the lobby, when Tess said, "I'll do it. I want to talk to Lizzie about tomorrow night."

Luis kissed me on the cheek. "Sleep well."

"Thank you. I had a wonderful time."

"I'll get back to you if my contacts have anything useful."

He stood by the car as we went into the hotel. Tess stopped as the bellman greeted us. She pulled me to one side.

"What about tomorrow night?" I said.

"Dinner at my house."

"I'd love to. I want to meet Elena."

She looked uncomfortable. "I would have insisted you stay with us, except—"

"Except we were still in our awkward stage?"

She pushed back a stray strand of the dark hair that she had let grow down to her shoulders. "No, it wasn't that. It's . . . uh . . . about Luis."

"What about him?"

"He's around a lot. I wanted you to meet him before—"

"In case, we didn't like each other."

"You and Michael—"

"I won't mention his name, if you don't."

"Deal."

We hugged and she waved as she went back out the door to Luis.

I went to my room and flopped down on my king-size bed.

It was almost 10:00 Chicago time and an hour later in Gallagher. Quinn ought to be home by now. I reached for my shoulder bag and dug out the cell phone that he had reminded me to bring along. I propped the pillows up against the headboard and settled back.

Waiting until tomorrow when Wade called Quinn about Nico and the limo ride was only delaying the inevitable.

He picked up on the fourth ring.

"It's me," I said.

"Hi, me. How's it going?"

"I should ask you that. Anything on the rape?"

"Still investigating. The victim hasn't been able to give us much. A man, not too tall, grabbed her from behind and shoved a wet towel over her head. He dragged her behind one of the barricades near the field house and pushed her face into the grass, never spoke. What she remembered vividly was the way he smelled."

"How he smelled?"

"Sweat and chlorine."

"The chlorine would explain the wet towel—if he's been using the swimming pool in the rec center."

"That's our theory. Only problem is, we've got a long list of male students and faculty, not to mention alumni and guests, who were in the rec center last night. And no sign-up is required to use the swimming pool."

"What's the mood like on campus?"

"Calming down. I did a press conference to discuss campus safety procedures. I pointed out that this is the first sexual assault of its kind we've had on campus this year."

"I assume you're not counting date rapes," I said.

"You assume right. Those we can't do a heck of a lot about. I made that distinction. How are things going there?"

I wanted to spill out everything that had happened, but I said, "I had dinner with Tess. Guess what. She has a new man in her life."

I told him about Luis. I managed to stretch that out for several minutes. When I finally dwindled off, Quinn said, "So you and Tess have worked things out?"

"We're making real progress."

"Good. I'm glad to hear that. Did you hook up with Kyle Sheppard?"

"Yes, this morning. He introduced me to Nick Mancini's cousin-in-law Sonny Germano. Sonny has been running the club since Mancini was killed. We had lunch with him, and then Sheppard took me to the courthouse to meet Robert Montgomery's lawyer."

"Why?"

"Because Montgomery has changed his mind about talking to me. We were hoping his lawyer might persuade him to reverse his decision. But she blames

Becca for what happened to her client, so she won't help. And now I'm waiting to find out if Sheppard can get Mrs. Duncan, the churchwoman who took Montgomery in, to use her influence with him. But right now, everything's up in the air."

"Getting back to Nick Mancini's cousin. Did you say you had lunch with him?"

"Cousin-in-law. At the club. It was a little strange. Sonny said that he knew Nick had cheated on his wife, Sonny's cousin. But Sonny said that he himself was sentimental about mothers because his died when he was born, so he wants me to find mine."

"That's magnanimous of him."

"That's exactly what I told him. Speaking of being generous, Wade arranged for a limo to pick me up at the airport. But there was a slight glitch."

"What kind?"

"Well, just a small one. . . ."

When I finished telling him about having Nico as my substitute chauffeur, he said, much too calmly, "I suppose it would be a waste of time to ask you to get on a plane in the morning and come home."

"I can't."

"Then I'll call Wade and ask him to put someone else on the case, someone who can do a better job of protecting you than this Sheppard guy has been doing."

"No, Quinn, you can't do that. Mr. Sheppard didn't know what was going to happen."

"That's my point, Lizabeth. He was having lunch with this Sonny character while you were—"

"I happen to like Mr. Sheppard, Quinn. I want him to stay on the case."

"And I bloody well want you safe. If you won't come home—"

"I don't want you to ask Wade to fire Mr. Sheppard. He's a nice man, and he knows what he's doing. He has over twenty-five years of experience in law enforcement and security. And he's been a private investigator for over fifteen years."

"How old is this guy?"

"I don't know. I didn't ask. He's old enough to be experienced. And he knows Chicago and about the people we need to talk to."

"And he seems to be doing a bang-up job of arranging for you to see Robert Montgomery."

"He can't force Montgomery to see me. He's doing his best to arrange it. And as for this morning, meeting Sonny Germano was quite useful. Now I have a better sense of the players involved." I paused. "Sonny has a poster with Becca's photo."

"He does?"

"It's from when she was performing at the Club Floridian. He showed it to Mr. Sheppard."

"But he didn't show it to you when he was telling you how much he wanted you to find your mother?"

"Maybe he would have if Nico hadn't come in. I left rather abruptly after that." I tugged one of the pillows out from behind my back. "Mr. Sheppard says I look like Becca. Apparently she really could sing. Of course, she was also a mistress to a married mobster, and she may have killed him. But that's another story."

"Are you handling all of this okay?" Quinn said.

"I think so. What else is happening there? What about your vandalism investigation? The gang graffiti?"

"Nothing yet. We're keeping certain areas under surveillance."

"Be careful."

"I'm the chief. I sit in my damn office."

"Would you rather be somewhere else? I've been thinking about Wade's offer. The partnership—"

"That's something else we can discuss when you get home."

"If you're bored with Gallagher or tired of being a university police chief—"

"When you're in Gallagher, Lizabeth, it's hard to be bored. And when you're in Chicago, being driven around by the son of a dead mobster—"

"I love you too."

"I'm glad to hear that, but I'm still going to call Wade."

"But you won't ask him to take Mr. Sheppard off the case."

"I'll suggest Sheppard might need some backup."

"But you'll make sure Wade doesn't hurt his feelings—"

"Hurt his feelings? Lizabeth, you are in the middle of—" A ringing phone interrupted what he was going to say.

"I think that's your cell phone," I said.

"I hear it. I'll get back to you in the morning. Keep your door locked and stay out of trouble."

"I will do my best, Chief Quinn."

I let him go. There was no point in telling him about the pruning shears.

CHAPTER · 17

I woke up when the clock radio came on at 8:00 A.M. I needed to call Kyle Sheppard, but I couldn't decide whether to wait until after he had talked to Wade or to call and warn him about what was coming.

I was brushing my teeth when the telephone rang. I picked up the bathroom extension.

"Kyle Sheppard, here, Professor Stuart. We're set for your meeting with Montgomery, but we need to hurry."

"Why do we need to hurry?"

"I finally caught up with someone in the Duncan household. I've been leaving messages for Mrs. D. to call either me or you since yesterday afternoon, but she never got back to me and, I assume, not to you either. I called a few minutes ago and got her son Tad. He was the one who was there the first time I went to see Montgomery. He says Montgomery had a bad night, and his mama's gone out to get his prescription filled. He says we'd better come over right now because Montgomery will be out of it after he takes his medicine."

"All right. Are you going to pick me up?"

"On my way as we speak. Meet me downstairs in ten minutes."

"Ten minutes . . . okay, I just need to get dressed."

"This may be our last shot. The kid says Montgomery is getting worse."

When I hurried out of the hotel twelve minutes later, Sheppard was double-parked with the engine running.

"Good morning," I said.

"Yes, it is." he said. He shifted into gear as I buckled my seat belt.

"So are we certain that Montgomery will talk to me?"

"We won't know that until we get there. At least the kid's going to let us in the door."

As we passed a high-rise building, I remembered Jason, the cruise narrator, had made a comment about even the ghettos in Chicago being clean. When I told Sheppard that, he laughed without humor. "They may look clean enough from the outside, but you wouldn't want to live there."

"Montgomery must have been grateful to receive another option."

"He'd probably rather not be dying," Sheppard said. "But he's doing it in a comfortable bed in a clean house in a nice neighborhood. Of course, even nice neighborhoods have a struggle to keep the garbage out. See those guys?" He pointed out some men in their late teens or early twenties standing on the corner, talking.

"What about them?"

"Drug dealers," he said.

"Are they? In the movies, they're always flashier." But I knew about movie stereotypes.

"They only get it about half right in the movies," Sheppard said, echoing my thought.

He pulled up in front of a white house with blue shutters. Morning glories grew along the walk leading to the door. We went up the walk, between the rows of flowers. At the door, Sheppard rang the bell and we waited.

After two or three minutes, the door flew open. A scrawny teenager in cutoff jeans and a Chicago Bears tee shirt said, "Yo! Sorry. I was busy." He looked at Sheppard and nodded in recognition, then he turned his inquisitive gaze on me. "Are you the lady who wants to talk to old Robert?"

"Yes." I held out my hand to him. "I'm Lizzie Stuart."

He shook my hand awkwardly, a little shyly. "I'm Tad. Thomas Jerome after my pops. He's dead."

"I'm sorry," I said.

He shrugged. "Weighed too much. Had a heart attack. Moms kept telling him he ought to lose some weight. But he was a good guy. Hard on Moms to have him gone."

I had the feeling that he was trying to explain something, but I wasn't sure what. "Yes, I'm sure it must be. But she must be glad to have you."

"I have a half-brother, but he's not around much. He and Moms don't get along."

I nodded. "Do you think I could go in and see Mr. Montgomery now?"

"He's not feeling good. He might say some stuff."

"I understand."

Tad led the way down the hall that smelled of lemon furniture polish.

"Moms fixed up Pops' den down here for Robert because he couldn't handle the stairs. You better let me go in first and tell him you're here." He opened the door and stepped into the room. "Yo, Robert? You awake, man?"

"Go away," a cracked voice said.

"Man, you got visitors. That detective who came before and the lady you said you'd see."

After a moment of silence, the voice, even more cracked, said, "She's here? Becca's daughter is here?"

"I'll bring her in," Tad said.

"Wait! Help me sit up."

We stayed in the hallway until Tad came back to the door and gestured for me to come. I glanced at Sheppard.

He shook his head. "I'll wait here. The man said he wanted to talk to you by yourself."

I nodded and licked my dry lips. Then I stepped forward, crossing the threshold of Robert Montgomery's room.

Tad said, "I'll be out in the hall with Mr. Sheppard." He slid out and closed the door behind him.

The odor of sickness and decay hung over the room, stronger than the disinfectant and room deodorizer that had been used to combat it.

My gaze locked with dark, pain-wracked eyes. Montgomery leaned against the pillows piled behind him, staring at me from his bed. He stared as if I were a painting that he was studying, looking out at me from a ravaged face that still bore traces of male beauty.

"Hello, Mr. Montgomery. I'm Lizabeth Stuart. Becca's daughter."

He smiled, a twist of chapped lips. "Yes, I can see that. You've got her eyes and her mouth. Who's your daddy, Becca's daughter?"

Outside, a bird chirped. Receiving no response, it chirped again. It seemed to be close to the window, through which sunlight poured.

Inside the room, Montgomery's harsh breathing punctuated the silence that had fallen between us. "I don't know," I said. "Do you know who my father is?"

His long-fingered hands moved restlessly on the white and blue comforter. "'Fraid not. She didn't tell me," he said. "But it mattered to me back then. I wanted to know what man she had cared enough about to have his child."

"Maybe she just couldn't get an abortion." The words came out. I wished them back. They had revealed too much.

"She left her mark on you too."

"Yes," I said. "I'm surprised she mentioned she had a child."

"It was only once, when she was explaining why she'd left home."

"What did she say about that? About why she left?"

"That she'd had enough of Drucilla, Kentucky, and she sure didn't want to be nobody's mama." He smiled, and his face looked like a death mask. "You might not believe it, but you were better off without her."

"What do you want to tell me, Mr. Montgomery?"

"Tell you? I don't want to tell you anything, Becca's daughter. I just wanted one more look at your mother's face. But you can give her a message for me if you should find her."

"What?"

"Tell her I'll see her in hell." He tried to laugh and began to cough. Deep, wrenching coughs that shook the thin shell of his body.

I backed toward the door. I couldn't help him, and I couldn't stay there in that room that smelled of death and bitterness.

Tad looked up, his expression anxious, as I stumbled out into the hall.

"He's coughing," I said over the sounds coming from the room. "Do you know what to do for him?"

Tad nodded, but he hesitated. "Did he tell you what you wanted to know?"

I shook my head and turned toward Sheppard.

At that moment, the front door opened and a woman stepped into the foyer. Her hair, streaked with gray, was trimmed into a sleek cap that framed her narrow-featured face. Her skin had a smooth, flawless gleam like a seal's coat. She wore a royal blue tunic and pants and carried a plastic grocery bag in one hand. She looked at us and then turned to Tad.

He said, "Moms, Mr. Sheppard called again about bringing over. . . ." His words dwindled away as some message passed between them.

When she turned to Sheppard and me, she had gotten her initial reaction to our presence under control. She smiled in a kind of frozen parody of politeness. "Mr. Sheppard?"

He nodded. "Pleased to meet you, Mrs. Duncan."

She laughed. "I feel as if we know each other after our chat on the phone yesterday."

"I was hoping to get to speak to you last night," he said.

"I'm sorry not to have returned your calls. Robert has been feeling worse than usual."

Montgomery was still coughing while we stood there in the hall. Tad caught my backward glance, and he slid away into the sickroom. I heard him say, "I'll get your oxygen mask, man." Before the door closed, I heard Montgomery's obscene response.

Tad's mother put her grocery bag down on the straight chair by the hall table. She held her hand out to me. "Naomi Duncan." She had a French manicure. Her palm was clammy.

"Hello, I'm Lizzie Stuart. I hope you'll forgive us for coming over like this."

"I hope it wasn't a wasted trip. As I tried to explain to Mr. Sheppard when we spoke, Robert . . . he's in a great deal of pain . . . and the medications he has to take . . . I hope he didn't say anything to upset you."

"No," I said. "He didn't have anything he wanted to say to me after all."

"I'm sorry you made this trip all the way to Chicago for nothing."

"Not your fault," I said. "We apologize again for barging in like this."

"Think nothing of it." She looked toward the sickroom. "It's a shame if he wasn't able to help you."

"Maybe seeing me helped him," I said.

Sheppard had been standing silent, listening to the conversation. Now he said, "We'd best be on our way, Mrs. Duncan. You must have to get to work."

"Yes, I'm afraid I do. Even if you own the place, customers expect you not to keep them waiting." She saw us to the door and closed it behind us.

CHAPTER · 18

In the car, Sheppard opened the console between us and took out a cigar. He unwrapped it and clipped the end. When he had it lit, he started the ignition and pressed the button to lower the front and rear windows on my side.

"Well," he said. "That was right interesting."

"Yes, it was," I said. "She seemed nervous."

"Yeah, she did, didn't she?"

I glanced toward the house. I couldn't tell if Naomi Duncan was looking out. "Why do you think Tad told us to come over?" I said. "Do you think he knew that his mother didn't want me to see Mr. Montgomery?"

"Guilty as he looked when she walked in, I'd bet on it. I'd better see what I can dig up on Mrs. Naomi Duncan. What did Montgomery tell you?"

"That he doesn't wish Becca well," I said. "Mr. Sheppard, I meant to ask, have you spoken to Wade since yesterday?"

"He called me this morning. He said your boyfriend's worried about you and for me to make good and sure nothing happens to you."

"Was that all he said?"

"He wanted to know if I needed help. I said no. He said to let him know if I do."

"I did tell Quinn you had everything under control," I said. "But sometimes he overreacts."

"I think he reacted about right. You told him about riding around in that limo Nico was driving, didn't you?"

"Yes, I thought it would be better if I told him first."

"And his reaction was to want my head and to put somebody else on the case. I think that reaction makes a whole lot of sense."

"So you aren't annoyed? I mean, you're taking it well."

"I'm taking it well because I didn't get fired when Wade heard about it."

"If you don't mind my asking, why didn't Wade fire you? He and Quinn are good friends, and—"

"Like I told you, Wade and I go back a long way, and he knows I'm not quite over the hill yet."

"No, of course, you aren't."

He threw me a glance. "If you don't mind me saying so, Miss Lizzie, you're a sweet woman."

"Thank you, Mr. Sheppard, that's nice of you to say. Would you mind dropping me off at the Chicago Historical Society? While you're checking on Naomi Duncan, I want to see what I can find in the newspapers from 1969."

Sheppard popped in a Nancy Wilson CD for the drive to the Historical Society. He left me to my thoughts.

As I was getting out of the car, I remembered the police report on Mancini's murder and asked about it.

"I've got a copy of it in my office," he said. "It doesn't say much, but you can have a look at it."

"Thank you. I'll call you when I get back to the hotel."

After I explained what I needed to the woman at the reference desk, she made several suggestions in addition to the *Chicago Mirror-Examiner* microfilm from 1968 and 1969. I decided to leave my examination of the scrapbooks and photos she supplied until after I worked my way through the crucial months of the newspaper.

I settled down at a microfilm machine and randomly selected a reel from 1968. I wanted to spot-check the issues from 1968 and then focus on 1969. As I started to read, I tried to sort out what I knew about Chicago in the late 1960s. How many times had I seen that documentary of the 1968 Democratic National Convention? Outside the convention hall, protestors were crashing with the police. Inside, Dan Rather was being roughed up by security guards as he broadcast from the convention floor. During the next two years, there was pandemonium in the courtroom during the trial of the Chicago Eight (later Seven), who were accused of inciting the riots.

Meanwhile, liberal activists were trying to remake Chicago's poor neighborhoods. In one of the first seminars I had taken as a graduate student at U Albany, we'd looked at the grassroots community organizing in Chicago in the 1960s and the efforts to recruit gang members and put them to work making positive changes in the community.

I straightened in my chair and reached for my shoulder bag. I needed my reading glasses. Eyestrain was always one of the side effects of reading old newspapers on microfilm. At the moment, I didn't need any more eyestrain.

The *Mirror-Examiner* had given extensive coverage to the US Senate probe involving one Chicago gang, the Blackstone Rangers. A minister at a Presbyterian church was alleged to have misused an antipoverty grant that was supposed to provide job training for former gang members. The allegation was that his church had, in fact, been a gang headquarters and that he had used the money to bribe gang leaders into keeping the peace in that area.

The minister, who was white, countered that the charges were a sham to prevent black people and white people from working together. His supporters agreed.

I scrolled through August 1968, pausing over a column about a Chicago commission formed by "a 14 member group of Negroes" to investigate the riots in the wake of the King assassination in April of that year. The commission blamed the city's power structure for what had happened. It had recommendations ranging from the makeup of the police patrol in black communities to street cleaning and consumer protection.

How had these respectable Negro citizens felt when the Panthers took to the stage later that year? Fred Hampton would turn up somewhere in these pages. He had become a charismatic leader of the Panthers in late 1968. A year later he was killed—assassinated, many people claimed—during a nighttime police raid on the apartment where he and other Panthers lived. I had often shown the *Eyes on the Prize* documentary to undergrads who were so young, they thought of the 1960s as ancient history.

In the documentary, the Chicago natives who were interviewed praised Fred Hampton and the Panther movement. But how had the program gone over with this group of fourteen who had investigated the riots? In the South, many respectable black citizens who had been on board with Martin Luther King and nonviolence had been downright nervous about "Black Power" and young black men who asserted their right to bear arms for self-defense.

I scrolled on, pausing here and there to browse. August 15, 1968. I stopped to look at some photos that surprised me, given what I had read so far. The photos were a montage of the visit to a dude ranch by an interracial group of Southside Chicago teenagers. A community association had sponsored the trip. Racial harmony in action.

Politics in action that year too. Mayor Daley had praised LBJ at a rally, even though the war-embattled Johnson had declared he did not intend to run for reelection. Meanwhile, the Republican vice-presidential candidate, Spiro Agnew, promised to tour the ghettos and listen to black leaders. Yeah, right.

In December 1968, Richard Nixon, finally on his way to the White House after his bitter defeat by Jack Kennedy back in 1960, was reported to be "a nervous father of the bride."

I rewound and reached for the first reel of microfilm from 1969. Then I glanced at my watch and started to fast-forward to April. But the headline from January 2 caught my eye. "Missing Girl Found Slain." I paused to scan the article. The dateline of the story was Hollywood, not Chicago. The dead girl was the daughter of an author and an actress. I didn't recognize the names of the people involved.

The big story in Chicago on the second day of the New Year was the weather. The temperature had fallen to 10 degrees below zero on January 1, breaking a record. The cold wave extended into the Deep South and had caused havoc in

Chicago and the vicinity the day before. Malfunctioning traffic signals led to traffic jams. People tried to stay warm in buildings with overstressed heating systems.

The front-page forecast for January 2 called for temperatures between fifteen and twenty degrees with a chance of snow or snow flurries. Still cold—cold enough to make a Southern girl shiver.

By the next day, Friday, January 3, international news dominated the front page. The bold, large-font headline announced, "Hanoi Snubs U.S. Offer." There had been a hotel fire in Lincolnwood—wherever that was—with hundreds fleeing. An Eastern Airlines jet bound for Miami from New York had been hijacked to Havana. A gunman who opened fire in a police station was shot by a sergeant, who was wounded.

"Two Blackstone Rangers Killed by Gunfire." I glanced at the article but did not stop to read it. I'd had more than enough of historical context. What was it that Malcolm McDowell had said to Mary Steenburgen in that H. G. Wells time-travel movie? "Every age is the same. It's only love that makes any of them bearable." I knew already that Becca and Nick Mancini hadn't made the turbulent '60s any more bearable for each other.

I needed to get on with it and find the article about his death. I had asked Sheppard for the date of Mancini's murder. It was the evening of Monday, March 31.

On Tuesday, April 1, 1969, the front-page story was about the death of Eisenhower, the thirty-fourth President. There were photos of mourners paying tribute as his body lay in repose at the Washington National Cathedral. There was a photo of Mamie Eisenhower in widow's weeds with a handkerchief to her face.

I searched the rest of the paper and found nothing about Mancini. He must have been killed after the newspaper's deadline.

Wednesday, April 2. Easter sales, spring fashions.

"Club Owner Found Dead in Office." I sat back, took a deep breath, and began to read.

Nicholas Mancini, age 47, was found dead in his office at the Club Floridian, on N. Wells early Tuesday morning. The police were summoned after the bartender, Albert Carterra, discovered Mancini's body at approximately 12:15. Carterra told police that he had last seen Mancini alive as they were closing up at midnight. Mancini went into his office, and Carterra stepped outside to help their last customer, who was inebriated, into a taxi.

The official report of cause of death is pending, but police sources say Mancini was stabbed in the neck and torso with pruning shears. A suspect, Robert Montgomery, age 24, a Negro piano player at the club, has been taken into custody. A Negro singer, Becca Hayes, age 22, is being sought for questioning.

Mancini, alleged to have ties to the syndicate, had assumed proprietorship of the Club Floridian after the slaying of Max Sieger, the club's former owner, by an unknown assassin. Mancini had been arraigned several times on charges related to extortion and gambling, but he served only one brief stint in prison in his twenties, avoiding further convictions.

Police sources are not linking Mancini's death to his alleged criminal connections. The motive for his slaying is believed to have been an argument between Mancini and the suspect Montgomery that occurred earlier in the evening. During the argument, Mancini was said to have threatened to fire Montgomery when the piano player intervened in a discussion Mancini was having with the singer, Becca Hayes, prior to her performance. Carterra, the bartender, reported seeing Montgomery come out of Mancini's office shortly before his discovery of the body. The police hope to obtain a statement from Montgomery that will allow them to close the case.

I searched through the next day's edition, but there was nothing else on the case. Then on that Friday, April 4, attention shifted to coverage of a matter of more concern to the majority of readers. The city was bracing for more rioting on the first anniversary of Martin Luther King's assassination. The front-page headline read, "City Quiet Under Guard." Eighty-nine people had been injured the previous day, cars wrecked, a wave of "unrest," but nothing to compare to the riots the year before. According to one article, several of the incidents occurred when students were let out of or left school. Having grown up in a small town, I didn't equate "quiet" with the journalist's description of what had happened.

By Saturday, city officials were breathing a sigh of relief, and the curfew was being rescinded. *The Smothers Brothers Comedy Hour* was about to be dropped by CBS. And there was nothing else that I could find about the Mancini case.

Even if Montgomery had confessed—when he confessed—wouldn't the media have followed it up? Wasn't Mancini enough of a big-time mobster to rate even a few more lines of print?

Dammit, I should have thought to ask Sheppard if he knew the date when Montgomery had been arraigned. I might have missed it.

I was hungry, but I wasn't ready to leave yet. I dug into my purse and found a roll of peppermint LifeSavers. I had made this trek out here, and I might not have time to come back before my flight tomorrow. I wanted to go through the folders that the librarian had pulled for me. There might be something there.

I had told her I was looking for information on organized crime in Chicago during the sixties and any photos from that section of the street where Mancini's club was located. I opened the first folder containing newspaper clippings. I had no idea what I was looking for, and the clippings were not in chronological order. I paused over an article from June 25, 1968. The Chicago Crime Commission had published a sequel to its historic report on the syndicate. It identified businesses and firms having connections with the crime syndicate, including names and addresses. The Commission had linked the syndicate to construction, bookkeeping, linoleum and tile, restaurants, hotels, and real estate.

The next article, from 1967, discussed the Chicago Crime Commission's founding forty-eight years earlier. Senator Percy had inserted the Commission's report on Chicago "hoodlums" into the Congressional Record. Well, that made sense. Bobby Kennedy, in his role as Attorney General, had vowed that he would destroy La Cosa Nostra. After Valachi had become an informant and given up his bosses, the federal government had been heavy into bringing down the mob.

Kennedy's attention to organized crime had compelled J. Edgar Hoover, as head of the FBI, to become more proactive in pursuing mob investigations. Hoover would undoubtedly have preferred to focus on "domestic terrorists." He had been unequivocal in his assertion that "terrorist" groups like the Black Panthers had to be destroyed. COINTELPRO, the agency's operation employing surveillance, misinformation, and planted informants, had gone a long way toward doing that.

I paused with my hand hovering over the file. Could the FBI have been investigating Nick Mancini? The newspaper article had been explicit in mentioning his alleged ties to the syndicate. If reporters knew that, then the feds certainly must have known. Carterra, the bartender—who had picked this week to go fishing—had told Sheppard that Mancini thought he was being watched. What if it was the FBI?

I thought about that for a moment. I couldn't quite imagine Becca as an FBI informant. She'd had a good thing going with Mancini, even if he was jealous. Why would she betray him? When he'd said he knew she was up to something, he had undoubtedly been talking about another man that she had on the side.

No, if anyone had reason to give Mancini up, it was Sonny. Sonny had gotten the club.

Okay, get back to what I could see in front of me. Just because Mancini was a mobster, that was hardly evidence that the FBI had been trying to bring him down. They had probably had bigger fish to fry than Mancini—like the mobsters who were featured in a February 1964 article from the *Daily News* about the "private lives of mob chiefs."

According to the reporter, they lived well, with houses in the suburbs and winter vacations in Florida. They kept a low profile for the most part. They were good neighbors who walked their dogs and golfed. Their wives went to church and their children were well-behaved. The article even included the names of the suburbs where famous Chicago mobsters lived, along with photos of their mansions. Oak Park. Elmwood Park. Melrose Park. North Riverside.

The names of the suburbs meant nothing to me. I would have to remember to ask Sheppard where Nick Mancini had lived with his wife and son. For that matter, where did Sonny and Nico live? Somehow, Nico struck me as more the condo type than a house in the suburbs . . . unless he, too, had a wife that he was cheating on.

I turned to the folder containing photographs. I wanted one of the Club Floridian in the 1960s. The librarian had explained that these were simply photos they had collected of various street scenes. She wasn't sure I would find anything useful.

I had about given up when I picked up a photo with an address on N. Wells. It was a building that must be almost directly across the street from the club. I closed my eyes, trying to remember that building and what it was being used for now. The photo, taken in 1964, showed an antique market in the building. Cars were parked nearby, but the street was almost empty.

Maybe it had been taken on a Sunday morning.

I glanced at my watch. It was after two o'clock, and I needed to get back to the hotel in case Sheppard was trying to reach me.

I collected the folders and took them up to the desk.

The taxi driver who drove me back to the hotel seemed to have trained at the same driving school as Sheppard. At least this time I was sitting in the backseat.

I checked the telephone as soon as I walked through the door of my hotel room. The red message light was on. I kicked off my sandals and sat down on the bed. With any luck, Sheppard had called with something more useful than what I had found.

"Yo, Ms. Stuart?" The voice was young and male and hurried. "This is Tad Duncan. Please don't tell my moms I called you. She'd kill me. But Pops would want you to know." There was a little pause, and then he breathed out a name. "Reuben James. He was killed, and Pops was almost killed too. She—your mother—she was there. Please don't tell my moms I told you."

A computerized voice offered me a menu of options for my voice mail message. I replayed it twice, and then one more time to check what I had written down on a hotel notepad. Then I deleted it.

Reuben James? Who was Reuben James?

CHAPTER · 19

I found the business card Sheppard had given me and gave him a call. He was not in his office. No sultry-voiced secretary answered his phone. I left a message on his answering machine, and then I tried his cell phone. There was no answer there either. I left another message. "I'm back at the hotel. Tad Duncan called. Do you know who Reuben James is? Or was?"

I hung up and called Tess. I managed to catch her at her desk. When I had given her a summary of my morning and Tad's message, she said, "Luis can check it out."

"That's what I was hoping you would say. But I don't want to bother him at work, and Mr. Sheppard may get back to me in a few minutes."

"In the meantime, Luis can get someone to search their archives at the newspaper. Reuben James." I could tell she was writing. "What about the other man? Tad's father. Do you have a name for him?"

"Tad said he was named after his father. Thomas Jerome. That would make the father Thomas Jerome Duncan."

"Okay, I'll get Luis on it, and he can tell us what he found tonight at dinner. I'll pick you up at six."

"Thanks, Tess."

"That's what friends are for."

I needed to get out of that hotel room. I rode downstairs in the elevator but hesitated in the doorway of the hotel restaurant. There were white cloths and silverware on the table, but no one was in sight. It was three o'clock, making it too early for dinner and too late for lunch.

I half turned toward the coffee shop. I could get a sandwich there. Or I could go for a walk. If I couldn't do anything about answering the Reuben James question, I could walk back over to N. Wells and have another look at the Club Floridian from the outside. I could try to get some sense of the "crime scene" that night when Nick Mancini was killed.

I went back upstairs to change. If I was going to be in the vicinity of the Club Floridian, I should try not to be too obvious about it. I hauled my suitcase out of the closet. I had put the baseball cap I'd bought for Quinn inside. Going into the bathroom, I tried it on and tightened it to fit my head. I exchanged my blue flowered skirt for jeans. I unbuttoned the bottom of my white blouse and tied it halter fashion over my belly and slipped on socks and running shoes.

After a glance in the full-length mirror, I unbuttoned the two buttons at the top of the blouse. I hesitated for half a minute, then reached up and unclasped the chain with Quinn's ring. I put the ring in an envelope and slipped it inside the wall safe in the closet. It was not as good as taking it downstairs and putting it in a hotel safety deposit box, but unless someone was lurking outside waiting for me to leave and could figure out I had used Quinn's birth date as the safe combination, it should be all right.

I took one last glance at myself in the mirror and tilted the cap a bit more. I wouldn't pass for a twenty-something member of Generation X, but I didn't look quite like a staunch almost-middle-aged professional either. I might just be able to walk by the Club Floridian without attracting attention.

When I got to N. Wells, I paused to reconnoiter on a corner a block down from the club. I decided it would be better to stay on the opposite side of the street rather than risk passing directly in front of the Club Floridian's window.

Pushing my sunglasses up on my nose and tugging my—Quinn's—baseball cap a bit lower, I ambled toward the Club Floridian. I passed a pub and a restaurant with a parking lot. I came to the corner directly opposite the club and continued across the side street, then I stopped there at the light.

Nothing seemed to be going on at the club. The door was closed; no cars were parked in front. But Sonny and Nico could have parked somewhere else. One or both of them might be inside.

The light changed, and I strode across the street like a woman with someplace to go. I glanced at the club as my feet touched the curb on the other side, but I kept walking down the hill on the opposite sidewalk.

There was a half alley behind the club. Was that the alley where Nick Mancini's killer had dropped the pruning shears? It was formed by the juncture of that building and the building behind it, but there was no place to park a car. A big green Dumpster occupied much of the space, buttressed by a low-slung gate that must be a property marker rather than a serious attempt to keep anyone out.

I walked on down the hill toward the el station. A car passed me going up the hill in the opposite direction. This street was one way, and the el steps turned out to be an exit from the platform above to the street below. A sign on one of the steps said, "Stop. No Entry."

A block or so farther down the hill was another set of steps that must be the station entrance. Had it been this way in 1969, that night when Becca walked out of the club? Or did she run? Had she been running away from Nick Mancini lying dead on his office floor?

I got to the corner and looked left and right along Franklin Street. Not as much traffic as up on N. Wells, but lots of parked cars and a respectable number of pedestrians out on the sidewalk. Across the street from my corner, a young couple carried on an animated conversation in sign language, apparently discussing something in the window of a kitchen-design store. A man in a business suit had stopped to extract a folder from his briefcase in front of a building that advertised retail office space for rent. A younger man, wearing blue jeans and carrying a canvas, darted around him and disappeared down the steps of the art gallery next door.

The street I had walked down seemed to become residential on the other side of Franklin. Straight ahead, I saw what looked like apartment buildings or maybe condos.

I turned and walked back up the hill. I waited until a car passed, and then I crossed over about a half block down from the club. When I got to the alley, I stopped to have a closer look. Both the brown brick Club Floridian and the building behind it had two floors and outer steps with a platform for the second floor. Windows in each building overlooked the alley and the side street. For all I knew, Sonny or Nico might be at one of those windows looking at me right now.

The only movement I saw was an orange marmalade cat sitting beside the Dumpster and cleaning his front paws with his tongue. He looked too working class for Precious, Sonny's Persian.

I wasn't sure what revelation I had expected to have when I came back to the "scene of the crime." The buildings on these adjacent streets might be the same ones that had been there in 1969, but the uses to which they were being put could well have changed. The only business that I knew was there that night was the Club Floridian itself.

I glanced behind me at the antique shop, across the street from the club. I'd better move along before people started to wonder what I was up to.

I got to the street light on the corner, and rather than crossing back to the other side, I decided to be bold and walk right past the club. Even if they saw and recognized me, what could they do? It was a public sidewalk.

If Sonny saw me, I would ask if I could see that poster with the photograph of Becca that he had shown to Sheppard. That was my excuse for being there. I wanted to see my mother's picture.

Sure enough, as I came abreast, the gleaming green door opened outward. I caught my breath, expecting to find myself facing Sonny or Nico. But the person coming out was a woman, plump, fiftyish, stylishly clad in a beige dress and matching pumps. She glanced at me, and then someone called to her from inside the club.

"Angela!"

I darted past her and into the alcove of the neighboring shop just as Sonny reached the door. I turned my back to them, hoping he wouldn't look in my direction.

"Sonny, we've talked about this already. I have to go."

"You could have waited until I got off the phone."

"You were taking all day. I'm meeting someone for drinks."

But you understand me?" he said. "I've made myself clear, right?"

"Yes, yes. But you have to be patient with him, Sonny. He has too much of his father—God rest his soul—in him. I've got to go. Dinner on Sunday?"

"If we have this matter under control by then."

"What's to control?" There was a shrug in her voice. "Leave it be."

"If your freaking son will."

"Don't speak like that. He loves you. You've been like a father to him."

"He never listens to me. All I ask is a little respect."

"I'll speak to him. I said I'd speak to him. Don't worry so much. Dinner on Sunday."

She walked past me without looking in my direction. I heard the door of the club close. I stayed where I was until Angela had gotten into a gray sedan parked half a block down the street. Why hadn't she parked in front of the club? Maybe someone else had been parked there when she arrived, maybe Nico. The conversation about him suggested he wasn't around.

What was it that Sonny and his cousin Angela wanted Nico to leave be? I walked back to the hotel thinking about that. Sheppard had said Nick Mancini's widow lived in Florida. What was she doing in Chicago? Was she here on vacation, to visit her son and cousin? Or had she made a special trip because Sheppard had been asking questions about her dead husband?

CHAPTER · 20

Sheppard still hadn't called by the time I finished getting dressed for dinner at Tess's house. Where in the heck was he? Suppose I had an emergency? Obviously he expected me to call 911.

I checked my cell phone to make sure it was still charged and put it back in my purse. Then I went downstairs to wait for Tess.

She was ten minutes late because she'd had to fix a scheduling problem that had come up as she was walking out the door of her office. But she had reached Luis right after she talked to me, and he was on the Reuben James mystery. She said all this as she was changing the radio station, guiding her SUV back into the traffic, and making sure I buckled my seat belt.

Tess had always been good at multitasking.

Her condo was in a complex off Division Street, near the Old Town Mall. "Convenient location, off-street parking, and a branch of the Chicago Public Library right down the street," she said by way of explanation of why she liked it.

We were greeted at the door by an efficient looking woman whom Tess introduced as Mrs. Silvia, Elena's nanny. Tess had worried that, as a single mother, she wouldn't be able to afford child care. Either her job as a travel channel producer was paying well or she was getting child support from Michael's family.

She led me into the bedroom where Elena sat on a braided rug in the middle of the floor, surrounded by several dolls with various skin tones and styles of dress.

"I gather you're teaching her about cultural diversity," I said.

"Sometimes," Tess said, "being PC makes sense."

Elena said, "Mama!" and scrambled to her feet, stepping on one unfortunate doll's head.

Tess swung her up and kissed her on both rosy cheeks.

"Lizzie, this is Elena. Elena, this is Aunt Lizzie."

Tess held her out to me. Normally, I was wary of holding small children, but Elena was well past the stage of being infant fragile. Her arms coiled around my neck with surprising strength. She had dark curls and big brown eyes with extravagant lashes. She was much more like her mother than her blond father.

"Hello, Elena. It's a pleasure to finally meet you."

Toddler talk was not my forte, but Elena beamed at me, apparently forgiving my inability to speak her language. She reached up her chubby hand and yanked on my left earlobe.

"Ouch!"

"Aunt Lizzie needs that ear," Tess said, taking her back.

"Ear," Elena said and giggled.

If I could sort out my Becca mess and if Quinn agreed, a baby might not be a bad idea. Assuming, of course, that I wasn't going blind.

Tess said, "Come on, let's go have a drink while I get dinner started."

"Mrs. Silvia doesn't do that?"

"Mrs. Silvia only does child tending, and she leaves when I walk through the door."

She was already gone.

I followed Tess into the kitchen. "Can I help?" I said.

"Yes. Keep Elena occupied."

I sat down at the table, and Tess put her daughter in my lap. Elena began playing with my fingers while singing a song that seemed to be of her own composition.

Tess took some vegetables out of the refrigerator and reached for a bowl. I watched as she began to chop.

"Now, if Luis puts in an appearance within the next half hour," she said, "we'll be fine."

"It's actually happened," I said.

"What?" she said, measuring oil into a cup.

"You've become domestic."

"Only as needed. I've got a guy who likes to cook."

"Good for you. And definitely a good thing for Elena." I brushed back the soft baby curls. "Isn't that right, sweetheart?"

She looked up at me and clapped her hands and laughed.

"So does the cop cook?" Tess said.

"Yes, as a matter of fact, he does."

Tess turned to look at me. She leaned back against the counter with her wineglass in her hand. "That was a lot of it, you know?"

"What was?"

"What I was upset about." She made a face. "I was pissed as hell that I invited you to join me for a vacation in Cornwall, my life fell apart, and you met a guy."

I was silent for a moment. "But Quinn and I didn't get together then." I didn't mention that kiss in the hospital waiting room.

"No." Tess pushed back her hair with her free hand. "But I could see it coming." She grinned. "You're as transparent as cellophane, buddy. And the way you looked at Detective John Quinn. . . ."

"But I felt awful about the way I was reacting to him when you—"

"I know you did. And that was a part of why you tried to put him off."

"I thought I had." I touched Elena's velvety cheek. "When I gave him my little speech about how it had just been an aberration, a passing attraction, he agreed."

"What did you expect him to do? You probably hurt his feelings. Cops tend to be sensitive souls."

I looked up. Tess looked back, smiling.

"Is it okay now?" I said. "Between us? Now that you have Luis."

"Even if I didn't have Luis. He's pretty terrific, and I'll probably keep him around for a while. But even if it didn't work out. . . ." She wrinkled her nose. "I wasn't being a very good friend when I made you feel guilty about Quinn."

"Well, you were having a pretty rough time right then. And if it makes you feel any better, one of the reasons I didn't like Michael in the beginning—before he gave me a whole bunch of other reasons—was probably because I was jealous that you were in love and had someone and I didn't."

"Why is it that women let men screw up perfectly good friendships? Tell me that."

"Because we're stupid. But we won't let it happen again. Deal?"

"Deal. Let's seal it with a toast." Tess raised her glass. "To the two of us. Men may come and men may go, but we will be friends until the end."

I laughed and raised my glass, returning her salute.

When Luis arrived a few minutes later, Tess was bringing me up to date on her family back in New York. "Perfect timing," she told him and slid the chicken dish she had made the night before into the microwave to reheat.

He kissed her on the cheek, said hi to me, and reached down to scoop up Elena, who was saying "Lou" and holding out her arms to him.

Over dinner, with Elena in her chair between the two of them, Tess turned to Luis and said, "What did you find out?"

"He didn't have a lot of time, Tess," I said. I had only managed to restrain myself from asking that question when he walked in because I didn't want to be rude. "Luis, if you couldn't find out anything—"

He held up his hand and said, "Just waiting until we were sitting down and comfortable."

"We are," Tess said. "Start talking."

Luis gave her his dazzling smile. "One of the things I love about you, *mi corazón*, is your ability to give orders."

"Please share your information with us, Luis," she said.

He turned back to me. "I'll start with Nick Mancini, since there's less to say there."

"But you did find something?"

"I checked out Mancini Sr. with my godfather."

"Your *godfather*?" I said.

Luis grinned. "Not that kind. Carlos and my father came from Puerto Rico together back in 1944. They both found jobs in a factory, but later Carlos quit to open a shoe-repair shop. That was the dream of every migrant back then, to have his own business."

I nodded my understanding of the Puerto Rican migration pattern and the American dream. "Why did you check with your godfather about Mancini?"

"Carlos has done quite well over the years. He has some other business ventures, including real estate development. Through his business dealings, he knows lots of people, including people who knew Mancini. He asked those people a question or two."

"And what did they say?"

"That Mancini was too slick for his own good. That he had his hand in a number of operations. Gambling in particular. Prostitution. Money laundering. Extortion. They thought the feds would have come after him if he hadn't been killed first."

"Did any of Mancini's associates have reason to want him dead?"

"Maybe. Especially the ones whose wives he had been banging."

"Luis!" Tess put her hands over Elena's ears.

He smiled at Elena and chucked her chin. "Sorry, sparrow, I didn't mean to offend your delicate ears."

Tess took her hands down. "I know she's too young to understand, but—"

"You're right," Luis said.

"Getting back to Mancini's extracurricular activities," I said, "I saw his widow today." I told them about going back to the club and seeing Angela with her cousin Sonny.

"You shouldn't have gone there," Tess said.

I knew she was going to say that. That was why I had waited until Luis arrived to mention it.

He said, "Probably no harm done. Now, would you like to hear what I found out about Reuben James?"

"Yes," Tess and I said in unison.

"Actually, it might be easier if I show you the article. Excuse me." He got up and went back into the living room.

Elena laughed and slapped at her high chair with both hands. Tess picked up the fish stick that she had microwaved for her and broke off a bite-size piece. Elena opened her mouth like a baby bird. Then she reached out for the fish stick. Tess broke the rest of it into pieces and put the saucer in front of Elena, who said something I couldn't translate and dug in.

She was chewing, face smeared with crumbs, when Luis came back. He smiled at her and handed copies of the article to Tess and me.

I glanced at the paper. "This is the article I saw when I was looking for the story about Mancini's murder. If I had bothered to read it, I would have known who Reuben James was."

"Understandable you missed it," Luis said. "You were looking for something else at the time."

"Blackstone Rangers," Tess said. "Reuben James was in a gang?"

"Finish reading it," Luis said, "and then I'll tell you what I know."

The article was brief:

Last night at around 11:30, Reuben James, age 26, was killed by a hail of gunfire from a speeding car. Another man, Thomas Jerome Duncan, age 25, was seriously injured. Duncan was rushed to the emergency room at Lincoln Memorial Hospital, where he remains in critical condition.

James, a leader of the Blackstone Rangers, was said to have recently associated himself with the Black Panther Party. Police sources report Duncan was also a member of the Negro gang and served as James's lieutenant. A young woman, Rebecca Stuart, age 22, was with the two men at the time of the shooting and described to police a black late model car that sped past, riddling the scene with bullets.

Police report that the men had gone to the house at 1254 E. Bonaventure Street for a peace summit with rival gang members, who fled the scene after the shooting. The three were standing outside the house waiting to be picked up by another gang member, Wesley Deavers, when the shooting occurred. Deavers has not been located.

I put the article down on the table beside my plate. "Tad was right. Becca was there. The question is, why was she there?"

"That I can't tell you," Luis said. "The story seems to have disappeared after this article. We searched but found nothing else on the investigation, no other mention of James. No more about Becca until three months later, when she resurfaces as Becca Hayes in the Mancini case—and we would have missed that if you hadn't told Tess she was using that stage name."

"What about Tad's father?" Tess said. "Did you find anything else about him."

"One more mention, in October 1969, when he was arrested for assaulting a police officer during a traffic stop." Luis opened the manila folder in his hand and found another printout. He handed it to me.

I glanced at it and then read it out loud to Tess:

Black Panther Arrested in Police Assault

Thomas Jerome Duncan, age 26, was arrested last night for assault on a police officer during a routine traffic stop. During the scuffle between Duncan and Officer Martin Ramsey, Duncan struck Ramsey with a tire iron. Ramsey's partner, Officer David Ames, came to his assistance, subduing Duncan at gunpoint.

A cache of weapons was found in the trunk of Duncan's car. In January

1969, Duncan was injured by shots fired from a speeding car as he and two companions stood on a street corner. That attack left Black Panther leader Reuben James dead.

"That's all." I put the printout down on the table. "Apparently, they couldn't decide how to describe Reuben James. In the two articles, he went from a 'leader of the Blackstone Rangers' to a 'Black Panther leader.'"

Luis said, "By October 1969, the press would have been more aware of the Panthers. I was able to find out a bit more. Duncan was charged with aggravated assault and with possessing unregistered firearms. He got fifteen to twenty-five in Stateville. He was a model prisoner and was paroled after he'd done the fifteen. He seems to have kept a low profile after that."

"What about Wesley whatever-his-name-is?" Tess said. "The one who was supposed to be picking up Reuben and Duncan and Becca the night of the drive-by?"

Luis shook his head. "There's no indication he was ever found."

"But even if he had been," I said, "you said there was nothing else about the drive-by in the newspaper."

"And I can't explain that," he said. "It could have been that other news—"

"Or lack of interest," Tess said. "It was a drive-by involving black gangbangers-turned-Black Panthers. Why would white newspaper subscribers want to know more?"

Luis shot her a glance as if he thought she had just insulted me.

Tess said, "Lizzie and I have known each other a very long time, Luis."

"And it's probably the truth," I said.

He said, "If it makes you feel any better, the powers that be weren't too enraptured by Puerto Rican gangbangers either."

"Puerto Rican?" I said.

He gave me his dazzling smile. "Forget about *West Side Story*. I'm talking about the Young Lords."

"Not to be confused with the Vice Lords," Tess said.

Luis said, "One of the chiefs of the Young Lords, an hombre named Jimenez, was in and out of jail, and he hooked up with the Black Panthers. He liked their agenda, their ten-point plan for community empowerment. He wanted to do the same thing in the Puerto Rican community. So, like some of the former black gang members who became activists and/or Panthers, the Young Lords also became politicized."

"That couldn't have made the Chicago PD or the FBI happy," I said.

"I did a research paper on the Young Lords when I was in high school," he said. "But it wasn't until I was in college that I really understood the game of 'divide and conquer' that the Bureau was deep into. They wanted to keep these groups from working together."

I nodded. "So they provided anonymous tips."

"Exactly," Luis said. "Concocted tips sent to groups like the Panthers and the Young Lords about the plots supposedly being hatched against them. The Bureau wanted to keep the warfare going."

"At the same time that Congress was enacting a bill to control crime and make the streets 'safe,'" I said.

Tess sighed. "If you think about it too long—"

"It isn't conducive to respect for the government," Luis said. "But getting back to your mystery, Lizzie, I think the question is what the drive-by assassination of Reuben James has to do with Nick Mancini's murder."

"Wait a minute," Tess said. "That's a big leap."

"But it makes sense," I said.

"Intuitive sense," he said.

"Quinn never appreciates it when I take intuitive leaps."

"Some of us," Tess said, "prefer to move in a logical path from one point to another."

Luis winked at me. "Makes you wonder why they hooked up with the two of us, doesn't it?"

"We keep them from missing what they can't see." I turned to Tess. "And what's illogical about assuming that if Becca was there when both men died, then there might very well be a link between the two deaths."

Tess opened her mouth. Then she picked up her wineglass and took a long sip.

"Go ahead," I told her. "Say what you're thinking."

"I'm thinking that if your mother was crazy enough to be involved with two men like that at the same time, then she was very lucky that she didn't end up dead herself."

"Yes." I took a sip from my own glass. "But maybe she was like a cat. A beautiful, dangerous cat with nine lives, and it was only the people around her who died."

"Then maybe you should stop trying to find her," Tess said.

"I told you, it's too late to go back now." I gestured toward my plate. "If I'm going to finish my wine, you'd better give me some more chicken, or I could end up dancing on your table."

Tess stood up and reached for my plate. "Not that I wouldn't enjoy seeing that, but I'd rather you didn't shock Luis."

"Luis is hard to shock," he said.

I smiled at the child sitting beside him. "So is Elena." She'd found our conversation so boring, she dozed off.

Luis stood up and began to ease her from the high chair. He really was good husband and father material.

I told Tess that when she came back with my plate.

"I'm thinking about it," she said. "Do you want a cup of tea?"

CHAPTER · 21

Luis offered to drive me back to the hotel. Tess said she'd talk to me tomorrow, gave me a hug, and sent me off with him.

As Luis was starting the car, I asked if we could make a detour on the way back. I told him where.

Even in the dim light, I could see that he looked concerned. "Are you sure you want to do that?"

"I'm sorry, don't worry about it. I can ask Mr. Sheppard to take me there tomorrow. He's the one who's being paid to—"

"I don't mind doing it, Lizzie. I only want you to be sure that you want to go there."

"I've seen the Club Floridian. I may as well see that too."

"And since it happened at night, it makes sense to see the street in the dark." He backed out of the parking place. "No problem. We can go there."

"I would have mentioned it to Tess, but it didn't occur to me until we walked out of the house."

His smile flashed. "We can tell her about it later."

We drove in silence. Luis did not seem to feel the need to talk, and I had nothing to say at that moment.

The night air rushed through the open windows. The route we traveled was unfamiliar to me, but our destination was the street corner where Reuben James had been shot down as my mother watched.

"This is it," Luis said about ten minutes later. "The street where it happened."

He slowed down, and I leaned forward. Some of the buildings were abandoned, boarded up. Even on a night in June, this street seemed darker and more forbidding than those we had left behind.

Luis pulled up at the curb. He pointed at the brownstone with the boarded-up windows and door. "That should be the building they came out of."

"Is it all right if we get out?"

He glanced around. "Only for a moment. This isn't the best neighborhood to hang out in at night."

"I just want to take a quick look. Promise." I opened the car door and stepped out on the sidewalk. A stray breeze caught a crumpled sheet of paper, dragging it along the pavement. I glanced back at Luis, who had gotten out too. "I'm just going to walk to the corner, okay? I'll be right back."

At the corner, I peered down the dark side street. Luis was walking toward me. I pointed at the sign and said, "This street is one-way. A car could have been sitting there with its lights off, waiting for them to come out."

"That's possible." He glanced down the narrow street. "The question is, who was in the car?"

The paper rustled along the sidewalk again. "I'm ready if you are," I said.

"Yes, I think we should probably move along."

"But thank you for bringing me."

We had gotten back into the Land Rover when a light-colored car drove past in the opposite direction. Luis followed its slow progress in his rearview mirror. I swerved around in my seat to look.

"Were they watching us?" I said.

"Quite possibly."

"Gang members?"

"Maybe." Luis started the ignition. "But they looked more like bikers."

"Bikers?"

"Two guys. One white. One black. Shaved heads."

My stomach clenched. "Then I think I know who they were. I took a river cruise yesterday. If it's the same two men. . . ."

As we retraced our path through the streets, I told him about Percy and Earl. "But they were being so obvious on the cruise . . . unless they were trying to be so visible that it would never occur to me that I was being followed."

We were back on a broad, well-lighted boulevard now. Luis said, "Maybe you should come back to Tess's."

"No, I can't do that. Not with Elena there. And I don't want to involve you and Tess in this any more than I already have. I'll be fine at the hotel."

"I don't like it that this detective of yours hasn't gotten back to you."

"He's probably hot on the trail of something. I'll give him another call."

"I think there's someone else you should call once you're safely tucked in for the night."

"Quinn?"

"I would if I were you. From what Tess tells me, he'd feel the same way I would about not being told what's going on."

"But I don't suppose Tess causes you nearly as much bother as I seem to cause poor Quinn."

"He must think you're worth it."

"I hope so."

At the hotel, Luis hopped out and assured the bellman he would be right back as soon as he escorted me up to my room. "The lady's feeling a little woozy."

Any inclination the bellman felt to point out that he was in a "no parking" zone was sidetracked by the bill Luis slipped into his hand.

We took the elevator from the lobby up to the eleventh floor without encountering anyone who looked out of place. In fact, we saw only one couple, a man and woman who got off on the seventh floor.

At my door, Luis waited for me to fish out my keycard and swipe it. The light turned green and I pushed the door open.

"Thank you very much," I said.

He raised my hand to his lips and bowed. "Sleep well, Lizzie." He let go of my hand and tapped the door. "And keep this locked."

"I will. Good night."

I decided to wait until morning to call Quinn. There was no reason to deprive him of a good night's sleep, when I was safe for the night.

I washed my face, brushed my teeth, and climbed into bed. I thought of calling Sheppard again but decided that could wait until morning too.

I was tired, really tired. I clicked off the television that I had turned on for background noise and slid down in the bed.

Sometime during the night, I began to dream. I knew I was dreaming, and I tossed and turned trying to free myself and wake up. But the scene played out in front of my eyes. It was a dark, cold night, and Quinn and I were standing on a street corner. A piece of paper scurried along the sidewalk. A car barreled around the corner, spraying gunfire. Quinn pushed me to the ground, and he fell.

I woke up gasping for air. For a moment, I thought someone was there in the shadows by the window. I fumbled for the lamp.

It was only the baseball cap that I had dropped onto the corner of the desk chair.

I reached for the remote control. The CNN entertainment reporter was reviewing a new Tom Cruise movie. I leaned back against the pillows I had propped behind me. It was 1:24, too late to call Quinn.

CHAPTER · 22

WEDNESDAY, JUNE 9

I seemed to spend my life waking up to phones ringing in my ear.

"Professor Stuart? Sheppard here."

I pushed myself up in the bed. "Where were you yesterday afternoon and last night?"

"I made a quick trip to Springfield. After that I was at the hospital."

"What happened? Are you all right?"

"I'm fine, but Robert Montgomery's dead. He was rushed to the emergency room at around eight o'clock last night, and he died a couple of hours later."

"Oh," I said. The word was inadequate, but I didn't know what I felt or should be feeling.

"I think we need to pay another call on Naomi Duncan."

"Did you find out anything about her?"

"She's Mama Lovejoy's daughter."

"Mama Love— The woman who owned the Shack? The place where Becca worked? Then Naomi must have known Becca."

"Yeah, she must have." He coughed. "Excuse me. Shouldn't be smoking a cigar this early in the morning."

"What time is it?" I said, leaning over to look at the clock radio.

"About seven-thirty. Can you be ready in half an hour? We don't want to miss Mrs. Duncan."

"No, we don't. I'll be downstairs."

"Did you see Naomi and Tad at the hospital last night?" I said, as Sheppard weaved his Caddie through downtown traffic.

"No, their neighbor told me that Montgomery had been taken away in an ambulance. I tracked him down, but he was dead by the time I got to the hospital. The Duncans had already left. I went to the house and waited, but they never came home."

"That's odd. Where would they have gone?"

"I called Mrs. Duncan's partner in the beauty salon at around six o'clock this morning—"

"Six!"

Sheppard laughed. "Hard-working businesswomen are up bright and early. She did seem a little grumpy, but I think that's because she didn't want to answer my questions about where I could find her partner."

"You think she knows?"

"I'd bet on it." He honked his horn at the car that had stopped in front of us. "But we'll see how this plays out. While we have a moment, let me tell you what I found out about Mrs. D. That'll bring us to who Reuben James was."

I grabbed the dashboard. "I already know a bit." I told him about Luis and what he had found.

Sheppard said, "The only thing I can add is that he was the son of one of Mama Lovejoy's close female friends. He and Naomi knew each other from childhood. They knew TJ too."

"TJ?"

"Thomas Jerome. Tad's father. That's what they called him."

I tried to put it together in my mind. "TJ, Reuben, and Naomi knew each other from childhood. TJ was Reuben's first lieutenant. Reuben was killed in the drive-by. TJ almost died in that same shooting. Later, TJ went to prison on aggravated assault and weapons charges."

"And when he came out, Naomi divorced the man she'd married and had a child with, and then she married TJ."

"She was married before?"

"Yeah. The guy was in his fifties when they said 'I do.' They had one son, Tad's half-brother. The first husband died a few years after the divorce. Naomi and her oldest son are still on the outs. That's why I went to Springfield."

"I'm sorry, what is?"

"That's where Naomi lived when she was married to her first husband. I wanted to see what else I could find out about her."

"What did you find?"

"Nothing much. Good wife and mother. Worked in the church. People who knew her were surprised when she divorced her husband and moved back to Chicago. They felt sorry for the husband because she took the son with her. Then after Naomi married TJ and got pregnant with Tad, her other son came back to Springfield to live with his father."

"But all of this really doesn't explain why she didn't want me to know about Reuben James."

"Nope. That's what we need to ask her about. But now we have a better idea of who we're dealing with."

We turned onto Naomi Duncan's street, which was quiet, as if all her neighbors were also early-rising hard workers who had gone off to their jobs. The only people in sight when we pulled up to the curb were three little girls in bright colored shorts and tee shirts jumping rope in a driveway a few houses down.

Sheppard rang the doorbell and we waited. No one came. The drapes were only half drawn over the living room windows, but no one was visible inside.

Sheppard pointed toward the side of the house. "Let's go have a look around back."

"Do you think we ought to do that? I mean—"

"We're concerned for the welfare of the occupants of the house," he said. "I haven't been able to reach them, and Mrs. Duncan's partner doesn't know where they might be."

I glanced toward the other houses as I followed Sheppard. No one seemed to be looking out at us. I would leave it up to Sheppard to explain if someone decided we were suspicious characters and called the police.

Or maybe they didn't do that in big cities.

Sheppard stopped and I almost barreled into him. "What?" I said.

He gestured for me to be quiet. Then he pointed at the back door.

The wood around the lock had been shattered. Someone had broken in. The door was ajar by an inch or two. Sheppard pushed it open a few inches more with the toe of his big brogue.

"Shouldn't we call the police?" I whispered.

"As soon as we know what we're dealing with," he whispered back. "Stay here."

"Mr. Sheppard, maybe—"

He scowled at me and gestured again for me to be quiet. Then he stepped inside.

I dug into my shoulder bag for my cell phone. *This man is supposed to be protecting me*, I thought, *and he goes into a house alone when—*

I heard shouts and a crash. I punched in "911" as I ran through the door. I had the phone in one hand, trying to talk to the dispatcher, and the skillet I'd grabbed from a kitchen trolley in the other, when I ran into the hallway.

I skidded to a stop. Sheppard, sitting on the stairs with a gun pointed at the man on the floor, was breathing hard but seemed to be all right. His opponent, who was clasping his midsection, was dripping blood from a split lip.

"Who are you calling?" Sheppard said.

"The police."

"Hang up."

"But—"

"Hang up. This is Percy. Naomi Duncan's other son."

CHAPTER · 23

The dispatcher asked my name and location.

"Sorry," I said. "Everything's all right. It was a mistake."

She asked if I was sure no assistance was required. I looked at Sheppard. He scowled at me again.

"Yes, thank you. Everything's under control." I pushed the button to disconnect the call and shoved the cell phone into my shoulder bag.

Keeping an eye on the man on the floor, I put the skillet down on the hall table and dropped onto the adjacent chair. "He may be Naomi Duncan's son, but he's also the man who was on the river cruise I took Monday afternoon. He has a running buddy."

Sheppard said, "Where's your partner, Percy?"

Percy rolled over on his back and glared up at Sheppard. "This is my mother's house."

"Seems she took your key away." Sheppard pointed with his gun toward a crowbar a few inches from my feet. "You had to use that to get in."

"I lost my key," Percy said. He groaned as he sat up. He reached into a pocket of his shirt and found a tissue and pressed it to his lip. "I have a right to be here. You don't."

"That depends," Sheppard said. "If there are two dead bodies upstairs—"

"I didn't kill anyone! You're out of your mind."

"So you limited yourself to housebreaking."

"I wanted to find out what was going on. She brought that old con here to die, and then as soon as he did, she and Tad took off."

"They're gone?" I said.

He pointed to the stairs. "See for yourself. Drawers pulled out, things yanked out of closets. They left in a hurry."

Sheppard nodded at me. "Go look while I keep our friend Percy company." He pointed at the crowbar. "Pick that up first. Percy might make me shoot him."

The crowbar was cold and heavy in my hand. "What should I—"

"Take it with you."

I eased around Sheppard on the stairs. When I got to the second floor landing, I stopped to sniff the air. A musky, exotic scent. Too heavy for room spray.

I found the source in the bathroom. Someone had broken an old-fashioned crystal perfume bottle. The atomizer, attached to a silver top, and chunks of glass were on the back of the commode. Another large shard of glass was in the sink.

I pushed open the door of a bedroom that must be Tad's. Baseball posters on the wall. Dirty socks balled up on the floor. Bed not only unmade but a mess. As Percy had said, the closet door had been left open, and the dresser drawers were pulled out with clothes dangling from them. A backpack had been tossed on the bed and left there.

"What do you see up there?" Sheppard yelled.

"I'm in Tad's room," I called back. "It does look like they left in a hurry."

They had left in such a hurry that Tad's computer was still on. The screen saver was an image of an African savannah. The main menu was displayed on the left. I clicked on the e-mail logo . . . and received a request for my password.

Well, that was just as well. I was turning away when I thought of the bookmark feature on my own computer. Still an invasion of privacy, but it was not as bad as reading someone else's e-mail.

Tad was like me; he saved the links to his favorite sites. I scrolled down the list. A lot them seemed related to baseball. He and Quinn would enjoy talking. I clicked on some of the other sites to verify they were what they seemed to be. Environmental justice. Animal rights. The Amazon. Africa. Australia. Emphysema. Death with dignity.

The last two sites on the list gave me pause. Robert Montgomery must have inspired both searches. Had he wanted to die on his own terms? Surely, he hadn't asked Tad to help him.

I didn't want to go there with that thought.

I scanned down the list again and clicked on one I hadn't looked at. Cape Fear? Why was he interested in Cape Fear? More environmental stuff?

"What are you doing up there?" Sheppard called.

"Be down in a moment. I just need to check Naomi's room."

I logged off the computer and watched the screen go dark, but just in case, I switched off the surge protector. There was no point in leaving equipment on that might set the house on fire.

Naomi's bedroom was next door. She was much neater than her son. The blue-and-white-plaid comforter on her bed was straight, and two blue precisely aligned armchairs flanked a small circular table by the window. But she too had been in a hurry. The closet door was ajar, not quite closed. The dresser drawers had been shoved back into place but were slightly askew. One of the black pumps she had apparently decided not to take was tumbled on its side. An empty hanger rested on the floor beside the bed.

I went back downstairs to tell Sheppard what I had found. He had put away his gun, and he and Percy were sitting there looking at each other. Percy sat with his back against the wall, his hands draped loosely over his knees. Blood stained his orange tee-shirt, but his lower lip had stopped bleeding. Now it was puffy and swollen, twisting his mouth up and to the side.

I sat back down in the chair and put the crowbar I had been carrying around on the floor beside my feet. I gave Percy my best impression of an intimidating stare. "What I want to know is why you've been following me."

He wasn't flustered. "I don't know what you're talking about."

"You and your running buddy. First on the river cruise, and then last night. It was the two of you in that car, wasn't it?"

"What car?"

Sheppard said, "Maybe we're gonna need the cops after all."

"I have a right to be in my own mother's house."

"Since you had to break in," Sheppard said, "Chicago's finest might not see it that way."

"So let's try it again," I said. "Why have you been following me?"

"I wanted to know what my mother was up to." He nodded his head toward Sheppard. "When Tad told me about him coming here, I started watching." He looked at me. "Then you turned up."

"So you started following me around."

"There was no point in following Mama. She wasn't going to give anything away unless she had to." He hawked and spat. The blood-tinged glob landed on his mother's shiny hardwood floor.

I stared from it to him. He looked back with a smirk on his blood-streaked face.

That was when the back door banged. Someone called, "Percy? Man, you in here?" It sounded like Earl.

Percy's eyes darted from me to Sheppard. "Stay out there!" he yelled back. "I'll be right there." He started to stand up, then glanced at Sheppard.

Sheppard nodded his permission and said, "We'll keep you in mind."

Percy glared at him. Then he darted off through the dining room.

Out in the kitchen, his buddy said, "What happened to you?"

"Tripped on the stairs," Percy told him.

"Your lip's a mess."

"It's okay. Come on, let's get out of here. They're gone."

"Gone where? Did you break the door like that? What—?"

The back door slammed, cutting off their voices.

I stared at the glob of spit glistening in the sunlight.

Sheppard laughed. "Well, he knew how to tweak your nose anyhow. You should have seen your face when he—"

"I hate it when someone does something to be deliberately disgusting. Why did you let him go?"

"Because I thought he'd told us about as much as he knew."

"Are we going to do anything else before we leave?"

"I'm going to go upstairs and look around. But I think we can assume that whatever Percy thought might be here ain't."

"What do you think he was looking for?"

"I'm inclined to believe his story that he was trying to find out what was going on with his mama."

"He didn't want his friend Earl to know we were in here," I said.

Sheppard grunted as he started up the stairs. "Why would he? Got beat up by an old man. Right embarrassing if you think you're tough. Don't want your man knowing you can't hold your own."

"Your—? Percy and—? You think so?"

"According to the folks I talked to in Springfield, young Percy's gay. We got us a bit of homophobia in the black community, and apparently Percy's sexual orientation didn't set well with his parents. Especially his mama. That could be why they're still on the outs."

"But didn't you say that Mama Lovejoy . . . if her own mother—"

"If she didn't appreciate it in her mother, she wouldn't appreciate it in her son. I'll be down in a few minutes."

While he was upstairs, I went out to the kitchen. I spotted the rubber gloves that Naomi used for dishwashing and pulled them on. Armed with paper towels, I went back out into the hall and scrubbed up Percy's glob of spit and the blood that had dripped from his split lip.

C H A P T E R · 2 4

I was washing my hands when I thought of Robert Montgomery's room. If Naomi and Tad had left quickly, maybe Naomi had overlooked something there, something that Percy hadn't found. I reached for the rubber gloves I had been about to toss. I might need them.

When I pushed open the door, that sweet stench still hung in the air. I walked across the room and unlocked the window next to the bed and shoved it up.

The bed was unmade, covers flung back to reveal crumpled sheets. A bedpan had been shoved almost out of sight under the bed, but I could smell the urine. A stained towel lay on the floor. I stepped over it and went around to the other side of the bed to the nightstand. I opened the drawer and saw a black, leather-bound Bible, the kind parishioners carried to church. This one had made that trip. A Sunday program from the All Souls Baptist Tabernacle was stuck in back.

The minister of the church was the Reverend Nathaniel Carter. Was he Naomi's minister? I folded the program to take with me and replaced the Bible.

The drawer also contained a transistor radio and a composition book, the kind children used in school. I took out the composition book and flipped through it. Nothing was written inside, but pages had been torn out, leaving ragged edges. Had Montgomery torn them out or had someone else? I shook the book to make sure nothing was stuck between the pages.

A small wicker wastebasket peeped out from behind the armchair near the bed. Inside were crumpled tissues, discarded cotton balls, and a torn prescription bag . . . and half of an old Kodak photo. I fished it out and shook the wastebasket until I found the other half. I put the two pieces together on the edge of the armchair.

I stripped off my gloves and dropped them in the wastebasket, then leaned closer to examine the photograph. A young man in a dark suit, white shirt, and tie sat at a piano. He was looking up at the young woman in a glittering black gown who leaned against his instrument. She wore an orchid in her hair.

Robert Montgomery . . . and Becca.

My mother and I had the same basic facial structure; I had looked at myself often enough in a mirror to recognize that. But that was where the resemblance ended. Even in this old photograph, Becca was sultry and sexy like the orchid in her hair.

I was a chrysanthemum to her orchid.

Sheppard spoke from the doorway, "What'd you find?"

I motioned toward the photo on the chair. "This was in the wastebasket."

He limped forward and peered over my shoulder. "That's your mama and Montgomery."

"His lawyer was right. Even in this old photograph, you can see that he. . . ." I shook my head. "He shouldn't have spent all those years in prison."

"Unless he did kill Mancini. You're assuming he was innocent because Gwen says he was." He nodded toward the photo. "I told you that you looked like your mama."

"A little." I plucked out a couple of tissues from the box on the nightstand and used them to wrap the torn photo.

"We'd better get moving," Sheppard said. Downstairs, as we left, he pulled the shattered back door closed behind us.

"Shouldn't we do something about the broken lock?" I said.

"It's not our job to have it fixed. What I think we ought to do is swing by the beauty parlor and let Mrs. D.'s partner know we found the door busted and Percy prowling around inside."

"And see what she has to say?"

"Now you got it."

"What time is your flight?" Sheppard said.

I glanced at my watch. "It's at 5:45. So I need to leave for the airport around 3:15. That should give me enough time if I take a taxi."

"I'll drive you out there. After the limo screw-up, I owe you one." He braked and swerved toward the curb. "Looks like the place. The Clip and Curl."

As we walked through the door, female gazes marked the entrance of a male into a female domain.

Sheppard nodded and smiled. "Ladies. Good morning to you."

A short, squat woman with a weave that gave her shoulder-length hair an abundance Diana Ross would have approved of came to the front desk. "May I help you?"

"Would you be Mrs. Bradshaw, ma'am?" Sheppard said.

"That's me. What can I do for you?"

"I think we might want to talk in private, ma'am. I'm Kyle Sheppard. I called you this morning."

"I thought you might be." She glanced at me.

"She's with me," Sheppard said.

"Come on in back." She led the way down the aisle past three stylists working on women in various stages of becoming beautified. Coloring, texturizing, hot-oil treatments—the strong smell of chemicals testified to the science involved.

Not that I was above that. The more gray hairs I found, the more I considered employing the marvels of science to put the color back where it belonged.

Mrs. Bradshaw gestured us into a storeroom stacked with boxes of supplies, wig stands, a castoff shampoo sink, and other items. She closed the door and turned to us with her arms folded. "What do you want to talk about?"

Sheppard said, "We thought you might want to get someone over to your partner's house to fix the lock on her back door. Her son Percy broke in."

Mrs. Bradshaw frowned. "Did you call the police?"

"No, we're telling you about it, so you can let your partner know. She might not want the police called on her son."

"I told you, I don't know where she is."

"Mrs. Bradshaw," I said, "I really need to speak to her. It's important. I'm leaving today."

"Like I said, I can't help you."

Sheppard said, "So you're saying Naomi took off and didn't tell you where she was going or when she would be back?"

"She must have had an emergency."

"Must have." Sheppard held out a card. "If she should check in—"

"I'll tell her you came by." She tucked the card into the pocket of the dusty pink smock she was wearing. "Thank you for letting me know about the door."

As we were on our way out, I saw the framed school photo on the counter at an empty work station. I slowed my step to take a closer look. It was Tad. A state certificate with Naomi's name and photo hung on the wall. I swept my gaze over the counter. Spray cans, brushes, clippers, combs in sterile solution. A notepad in a crab-shaped caddy. I leaned forward to read the words on the caddy.

Mrs. Bradshaw stepped in front of me.

I smiled at her. "Nice picture of Tad." I touched my fingers to my hair. "I don't suppose you could fit me in for a quick trim?"

She shook her head. "We're booked solid. And I would suggest you wait another two or three weeks before you have another trim."

"Would you? Well, you're the expert."

Outside, Sheppard said, "What was that about?"

"Cape Fear and Wilmington, North Carolina. Tad had a bookmark on his computer for a Cape Fear site. Naomi had a notepad caddy from Wilmington on her counter."

"Wilmington." Sheppard looked at me over the roof of the car. "It's worth checking out."

"Of course, they could still be here in Chicago."

"But then again, they might have decided to get out of town for a while. I'll see what I can find out before your flight."

CHAPTER · 25

It was ten minutes to noon when I got back to the hotel, and I hadn't packed. I went to the front desk and explained that I was running late. The desk clerk assured me that the hotel would be happy to give me an hour's extension on my checkout time and to store my luggage until I was ready to leave.

When I got upstairs, the maid was two rooms down with her trolley. I ducked into my room and put the privacy sign on the door.

The telephone message light was on. I had a message from Tess: "Call me before you go."

I dialed her office number. Her assistant answered and asked if I could hold.

"Did I catch you at a bad time?" I said when Tess came on.

"We're doing a lunch meeting. You certainly were out and about early this morning."

"Mr. Sheppard came by to pick me up. Robert Montgomery died last night, and— Do you have time for this now? I can call you back later."

"No, I want to know what's happening. Hold on." She spoke to someone and then she came back. "I told them to start without me. Go on."

I gave her a two-minute update.

"So even Naomi Duncan's son thinks she's up to something," Tess said.

"Whatever it is, I'm not likely to find out unless we can locate her."

"Your Wilmington clue sounds like a long shot, Sherlock."

"I know. But it's the only one I have at the moment. I suppose if Mr. Sheppard has more time, with Wade's high-powered connections, we should be able to track them down eventually." I reached for Quinn's baseball cap on the back of the chair so I wouldn't forget it. "But I'd like to get this resolved now. I'd like to know what this is all about and where Becca went and who. . . ."

"Who what?"

"The question I started with. I want to know who my father is."

Tess was silent on the other end of the line.

"You still there?" I said.

"Yes, I'm just thinking how to put this."

"The way you usually do. Just blurt it on out."

"Lizzie, even if you do find Becca, she might not be able to tell you what you want to know. I hate to say this about your mother, but if she was involved with lots of boys when she was a teenager, keeping track of who—"

"I've thought of that, but I don't think we're talking about a high school kid. Hester Rose said 'that man,' not 'that boy.' And why would it be such a secret if it was just a boy who—"

"Have you thought about the whole secret thing? It was something your grandmother kept even from your grandfather. So why would Becca tell you?"

"To spite Hester Rose," I said. "Because my grandmother didn't want me to know."

Tess's sigh came across the line. "Lizzie, it's been forty years. Becca may have gotten over her teenage rebellion against her mother. After what happened here with Mancini and Reuben James, she might have decided to clean up her act."

"And in that case," I said, "she might want to make up for past mistakes by telling her daughter the truth."

"You're pinning a lot— Hold on."

I heard a muted exchange in the background.

"Okay, I'm back."

"You've got to go," I said. "And I need to get moving too."

"Do you have a ride to the airport?"

"Mr. Sheppard's taking me."

"Call me tonight and let me know you got home okay."

"I will. Thanks for everything, Tess. And thank Luis for me."

"We'll see you soon. Maybe we'll come visit."

I laughed. "You're actually thinking of coming down South to visit me in Gallagher?"

"We might. The place can't be too bad if your cop's willing to live there. Talk to you later. I've got to go before someone makes a decision that I'm stuck with."

"Have fun," I said.

I hung up and got my suitcase out of the closet. After I packed the few clothes I'd brought, I gathered up the things I'd put out on the bathroom counter. Then I opened the safe in the closet and took out Quinn's ring. I started to put the envelope in the zippered inside pocket of my shoulder bag, but my fingers touched the torn photo of Becca and Robert Montgomery wrapped in tissue.

No, not there beside that photograph. It was much better to wear Quinn's ring around my neck than have it contaminated by a torn photograph that symbolized a relationship that had ended in betrayal and pain.

I pulled my suitcase over to the door and then stood there considering my options. Sheppard was going to pick me up at 3:15, but he had my cell phone number so he would be able to reach me if he needed to. I could go downstairs, have a leisurely lunch in the restaurant, and then take a walk along the Magnificent Mile and window shop until around three. Then I could come back and sit in the lobby until he came.

But first there was one more lead I wanted to follow up. I sat down at the desk and reached into my purse to get the Sunday church program I had found in the Bible. What should I say to the Reverend Nathaniel Carter? Could I just call him up and ask if Naomi Duncan was one of his parishioners?

I could ask about the service for Robert Montgomery.

I dialed the number on the back of the program, hoping it was for the minister's home. If it was for the church, no one would likely be there on a weekday unless it was one of those urban churches that was large enough to have a full-time secretary. The name of the church didn't suggest that.

The telephone was on its third ring when someone picked up. A man, sounding breathless, said, "Hello. Reverend Carter here. How may I help you?" In spite of being out of breath, he sounded delighted to answer this call from whomever it might be.

"Hello, Reverend Carter. I'm so sorry to disturb you—"

"Not at all. Not at all. What can I do for you?"

"I'm a friend—an acquaintance—of Naomi Duncan. I believe she's a member of your church."

"Of course, Sister Naomi, a fine, hard-working member of our fellowship."

"Yes, well, I've been trying to reach her because I had heard that Robert Montgomery— Do you know about Mr. Montgomery?"

"Of course, of course. Naomi brought him to church on his first Sunday after his release from that awful place of confinement. He stopped attending as he weakened, but I hope our message had reached him."

"So Naomi did her prison missionary work through your church?"

"Yes, I'm pleased to say that it was Sister Naomi who urged us to take the message of God into the prison. She reminded us that even those who had sinned so gravely needed God's comfort and forgiveness."

"And I understand she took on Mr. Montgomery as her special project."

"Yes, when she met him there in that sad place, she was deeply moved by his story. He was a man who had spent much of his young manhood in prison, grown sick and old before his time."

I was still back on the first thing that he'd said: *when she met him there*. But Naomi must have known who Montgomery was when she met him. How could she not have known that he was the man who had gone to prison for Nick Mancini's murder. Becca had worked at Mama Lovejoy's place. Naomi was Mama Lovejoy's daughter. How could she not have heard about Mancini's murder and who had been charged with it?

But maybe Naomi had already married and moved to Springfield when Mancini was murdered. Or maybe, even if she had known who Montgomery was, she hadn't been comfortable telling her minister and the members of her congregation about her mother, Mama Lovejoy, and the people she had known before she became a respectable churchwoman.

Reverend Carter was saying, "Hello? Hello, are you still there?"

"Yes, I'm sorry. Did you say Naomi met Robert Montgomery in prison? For some reason I thought she knew him—knew of him—"

"No, he was a stranger that she took to her heart and eventually brought into the warmth and comfort of her home to live out his last days."

"That was so good of her. We never really talked about. . . . Do you know if she believed he was innocent? That he had been wrongly convicted?"

"She never asked him that," Reverend Carter said with great confidence. "We came to bring comfort and salvation to the lost souls like Mr. Montgomery, not sit in judgment. It was not our place to ask."

"But you said she was moved by his story."

"She learned much of it later from his attorney, another fine woman. Mr. Montgomery's attorney came to commend us for our work and to share with us the stories and the needs of those who were imprisoned."

"About Robert Montgomery—his attorney believed he was innocent."

"So she told us. But no one in our fellowship of souls asked Robert to declare his innocence. We sought only to bring him to God's way." He paused. "Forgive me, young woman, I've been going on. You had a reason for your call."

"I was wondering if you had been in touch with Naomi recently."

"Certainly. Certainly. She called me to come to the hospital because she feared Brother Robert was passing."

"So you saw her there?"

"No, the nurse informed me that Naomi had been called away and had needed to leave before I arrived. And I had also arrived too late to pray with Brother Robert."

"But I'm sure he would have been grateful to know you came. Have you spoken to Naomi since she called you last night?"

"No, I have not. Is there a problem?"

"The funeral. I was wondering about Mr. Montgomery's funeral."

"Brother Robert did not wish a service. His body is to be cremated. Sister Naomi will claim his ashes and sprinkle them on his mother's grave."

"Would you happen to know where Naomi is right now, Reverend Carter?"

"Where she is? No, is something wrong?"

"I hope not. I just want to reach her. Thank you very much."

"Who did you say you—"

"Reverend, would you happen to know if Naomi has relatives in Wilmington, North Carolina?"

"Wilmington? I know she has gone there on vacation. I can't recall if she mentioned relatives." He chuckled, a kindly sound. "But then we all have our roots in the rich soil of the South, don't we?"

"Yes, we do," I said. "Thank you so much, Reverend."

"Please join us for services on Sunday, young woman. Come with Naomi."

I said good-bye and hung up the phone.

Well, I'd learned more than I expected.

But I wasn't sure what to make of the fact that Naomi had pretended to know nothing about Montgomery before meeting him in prison. Had she pretended to Montgomery too that she knew nothing about him, had never heard of Becca? And why would she have done that?

I reached for my purse and put the church program back inside. It was time to vacate my room.

CHAPTER · 26

After I stored my suitcase with the bellman, I came back up to the restaurant. While I was waiting for the clam chowder and the seafood salad I had ordered, I took out a notepad and started writing down key points. It was what I always did when I was stuck.

I must have had a scowl on my face and looked either like a racial discrimination investigator or a restaurant critic who was making notes for a scathing review. My waitress rushed over to apologize for the delay in the kitchen and to assure me that my chowder would be right out.

I smiled and told her that I wasn't in a hurry.

She seemed to relax. Maybe she had thought I was someone from the home office doing an evaluation of her job performance.

I went back to my notes. Three months between the two killings. Reuben James on January 2. Nick Mancini on April 1. April Fool's Day, no less.

Becca had been there in front of that house on the night Reuben was gunned down. She had been there in the club on the night Mancini was stabbed to death in his office. Montgomery had confessed to killing Mancini and been sent to prison. Years later, he had been befriended by a prison visitor, Naomi Duncan, who just happened to be TJ's widow.

Her son Percy wanted to know why she had taken Montgomery in. He suspected that her motives were not as pure as they seemed. She might be a good Christian. But being a good Christian might also have been a cover for something else she was up to.

"Here's your chowder," my waitress said. "Sorry again for the delay."

"No problem," I said, moving the notepad aside so she could put down the steaming bowl.

"Your salad will be out shortly."

"Thank you."

"Anything else you need right now?"

"No, I'm fine."

She left, and I tried to find the thought that had scampered away.

I opened my packet of oyster crackers and shook them into my chowder.

Naomi Duncan. Robert Montgomery. What was the connection? Naomi and

Becca must have gotten to know each other when Becca was working at Mama Lovejoy's. Naomi had grown up with Reuben and TJ.

But it was Becca, not Naomi, who was with Reuben and TJ when the drive-by happened. What did the drive-by have to do with the Mancini murder and Robert Montgomery?

I dropped the spoon, splattering chowder.

"Is something wrong?"

I looked up at the waitress, who was back again. "What?" I said.

"With the chowder?"

"No, it's fine. My spoon slipped."

"I brought some more hot water for your tea."

"Thank you."

"You're welcome. Just let me know if you need anything else."

She left and I poured more water into my cup. Then I wrote down the thought that had made me drop my spoon. A triangle: Reuben James, Becca, Nick Mancini.

Tess had said if Becca was crazy enough to get involved with two men like Reuben and Nick, she was lucky to have gotten out of it alive. That was what I should be focusing on. I should be playing out that scenario of Becca and those two men, the mobster and the gang-member-turned-Black Panther. Suppose Becca had taken Reuben as a lover, and suppose Mancini found out. Suppose Mancini, in a rage, ordered a hit on Reuben. Her lover was gunned down in front of her eyes, and Becca knew Mancini was responsible. She decided to avenge Reuben's death.

The only problem with that theory was that Becca herself could have been killed in the drive-by. Would Mancini have been in such a rage that he would have risked killing his mistress too? Had he wanted her dead? And if she thought that, then why on earth would she have gone on working at the club?

She might have been afraid to leave, but nothing about the way the bartender had described her behavior when Mancini confronted her suggested that. She seemed to feel in control. Presumably at that point, she was still his mistress, because Mancini had gone to her apartment and expected her to be there. He had waited outside in his car. That must mean he didn't have a key. He was paying for the place and hadn't insisted on having a key? How had she pulled that one off?

Okay, say she did suspect him of arranging the drive-by. But she went on working at the club. Maybe that had been the whole point. Maybe she had been lulling Mancini into a false sense of security, letting him think he had reclaimed her . . . and then she killed him.

Could that be what Naomi Duncan was afraid of? Could she know that Becca had killed Mancini? Maybe she had always known, or maybe she had found out the truth from Montgomery. And now I had come around asking questions, and she was making herself scarce until I went away.

I spooned chowder into my mouth and reached for the pepper shaker.

But it was Tad, Naomi's son, who had given me Reuben's name. He knew that his mother didn't want me to know about Reuben. Yet, for some reason, he thought that his father, TJ, would have wanted me to know. Why?

Maybe if there was some danger, Naomi hadn't told Tad what it was, hadn't explained why I needed to be kept in the dark. And Tad, who seemed like a nice kid, had felt sorry for me, wanted to help me find my mother.

But why had he thought knowing about Reuben's death would help me do that?

I ate another spoon of chowder and stared at the names I'd scrawled on the page. Reuben. TJ. Naomi. Becca. The one thing they all had in common was Mama Lovejoy. But Mama was dead and the Shack was gone.

Mancini had met Becca at the Shack. Was that where Becca had met Reuben? But if she had met Reuben at the Shack, wouldn't she have met him before she met Mancini? And, in that case, why had she become Mancini's mistress, if she was already involved with Reuben?

But this was Becca I was talking about. Nothing I knew about her suggested she had ever felt it necessary to be monogamous. Mancini had money, and according to Sonny, he had been charming. He had offered her a chance to be his featured performer.

As for Reuben, maybe she had been raising her political consciousness with him. Who knows? She could have been thinking of becoming a Black Panther. She could have hung with Elaine Brown and Angela Davis.

"Here's your seafood salad," my waitress said. "Are you done with your chowder?"

"Yes, thank you."

She picked up the empty bowl. "Just let me know if you need anything else."

"I'm fine, thanks."

It was possible that I was underestimating Becca's cunning. She had been smart enough to play whatever game she had been playing with Mancini and still get out of Chicago alive. Of course, I was assuming she had left Chicago on her own steam and not in the back of a garbage truck.

I picked up my fork and speared a shrimp in my seafood salad. Why couldn't I have had a June Cleaver mother who did the housework wearing pearls?

At 3:30, I started getting anxious. I tried Sheppard's cell phone. There was no answer. I left a message, reminding him that I was waiting to be picked up for the airport.

I called back ten minutes later. Then I tried his office phone.

Now I was not only concerned about missing my flight, I was beginning to worry about Sheppard.

The bellman, who had been watching me pace, asked if I'd like a taxi. I called

Sheppard's cell phone again and left a voice mail telling him that I was taking a taxi to the airport and would call him when I got home.

In the taxi, I called Tess. She was away from her desk. I didn't leave a message. There was no point in worrying her. I couldn't ask her to send Luis out to look for Sheppard.

I would call Sheppard when I got home. If I still couldn't reach him, Quinn could call Wade and Wade would get someone to make sure he was all right.

It was probably like last night when he had gone off to Springfield and then been busy checking hospitals for Montgomery and hadn't bothered to return my calls.

But today he knew I was waiting for him to take me to the airport. I couldn't believe he wouldn't pick up his cell phone and tell me he had been delayed or couldn't make it.

I squirmed on the taxi seat that was nowhere near as cushy as the limo I'd taken in from the airport when I arrived. Where was Nico Mancini? He had been keeping a surprisingly low profile for the past couple of days. I glanced at the photo of the cab driver and then at the man behind the wheel. They matched. We were headed to the airport.

But where was Sheppard?

C H A P T E R · 2 7

An accident less than a mile from the terminal had tied up traffic in both lanes. My taxi driver looked at me as if I were crazy when I said maybe I should get out and walk the rest of the way. But from the number of people climbing out of their cars and glancing at their watches, I didn't think I was the only one considering that course of action.

Before it could come to that, the police got things moving again.

I huffed my way to my departure gate but managed to make it in time.

While we were waiting for the door to close, I got out my cell phone and tried Sheppard one more time. Still no answer. Where was he?

"Problem?" my seatmate asked.

She looked chatty, and I didn't feel like chatting. I shook my head. "I was calling to say good-bye to a friend."

I made a production of leaning back in my seat and closing my eyes. She took the hint.

The nap I pretended to take turned into a real one. When I opened my eyes, the flight attendant was announcing our approach to Greensboro. We came down through puffy clouds to a bright sunny early evening. I would be home well before dark. That was the upside of summer—or rather late spring—travel.

As soon as the flight attendant gave the all clear, I dug out my cell phone again. I had a text message to call a phone number that I didn't recognize. It could have been left by someone who misdialed, but it was a Chicago area code, so I punched in the numbers.

"Hello?" a scratchy, groggy male voice answered.

"Hello, this is Lizzie—"

"Professor Stuart? Sheppard here."

"Mr. Sheppard? Are you all right? You sound—"

"Good painkillers."

"Painkillers!" I said the word too loud, and my seatmate shot me an uncertain glance. "Where are you?" I said into the phone. "What happened?"

"Hospital. Had a little run-in with Percy and his partner."

"A run-in? What did they—"

"Waiting for me when I came up the stairs to my office—"

"Oh, no!"

"I got in a few more licks than they expected." He laughed and then groaned. "Shouldn't have done that. Got a couple of busted ribs. And a headache."

"A headache? What did they do? Did they—"

"No, I fell down the stairs on my own. Be out of here in a day or two. Just wanted to let you know what became of me."

"I'm so sorry. I should have made sure you were all right before I left."

"Client's not supposed to be watching out for the PI."

"Do you need . . . should I call Wade?"

"Called him already. Everything's under control."

"What about Percy and his friend?"

"Could have got them when they ran by me down the stairs. Didn't want to shoot them."

"They got away?"

"They didn't make it far. Cops picked them up. Cooling their heels in jail."

"Well, I'm glad to hear that. I'm so sorry this happened, Mr. Sheppard."

"Not your fault. I hurt Percy's pride."

"So he and his friend responded by beating you up?"

My seatmate was staring at me openly now.

Sheppard said, "They were trying to get into my office. I came back too soon. So they jumped me."

"Are you sure you're all right?"

"Been a lot worse than this." He grunted as if he might be changing positions. "Just called to tell you about Wilmington."

"Wilmington?" I had almost forgotten. "You had time to find out—"

"Not much. Just that Mama Lovejoy was from there. That don't mean Mrs. D. and Tad went there. But Percy and his pal seemed to think they weren't to be found here in Chicago." His voice was fading out.

"You get some sleep and take care of yourself," I said. "I'll call and check on you later."

"You don't have to—"

"I want to and I'm going to. Thank you for everything, Mr. Sheppard."

"Just doing my job," he said.

As I clicked my phone off, my seatmate said, "Problem with your friend."

"Job-related mishap."

"But I thought I heard you say something about someone beating—"

"Did you? Then you must have been shocked."

She looked at me. She opened her mouth, then closed it.

I felt bad about being rude. She had been a captive audience to that call, and I couldn't blame her for being curious. But I couldn't deal with her curiosity right now. I had to decide what to do about Naomi Duncan and Wilmington.

C H A P T E R · 2 8

All I had to do was keep walking through the airport and out the door. I could pick up my car from the parking lot and be home in time to spend the evening with Quinn. I pulled my suitcase over and sat down in an empty row of seats by one of the gates that wasn't in use. I needed to think about this some more.

I could get in my car and go home. But I might not have another chance to go on with my search. I needed to have that eye exam. In fact, as soon as I told Quinn, he would insist I get in as soon as possible to see the optometrist. If there was a problem, I would have to focus on that, on dealing with it. I would have to depend on someone else to find Becca.

The truth was, a PI might be better equipped to find both Naomi and Becca, but what would a detective say to either woman when he found her. This search was something I needed to do myself. I could use all the help I could get, but I needed to be there when the trail ended. With Naomi, I had the feeling I needed to be wherever she was as soon as possible because she was panicked, running. I needed to go with this lead because it might be my only opportunity to find her and talk to her again.

I touched the ring on the chain around my neck. If I went home now, I would also have to give Quinn an answer about which hand. Even if it turned out I wasn't going blind, I couldn't lie to him and say, "I'll forget about my mother, if you will. Let's go on from here. The two of us."

Happily ever after only happens in fairy tales. Real life has challenges and pitfalls, and starting with a lie would be building on a shaky foundation. Telling Quinn that I could forget about Becca was a lie. It would be there between us. He would know and I would know, and it would wear us down.

I couldn't live that way. I wouldn't bring a child into the world and make him or her live that way. I wanted no child of mine to feel that I was watching him or her for signs of delinquency or something worse.

Hester Rose had done that with me. I knew she loved me, but she had watched me so closely, been so concerned that I always be well-behaved, that I had known that she was afraid I would turn out like Becca. I had spent my childhood and much of my adult life being good to prove to her that I was different from my mother.

I never wanted to do that to a child of mine. But I might end up doing that if I didn't follow this search to the end. If I was afraid of what was inside of me because of Becca and my father, wouldn't I have that same fear about a child I produced?

If Quinn wanted children, I couldn't deprive him of having them because I was afraid. I had to try to find Becca so I would know rather than fear the unknown. I had to find her so I could stop hearing Hester Rose's voice in my head telling Becca to pray for herself and the child growing inside her.

I was that child grown up, and I'd damn well had enough. I wanted answers. Someone was going to give me some answers.

If I found Naomi, she might be able to give me another lead on Becca.

Wilmington would be my last attempt. If Naomi wasn't there, I would have no more leads to follow and I would go home and leave this search to the professionals. But I had to at least try.

I got up and grabbed my suitcase by the handle. All right, decision made. I was going to Wilmington.

First, I called my dean's office and left a message in his secretary's voice mail to the effect that I had a personal emergency and I would need to reschedule tomorrow afternoon's meeting with the provost and the VP for Academic Affairs. Amos Baylor, my dean, was not going to like that, but there was nothing he could do about it except complain about the timing of my emergency when I returned on Monday. The funding for the Institute was coming from an endowment to the School of Criminal Justice, and a part of the bargain was that I would serve as executive director. There was nothing Amos could do to change that unless I made a mess of it. Missing a meeting was not sufficient.

My next call was to Quinn. I left a message on his answering machine at home. I said I had to go to Wilmington and would call later that evening and explain.

He was not going to be happy with me either. If we were discussing this matter now, he would point out that my theory that Naomi and Tad had gone to Wilmington was based on nothing more substantial than a bookmarked Web site and a crab notepaper caddy.

I would answer that Mama Lovejoy had come from Wilmington. Maybe it was a place that her daughter thought of as "home" the way migrants from the South often did. "Going home." "Going down home to see the folks." "Sending that boy down home before he gets into any more trouble." "Going home because I can't live up here in this city no more."

Maybe Naomi had gone "home" and taken her son with her.

I didn't have time to wait for Sheppard to get up out of his hospital bed or Wade to check it out using his resources. I needed to follow the trail myself.

C H A P T E R · 2 9

I tried not to wince as I handed over my credit card for an expensive seat on the commuter plane to Wilmington. Driving would have been cheaper, but I didn't have that kind of time.

The flight was short. I spent most of it not looking out the window. When it comes to flying, I prefer to see the ground only during take-offs and landings. And I prefer not to have to bend my head to make my way down the aisle to my seat.

To keep from listening for engine problems, I started developing a game plan. I ran through the few bits of information I had about Wilmington. My grandfather, Walter Lee, who had been a huge fan of the Harlem Globetrotters, had once told me that Meadowlark Lemon was born there. And I knew that Wilmington had a state university and a famous historic district. The city had also been the scene of a race riot in 1898. I knew that because I had looked at the Wilmington riot in conjunction with the riot in Gallagher fifteen years earlier. Both had been episodes in the post-Reconstruction return to the racial status quo.

What else did I know about the area? The Cape Fear region had provided the title for the John D. MacDonald suspense novel. I'd seen both movies, original and remake. I liked the original best. Great, that should help with my search.

But my impression was that the city wasn't that large. I could rent a car and drive myself around rather than relying on taxis. So first get a car. Then find a hotel.

And then if I had to, I would stop black people on the street and ask if they had ever heard of Mama Lovejoy and knew of any of her relatives. Was that her real name? Lovejoy? It sounded like a raunchy blues woman name.

All right, after car and hotel, that should be next on my list. Call Sheppard and ask about Mama's name. I would leave out the part about being in Wilmington. With a concussion and busted ribs, the poor man had enough to occupy his mind.

And I would have to make sure Quinn understood that Sheppard had not suggested I go off on my own.

At the rental car counter, I got a map and directions to the hotel I had located at the airport courtesy desk. The car I had been assigned was a red Cavalier. It occurred to me as I was loading my suitcase into the trunk that a less conspicuous color might have been in order. With Percy and his partner in jail, it was unlikely that anyone else would think of coming to Wilmington to look for Naomi. But I was a little concerned about the fact that Nico Mancini was doing something of which his mother and Sonny disapproved. When I imagined myself in his place, I would have been following me to see if I would lead him to the woman who had been involved in his father's death and might be able to tell him what had really happened. If I were Nico, I would want to find Becca too.

That worried me. But he certainly hadn't been on my commuter flight, and even if he did have a pilot's license, he would have to get here. Then he would have to find me before he could follow me. Just the same, I almost went back inside and asked for a fade-into-traffic beige car.

I was glad I had arrived after rush hour when the highway I was following via the Martin Luther King Jr. Parkway came to a confusing four-way intersection. I was saved by the fact the young woman at the rental car desk had written out her directions on the map she had given me. I was still a little unsure until I saw the Landfall gated community that she had told me to watch out for, followed by the traffic lights with the shopping mall on the right.

I waited for the light and then turned into the driveway leading to the hotel. It was tucked away behind a steak house and across from an office complex. Once my red car was parked, no one was going to spot it from the highway.

I checked in at the desk and maneuvered my way around the cozy seating area and down the hall past the breakfast room. Seeing the empty tables reminded me that I should have stopped for food. But it had been getting dark fast and I'd wanted to find the hotel. Besides, I needed to call Sheppard before he went to sleep for the night.

He was already asleep. His voice was even groggier than before when he answered.

"I'm so sorry to bother you again tonight, Mr. Sheppard."

He grunted. "No bother. You get home okay?"

"Actually, I'm calling because I have a question. I was wondering if Lovejoy was Mama's real name?"

"Her real name? Let me think . . . Reed. Catherine Reed."

"Do you know if she still has relatives in Wilmington?"

"Don't know. Didn't have time to check."

"Thank you, Mr. Sheppard. Go back to sleep."

"Hold on a minute. Why do you—?"

"Everything's fine. I'll call tomorrow."

I hung up and wrote down the name he had given me. Then I took out the telephone directory. I saw quickly that calling all the Reeds in Wilmington would take a while. If she had relatives, they might not be Reeds anyway. Besides, I was hungry and tired, and it was getting late.

The public library, that's where I should start. Librarians always either had the answer or knew the right person to ask. I returned to the hotel lobby.

"There's one on Military Cutoff Road," the desk clerk told me. "But it's closed by now."

"Thank you, I'll try it in the morning," I said. "Right now, I'm going to find some dinner."

"The steak house is good," she said.

I shook my head. "I need fast and to-go."

The Chinese take-out I had noticed near the entrance to the shopping mall across the road was still open. I ordered shrimp and cashews and then added won ton soup.

Back in my room, I turned on the television and stared at a reality dating show while I ate. I couldn't quite get into the problems that the twenty-something Atlanta singles were having as they tried to make "love connections."

Reality was the argument that I was about to have with Quinn.

I shoved the rest of my rice and the empty soup container back into the plastic bag and squashed the whole thing into the wastebasket beside the desk.

"Lizabeth?" he said when he picked up the phone.

"ESP?" I said. "Did you get my message about Wilmington? I'm here and checked in. Let me give you the hotel information."

He was silent as he wrote down the hotel name and telephone number. Then he said, "I bite. Why did you go to Wilmington?"

"That's what I called to tell you about."

"Then tell me."

I told him about Robert Montgomery's death and the disappearance of Naomi Duncan and Tad. I told him about Mama Lovejoy's connection to Wilmington and why I thought Naomi and her son might have come here.

When I finished my recital, he said, "Where's Sheppard?"

"Well, that's another story. He's in the hospital. He was attacked."

"Attacked! Were you there when it happened?"

"No, and the two men who did it are in jail." I told him what had happened at the Duncan house and that Percy and Earl had gone to Sheppard's office. "But he's going to be all right."

"And hearing the news, you decided to get on a plane and go to Wilmington to look for the mother of one of the men who put him in the hospital."

"Since Percy and his partner are in jail, it should be safe to look for Naomi. All I'm going to do is ask around for Mama Lovejoy's relatives. If I can't find them, I'll be home tomorrow."

"And what if you do find these relatives? What if you find Naomi Duncan?"

"Then I'll ask her about Becca and Reuben James. I'll ask her if she knows where Becca might have gone. Maybe she can give me a lead."

"And what if she does give you a lead, Lizabeth?"

"If that happens . . . if I have a lead, then it makes sense to follow it."

"Sense? It makes sense when the PI who has been investigating this—"

"I told you that Percy and—"

"I heard what you told me. And what do you expect me to do while you're out playing detective, Lizzie?"

"I'm not playing at anything Quinn. This is serious. This is my life."

"What about our life together?"

"This has nothing to do with—"

"Do you happen to remember that I gave you a ring before you left for Chicago?" he said.

"Yes, I do remember that. You said we would talk about it when I got home."

"I didn't know then that you would decide not to come home after Chicago."

"I didn't know that either. Quinn, this is really important to me . . . to us."

"To us? Lizabeth, I don't give a bloody damn about your long-lost mother."

"That's too bad, because I do. I want to find her."

"And I want you to come home."

"I'll be home as soon as I've done all I can do about finding Becca. Quinn, I need to do this. I—"

"Right." The phone clicked in my ear, and I stood there staring at it.

That had gone well.

CHAPTER · 30

Thursday, June 10

I didn't sleep much Wednesday night. I felt guilty because I was making Quinn worry about me. And I was mad at him for not understanding how important finding Becca was to me, even if I hadn't told him all the reasons why it was important.

Why couldn't he trust my judgment? My good sense?

At 7:30, I got up and showered and went down to breakfast. In the self-service dining room, I popped one of the omelet packets into the microwave and helped myself to a slice of whole wheat toast and an apple. Then I carried my food and a Styrofoam cup of herbal tea to one of the tables. My fellow guests were much too bright and cheery to suit my mood. I focused on the presidential campaign news on CNN.

I made a quick stop back in my room to brush my teeth and pick up the Wilmington guidebook I'd bought in the airport. Then I headed out the door.

"Have a good day," the desk clerk called out as I passed.

That remained to be seen.

I was pulling out of my parking place when my cell phone rang. I slammed on the brake and reached for my shoulder bag. "Hello?"

"What's wrong?" Quinn said. "Why are you answering your phone like that?"

"Like what?"

"Like you're worried about who it might be."

"Well, after the way you hung up on me last night—"

"Dammit, Lizzie!" He paused for a five count. "I'm sorry I hung up on you."

"You were upset. Quinn, I know that this—"

"Let's not get into that again, Lizabeth. I've got a meeting in ten minutes. But I want you to call me if—"

"If anything at all happens. Yes, I'll do that."

"And I want you to be careful."

"I will. Promise."

"Lizzie, I really can't get away right now. One of the academic buildings was vandalized with gang graffiti last night. I've got a surveillance going on, and the *Gazette* ran a front-page story this morning about gangs spreading to the campus. We haven't caught a break yet on the rape investigation, and I've got parents calling about—"

"I understand, Quinn. You don't have to explain. You're the university police chief. Twenty-six thousand students, plus faculty and staff, are depending on you to keep the campus safe."

"Thank you, Professor Stuart, for reminding me of my responsibilities," he said, his voice bone dry. "And for being so damn understanding."

"I was agreeing with you about your responsibilities. And are we going to fight now because I'm understanding?"

"I don't have time for another fight. I have a meeting. I'm trying to get through to Wade to see if he has anyone in the Wilmington area."

"Quinn, I don't need—"

"I don't want you out there alone."

"Thank you. I love you too."

"Leave your cell phone on."

"Yes. It's fully charged and in my purse."

"I'll call you back after I talk to Wade."

"If I don't pick up, it'll be because I'm in the library doing some research. No cell phones allowed."

He made a profane observation about library policies and hung up.

I squinted at the bright morning sunlight and breathed a sigh of relief. Quinn grumpy and not thrilled was better than no Quinn at all.

What had I done with my sunglasses?

The branch library on Military Cutoff Road was called the Northeast Regional Library. The reference librarian on duty listened to what I was trying to find—I told her it was a research project on Mama Lovejoy—and then suggested I try the Main Library downtown. She gave me the names of the two archivists who could help me with the special collection on African-Americans in Wilmington. She thought that collection would be a good starting point.

She suggested that while I was at her library, I should look at the local black newspaper. She pointed out the newspaper in the periodicals section, and I gathered up the several issues on display and took them to a table nearby.

No Reed family related to Mama Lovejoy leaped out of the pages and said, "Here we are." But after reading the political commentary and editorials and society news, I began to get a better sense of the black community in Wilmington.

I read the ads too. Funeral home directors always knew everyone and their business. That was a definite possibility. So were beauty shops and restaurants. I could try a couple of those. I wrote down business names and addresses. I was about to close the newspaper when it occurred to me to add the newspaper's own office address and telephone number to my list.

While I was at it, I decided to have a look at an issue of the *Star-News,* the city's main newspaper. The front-page story was about the impact of the weather on beach erosion. It seemed erosion was a major concern for owners of beachfront homes, and a photo showed a house that had been condemned. I flipped through the rest of the paper but saw nothing that seemed related to my search.

I closed my notebook after jotting down the address and telephone number for this newspaper too. Better to have a notebook full of information you didn't use than not to have what you needed when you needed it.

I walked out of the air-conditioned library and discovered that the day had warmed up much faster than I had anticipated when I was dressing this morning. I would just have to think cool thoughts. When out doing academic research, I usually found it wiser to opt for a skirt and jacket rather than more casual attire. It seemed a good idea to adopt the same dress code here, where I was asking questions and wanted people to believe what my business card said.

Following the directions the librarian had given me, I headed toward downtown. This stretch of highway was much more congested. Not just more cars, but restaurants and strip malls and motels. I was lucky that the tourist season had not yet gotten into full swing.

I almost drove on past. Then I made a snap decision and turned into the parking lot of the Beachcomber Café. I was ready for an early lunch because I was starving again—a combination of nervous energy and lack of sleep. Besides, if I ate before I went to the Main Library, I wouldn't have to cope with a grumbling stomach while I was looking for Reed relatives.

The first thing I saw when I walked through the door was the pitchers of tea sitting on a table under an easel board with the day's specials. The TV over the bar was tuned to CNN.

I asked for a booth, non-smoking. The globes covering the lights had the names of rival teams: UNC-Wilmington's Seahawks, Duke's Blue Devils, Georgia Tech, Clemson, William & Mary, NC State, USC. I entertained myself reading through the globes and looking at the seaport/seashore art on the wall until my chowder arrived.

The man in the booth behind me was telling his friend a story about a fishing trip. He had been twelve miles out when he opened a can of Vienna sausages and his inexperienced fishing companion turned green.

I had never actually seen anyone turn green. When I realized how much thought I was giving to that, I pulled out my Wilmington guidebook.

By the time I finished my chowder and the fish platter I'd ordered, I was well versed on the tourist attractions I didn't have time to see. A tour of the *Battleship North Carolina* would have been fun. On the other hand, after being trailed by Percy and his buddy Earl when I did the river cruise in Chicago, I was probably better off staying on dry land.

I thought about dry land again when I was back on the highway. As I got closer to downtown, a round blue sign pointed out the hurricane evacuation route. A sign for the trauma center came soon after. I hoped to avoid both while I was in Wilmington.

I passed down a tree-lined street with stately homes. I saw churches and the science museum. Then I came out into the central downtown area that I had seen on the map. Here the streets were laid out in grid fashion. If I got confused, it looked like I should be able to head downhill toward the river and reorient myself.

A red brick and gray granite building with a clock tower turned out to be the New Hanover County Courthouse. Next street up was the New Hanover County Law Enforcement Center. Now I knew where to find county records and the police. I parked and walked the couple of blocks to the library on Chestnut.

When I asked about the archives, I was directed to the second floor. I knew I was in the right place as soon as I opened the door. A man and a woman were engaged in one of those conversations about genealogy that must take place dozens of times a day in libraries across the South. They probably do in other parts of the country as well, but I only know how they go in Southern libraries: "His brother's daughter married my grandmother's third cousin. That's how they got in our family."

I went up to the desk and explained my mission, mentioning the name of the librarian at the Northeast Regional Library. The archivist nodded her head. Before she could speak, a patron going through a bound book at one of the tables nearby looked up and asked, "How far back does that collection of African-Americans in Wilmington go anyway?"

"The Civil War," the librarian said. "The man who started it clipped newspapers all his life. Then after he died, other people in his family continued it."

She then led me into a small room, where she pointed out several boxes in alphabetical order by family name.

"I need the Rs, please," I said.

"Here you go." She handed me a box. "Just help yourself if you need another one."

I took the "R-Smythe" box out into the main room and claimed a table. As I was settling down, it occurred to me that I might have saved some time if I had called the black newspaper and spoken to the society editor. Mama Lovejoy might even have performed in her hometown. If I had gotten a halfway decent night's sleep, I would have thought of that when I was going through the newspapers at the branch library. But I was here now, so I might as well see what I could find, just in case I drew a blank everywhere else.

I would be able to tell Amos Baylor, my dean, that even in the midst of my personal emergency, I had been doing research on collections we should know about for the Institute.

The items were taped or glued onto index cards. Some were brown with age, the date written in with ink. Census enumerations, obituaries, marriage notices, purchases of lots. Deaths by accidents and mischance. I worked my way through the cards, moving from the 1860s into the twentieth century. An article from 1902 gave me pause. Titled "Bitten by One of the Blue Gums," it was about the arrest of a colored man with blue gums (as a result of pigmentation, not disease) who had bitten a blind colored woman. According to the article, it was generally accepted in the South that the bite of a "blue gum nigger" was as poisonous as that of a rattlesnake.

What medical treatment did they give the woman who had been bitten? The article didn't say. Maybe they just waited to see if she survived.

I grabbed my notebook and pencil. This one should definitely be included in the exhibit we were going to do at the Institute on crime and folklore.

An article from 1979 had a more positive tone and more relevance to the reason I was there. The story was about the Willis Richardson Players, a black drama group named after a Wilmington native whose family had left town following the 1898 race riot. According to the author, Richardson had been the first black playwright to have a one-act play on Broadway. The article announced a production by the Players at the Community Arts Center. "Jive, Jazz, and Blues." Saluting the great composers Waller, Blake, and Ellington and performers like Billie Holiday, Bert Williams, and Cab Calloway.

Mama Lovejoy was not listed among the luminaries. I hadn't really expected her to be.

I had gone through the box, and the only Reed I'd found mentioned was an 1860 census entry for two mulattoes, age twenty and twenty-three, a brick layer and his wife.

"Find anything?" the librarian asked me when I came up to the desk.

"I'm afraid not. But the entries were fascinating."

"You know, we were just talking." She nodded toward her coworker behind the desk. "What you might want to do is stop by DeLong's Restaurant. Someone there might be able to help you."

The other archivist said, "There's a section of town you might want to try too. There's a fish market over there. They fry up what they sell, and people from the neighborhood are in and out all the time."

They gave me the directions and agreed that a call to the black newspaper might also be useful. The patron at the table piped in that I might find someone right out on the street who could tell me what I wanted to know.

Well, yes, I had thought of that. As I was walking back to my car, I decided to put it to the test.

The middle-aged black man I was walking toward nodded as we came abreast. "Excuse me, please," I said. "I wonder if you could help me with some directions?"

He stopped. "What are you looking for?"

"I'm trying to find the relatives of a friend of mine. She told me that they used to live here in Wilmington. My friend's mother was a blues singer who ended up in Chicago. Mama Lovejoy."

He shook his head. "Can't say I know the name."

"The relatives would be Reeds."

He smiled. "Lots of Reeds around here."

"Then maybe you could tell me, is there a black part of town?"

"People are scattered around, in different sections. But there's one place you might want to try." He started to give me the same directions the librarian had.

I mentioned the fish market.

"Yes, that's a good idea," he said. "They might know in there."

I tried DeLong's Restaurant first. After making a wrong turn and going past the street, I found it. But according to a handwritten sign stuck in the window, the restaurant was closed for the day because of a family emergency.

The fish market wouldn't be busy yet, and I wanted to go when the maximum number of people would be around—adults stopping to pick up dinner on their way home from work, kids hanging out with their friends. That meant I had an hour or so to kill.

I drove back down the hill toward the river. Water Street ran adjacent to the wharf and the river walk. A tidy little park looked out over the water, with shops and restaurants along both sides of the street. I pulled up at a meter in front of a shop that advertised its products as "A Taste of Wilmington." That sounded intriguing, but I had another matter to take care of.

I flipped through my notebook and found the phone number for the black newspaper. The receptionist transferred me to the society editor, but she was away from her desk. I left a message identifying myself as Professor Lizabeth Stuart and explaining I was doing some research on a blues singer from Wilmington named Mama Lovejoy. I said that I hoped she might be able to put me in touch with relatives in the city. I said I would be in town until tomorrow morning.

The park was calling to me. I got out of the car and put money in the meter and walked over. Benches provided seating for those who wanted to sit and watch the Cape Fear River as they chatted or snacked. I sat down and looked up the river at the bridge and across in the other direction at the *Battleship North Carolina*. I could imagine this plaza later in the summer. Tourists would be as common as the pigeons that had flocked around the woman feeding them bread crumbs from a brown paper bag.

But it was a peaceful afternoon. A fiddler farther down the wharf had his case open for tips. He was singing "Oh! Susanna." I could have drowsed there in the sun with the light breeze off the water.

I got up and walked back the way I had come, past the Hilton Hotel, and across the street to the Cotton Exchange. There was a parking lot out in front. According to the guidebook, this was the first shopping complex in North Carolina to make use of existing buildings. I wanted to poke around a little inside. The buildings were supposed to date back to the nineteenth century.

The interior had wooden floors and beams and twisting corridors. The buildings were linked by walkways and courtyards. I ended up in a jewelry store upstairs and found a pair of silver clip earrings. Back downstairs, I had a look inside a shop specializing in Celtic merchandise and bought Quinn a CD of Irish ballads.

That was it. Enough playing tourist. I resisted going into the shop that sold Wilmington food items. I would end up buying the salsa I saw in the window or something else that I would have to figure out how to pack.

I got out my directions and headed back up the hill from the riverfront. I thought I had seen the street I was looking for on my way downtown.

CHAPTER · 31

I had been right about the fish market. It was busy around dinnertime. I squeezed inside. The three metal chairs for customers waiting for their orders to be fried up were all occupied. All the customers were black, and a black woman worked the cash register. A white man in rubber boots passed through, greeting customers.

Behind the fish counter, a black man cut and filleted fresh fish and weighed up orders. He and the other man moved between the metal freezer and the metal sinks. I pretended interest in the fresh fish for a few minutes. Then before they could get to me, I went back to the counter and looked at the fish fry menu.

The place had a clean fishy smell. The cement floor was well scrubbed.

I watched the other customers while I waited for my turn to order. I wasn't quite sure how to go about identifying my would-be source of information. Should I pick out someone and ask my question, hoping anyone in hearing distance would chime in?

I placed my order for fried clams and claimed one of the metal chairs when it was vacated. The door opened and a woman came in, leaning on a cane.

The woman behind the counter and a couple of the younger customers greeted her as "Miss Evelyn." She acknowledged the greetings with a brisk "good afternoon." The woman sitting beside me got up and insisted Miss Evelyn take her chair. Miss Evelyn did with a regal nod of her head.

And I knew I had found my source.

I received my order before she did. I walked up the street and got in my car and sat there eating my clams while I watched the entrance to the market. When I finished, I found a moisturized wipe in my purse. Then I walked back down the street and back into the fish market.

Miss Evelyn was still waiting for her order. I found some bottled water and looked around some more. I was wondering how much longer I would have to stall, when the woman at the cash register came out from behind the counter with a brown paper bag. As she delivered it to Miss Evelyn, still seated in her chair, she apologized that the special order had taken so long to fry up.

I almost laughed. Dignified elderly women could put you through your paces.

Miss Evelyn rose and started for the door. I paid for my bottled water and followed her out of the market.

She turned her head, catching me by surprise. "Yes?"

"Uh . . . excuse me, I—"

"Speak up, young woman. I saw you hanging round in there watching me. What you want?"

"I was wondering if you could help me, ma'am." I glanced after two boys in low-rider jeans who bopped past us. "I'm looking for a friend of mine and her son. My friend told me she has relatives here in Wilmington."

"Who is she?"

"Naomi Duncan."

"Don't know her."

"Well, maybe you know of her mother. Her mother came from Wilmington. Her name was Catherine Reed. She moved up to Chicago."

"Chicago, you say?"

"Yes, ma'am. She was a blues singer and called herself Mama Lovejoy."

Miss Evelyn shook her head. "Don't know her either." Her gaze narrowed. "You say this friend of yours got a son?"

"Yes, ma'am. He's about fifteen years old. His name is Tad."

She gestured with her cane. "You see that street up there by the garage?"

"Yes, ma'am."

"You go up that street about two blocks. It'll be a gray house with a big crack in the sidewalk in front of it. Green chairs out on the porch that need painting. You ask them there."

"Ask them what?"

"About that boy they got staying there. He's from Chicago."

"Who are the people who—?"

"They ain't Duncans or Reeds. But they got a boy staying there. You ask about him."

"Thank you, ma'am."

"You're welcome." She gestured with her cane again. "Go on, you don't have to walk slow as me."

C H A P T E R · 3 2

Tad was out on the front porch, sitting in one of the green chairs with the peeling paint. He was hunched over a book. He looked up and our eyes met.

I was as startled to find him sitting right there as he was to see me.

I opened my mouth to speak, and he scrambled to his feet.

"Tad! Wait, I need to talk to you."

He grabbed the handle of the screen door. "I can't talk to you."

"Is your mother here?"

"She left."

The screen door banged. The wooden front door closed behind it.

I climbed the three steps and knocked on the door. No one came.

I kept knocking. Then I started ringing the bell.

The woman who flung the door open looked nothing like Naomi Duncan. She was big breasted and big hipped and café au lait. Her short hair had been bleached blonde. She said, "If anyone here wanted to talk to you, we would have opened the door."

"I'm sorry to intrude, but I need to speak to Tad."

"He has nothing to say to you."

"I need to ask him about his mother."

She put her hands on her hips. "Did you hear what I said to you, girl? Get the hell off my porch before I call the police."

"Maybe you should ask Tad if his mother would want you to do that."

She glared at me, but she hesitated. "What does that mean?"

"Did Naomi tell you why she left Chicago?"

Her hesitation had passed. "It's none of your damn business what Naomi told me. Get the hell off my porch."

The door slammed. I knew she wasn't going to open it again.

I turned away and walked back down the street. When I came out on to the main thoroughfare, I was hoping I would see Miss Evelyn, but she was nowhere in sight. Wherever she had been going, she had gotten there.

Plenty of other people were out on the street. I thought of asking them about the woman, but knowing about her was not likely to get me through her door. She seemed to know who I was and that Naomi wouldn't want me to talk to Tad.

I sat there in my car thinking, and then I decided to play a long shot. I started the car and drove past the house and parked down a block. I didn't have an envelope, so I wrote my note and folded it. I put Tad's name on the outside, but I assumed the woman would grab it first.

I wrote, "Your brother is in jail. Urgent that I talk to your mother about him. Your mother may be in danger." I went up the steps and slid the note under the door. Then I sat down in one of the chairs to wait.

I heard voices raised inside. Then the front door was thrown open. Tad shot out on the porch with the woman right behind him.

"You get your skinny ass back in here," she said.

"No! I want to talk to her, Cousin Darlene. I'm worried about my moms and Percy."

I stood up.

Darlene, hands on hips, looked like she was ready to deck me. "I told you to get the hell—"

"I need to talk to Tad."

"I want to talk to her too," Tad said.

Darlene looked from me to him. Then she threw her hands up. "Your mama goes off and leaves me to watch you. What does she expect me to do?" She went back into her house and slammed the door.

I gestured toward the chairs. Tad and I sat down next to each other.

"Why's Percy in jail?" he said.

"He and his buddy beat up Mr. Sheppard."

"Da-a-amn." He drew the word out, looking disgusted. "Sometimes Percy does stuff he ought to know not to do." He looked down at his hands, then at me. "That's why him and my moms don't get along."

I let that one pass. "I need to talk to your mother, Tad."

"What did you mean about her being in danger?"

"I was trying to get you to come out."

"You mean you were lying?"

"Stretching the truth. As far as I know, your mother's not in danger. But there is a situation that I need to discuss with her."

"About your moms?"

"And Reuben James. Thank you, by the way, for calling and leaving me the message about Reuben."

He looked away, down the street. "My moms flipped out when she found out about that."

"You told her what you did?"

"I figured you'd ask her about it and she'd find out."

"Was that when she said the two of you had to come here?"

"No, that was after old Robert died." Tad cleared his throat and blinked. "She said she had to go do something and she wanted me to stay here."

"But you're worried about her, aren't you?"

His glance darted toward me and away. "Something's been down with Moms ever since Robert came to stay with us."

"But she hasn't talked to you about it?"

"All she said was it was going to be all right. Just stay here and wait for her."

"And don't talk to me if I turned up?"

"She thought with that detective, Mr. Sheppard, you might be able to find out where we went."

"Did she tell you where she was going, Tad?"

He shook his head, but he looked away. "No."

"Sure about that?"

"Yeah, I'm sure. She didn't tell me where she was going."

"But you're a smart kid. You pick up on things."

He half smiled, pleased at the compliment. Then he shrugged. "Even if I did know, Moms wouldn't want me to tell you."

"Tad, I don't want you to do anything that would hurt her." I held his gaze. "I just want your mother's help in finding mine."

He shook his head. "She said she couldn't help you. She said she didn't know anything."

"Maybe if I could talk to her, she would remember something." I paused. "You said your father would have wanted her to help me."

He nodded. "Pops always had Reuben's back. If your moms was Reuben's woman, he would have wanted Moms to help you."

"Then you help me, Tad. Where did your mother go?"

He leaned forward with his hands dangling between his bony knees. "I don't understand this. I don't understand what my moms is so upset about. Ever since Robert moved in with us . . . Percy said there was something wrong there."

"I don't know what's wrong. But maybe it's something that I can help your mother with."

He sat back in his chair. "You'd really try to help her?"

I nodded.

He looked at me, into my eyes. And then he said, "My pops . . . he said you have to go with your gut about people."

What had TJ's gut told him about Becca? Obviously nothing that he had shared with his son.

"Will you help me?" I said.

He got up. "I have to go get it."

He went inside. I waited, feeling guilty about this kid. But I had told him the truth about not wanting to hurt his mother.

I heard a muffled conversation beyond the screen door. The cousin still sounded displeased.

Tad came back out. He sat down and held out the photograph in his hand.

It showed three young women sitting at a bar, dressed to the nines, drinks in hands, laughing for the camera. It took me a moment to recognize Naomi Duncan on the left.

And the woman in the middle—Becca?

Tad said, "It's my moms and your moms and a friend of theirs."

"Who?"

"Her name's Josephine Gilbert. But Pops said they always called her JoJo. She used to work at the Shack. But then she got a job singing with a band and she moved to New Orleans."

I raised my eyes from the photograph. "And you think that's where your mother went? To New Orleans?"

"Before we left Chicago, I heard Moms on the phone. She was asking about flights from here to New Orleans." He nodded toward the photograph in my hand. "That was in an album that belonged to Pops. My moms brought it with her. She forgot and left it on the nightstand beside her bed."

"Then I think you may be right."

"You do?"

"Yes. May I hold on to this photograph for now? I'll return it to your mother when I see her, okay?"

"Okay." He frowned. "You think you'll be able to find her? New Orleans is a big place, right?"

I waved the photograph. "But I've got this. Your lead."

He smiled. "Will you ask my moms to call me when you find her?"

"She hasn't called you since she left?"

He shook his head. "I left a message on her cell phone, but she didn't call back."

I reached out my hand to him. "If and when I find her, I'll tell her to call you."

I left him sitting there on the porch. As I was walking away, he yelled after me, "Yo! I hope you find your moms too."

CHAPTER · 33

I had turned my cell phone off because I didn't want to be interrupted during my conversation with Tad. When I turned it back on, I had two voice mail messages. The first was from the society editor at the black newspaper. She said she had only been on staff for three years and wasn't a native of Wilmington, but she would see if anyone else at the paper could provide me with information about Mama Lovejoy. If so, she would get back to me by tomorrow morning.

The other message was from Quinn. Wade was trying to line up an investigator in the Wilmington area to help me. Quinn would get back to me with a name and telephone number.

Oh, shucks! I'd better call him right now and tell him I was on my way to New Orleans.

His greeting was abrupt. "Quinn."

"Are you busy? Should I call back later?"

"I'm in a meeting. Just a moment." I heard him excusing himself, saying he needed to take this call. "Okay," he said. "What's happening?"

"Good news. I've found Tad Duncan."

"I would congratulate you on your sleuthing, Lizbeth, but—"

"But you don't want to encourage me?"

"You said you've found the kid. What about his mother?"

"She left him with her cousin while she went to take care of something. Tad and I are pretty sure she went to New Orleans."

"Lizzie, if you're thinking of—"

"So I won't need an investigator here in Wilmington after all."

"We have a lead on the rape case. If it pans out, in two or three days I'll be able to get away and—"

"I can't wait that long, Quinn. I told Tad I'd make sure everything's all right with his mother."

"You told him that you'd do what?"

"He's worried about her. I should let you get back to your meeting."

"Lizzie—"

"Quinn, I have to—"

"Will you marry me?"

"What did you say?"

"I said will you marry me?"

"I . . . we can't talk about this now."

"Since you won't come home, we can't have the conversation in person. I'm proposing now because I want official standing. If you should disappear into the bowels of New Orleans—"

"That's a really cheerful thought, Quinn."

"You're going to a city where things like that happen. So what's your answer, Lizabeth? Will you marry me?"

"Will you ask me again when I come home?"

"Maybe. Call me when you get to New Orleans."

"As soon as I get there."

CHAPTER · 34

I couldn't get a flight to New Orleans until Friday afternoon. I arrived during one of those thundershowers that I remembered from my last visit. Then it had been August, humid, and miserable. The only other time I had visited, it had been November and unseasonably cold.

New Orleans and I were not in sync.

I flinched as lightning flashed outside the airport shuttle bus. Inside the bus, the woman in front of me was reading a newspaper. "They found a dead woman in a motel room on Rampart Street," she said to her companion.

"So we'll stay off Rampart Street and out of cheap motels," he said.

"It says her body was mutilated."

"I doubt she was a tourist," he said.

"How do you know? They don't know who she was yet."

"Helen, we aren't going to be mugged or murdered."

"I don't know why we couldn't have just gone to Atlanta."

"Because I don't want to spend my vacation with your mother."

She shook the pages of her newspaper. "It's my vacation too."

"Then try to have some fun," he said.

She sniffed and chose not to respond.

Obviously, she and Quinn had been reading the same statistics on crime in New Orleans.

The thundershower had passed by the time we got into the city, but the sky was still gray and depressing. Or maybe I was just feeling that way because I had come to New Orleans without a very good plan.

I had thought of calling Miss Alice back in Gallagher. She had relatives down here, including a nephew who was a detective in the New Orleans police department. But if I had called Miss Alice, she would have called Quinn and demanded his presence at the Orleans Café to explain why I was in New Orleans getting into trouble while he remained there in Gallagher. So I had decided to save Miss Alice's nephew until I really needed him.

And I might not need him at all since by now Quinn had undoubtedly called Wade and gotten the name of a PI for me to contact here in New Orleans. And that might be just as well, since my own plan for finding Josephine Gilbert hinged on my proposed source's workaholic habits.

The airport shuttle driver closed the passenger door and slid back into his seat. "Cheer up," he said with a big grin. "Your hotel's next."

I'd booked my hotel during a quick trip back to the Wilmington library to use the Internet this morning. It was located in the French Quarter, three blocks from Bourbon Street, two blocks from Jackson Square. Since I suspected I was going to be spending time around Bourbon Street looking for Josephine Gilbert, it had sounded like a good location.

"Your hotel's right next door to the French Market," the driver said, as if he had read my thoughts. "You can walk over for breakfast tomorrow at Café Du Monde."

I caught myself before I could blurt out that I didn't drink coffee and found the beignets that left the diner covered in powdered sugar highly overrated. Instead I said, "What I'm really interested in is music."

"No better place for music than the Big Easy," he said.

"A friend of my mother's came here from Chicago in the late '60s. Her name was Josephine Gilbert. People called her JoJo. She was a blues singer with one of the bands. Have you ever heard of her?"

He gave me a look of mock horror. "I'm not quite that old, my lady. Before my time."

"Yes, I know she was before your time. I was hoping she might have become such a legend that she was still around or people still talked about her."

"Not unless she has another name. And you know we have our own home-grown legends. 'Jelly Roll' Morton and 'Satchmo.' Mahalia Jackson, 'Fats' Domino—"

"Not to mention the Marsalis family and the Neville Brothers."

"Now you're talking."

This morning when I was on the Internet, I'd looked for JoJo Gilbert among those New Orleans legends. Nothing.

I'd looked for Becca too. When she fled Chicago, she might have gone to a city where she'd known someone, where she had a friend. So I'd searched for a Becca Hayes in New Orleans. Nothing there either.

But she'd probably changed her name from both Hayes and Stuart if she thought the police and Mancini's friends might be looking for her.

We pulled up in front of the hotel. It looked unimpressive from the outside, but according to the Web site, it was listed in the National Register of Historic Places. I had a glimpse of the interior courtyard as I collected my suitcase from the driver and stepped into the small lobby/office to check in. Umbrella-covered tables provided casual seating at one end; a swimming pool was at the other. Facing into the courtyard was the restaurant that several former guests had given high marks for its creative cuisine.

The hotel had two stories. The rooms on the ground level opened directly onto the cobbled courtyard. My room was two doors down from the office on the ground floor. That was good from the standpoint of security. The only downside would be if folks tended to sit out in the courtyard at night. Or, even worse, if they had a few drinks in the bar and then decided to go for late night swims in the pool.

I unlocked the door to my room, pausing to study the design of the door. It was an interesting example of New Orleans architecture. The bottom half was wood, and the upper half was made of horizontal wooden slats that could be opened or closed.

But as much as I might admire the architecture, I was not about to get into the festive spirit of New Orleans. That wasn't going to happen.

My room was furnished with antiques, from the bed with the corn-stalk posts to the heavy frame around the painting hanging on the wall. I closed the door and went over to study the painting. It was one of those opulent renditions of a woman in a low-bodiced gown. The strange aspect of this painting was the man standing behind her. Was he a dashing cavalier or a menacing predator?

The painting reminded me that one guest who had reviewed this hotel on the Internet had said it was supposed to be haunted. It had been the site of a hospital during the Civil War. The guest didn't report seeing anything, but if she'd had this room, that painting in the moonlight might have given her ideas.

The rest of the room was lovely. I would just throw a towel over the painting.

I unpacked, shaking out my clothes and hanging them in one of the two closets. The state of my clothing was reaching the point when I was either going to have to find a Laundromat or go shopping.

I shoved my emptied suitcase into the closet and dropped down into the paisley print armchair. It was almost three o'clock on a Friday afternoon. I had given some thought to my options, but I still hadn't decided on the most efficient approach.

New Orleans must have a musicians' union, but I wasn't sure if singers generally belonged. And even if they did, JoJo Gilbert might have retired years ago. I needed someone with either a long memory of the 1960s and '70s or an in-depth knowledge of New Orleans music history.

I decided to start with a colleague of mine who lived in New Orleans and taught at a local university. We had been at grad school together in Albany and saw each other once or twice a year at criminal justice conferences.

When I'd seen him in March, Gary had told me that he was working on a book that he wanted to get finished this summer. He was the kind of guy who would work in his office at school and go in on his regular schedule even in June.

And I was the kind of woman who still relied on an address book. I had a small one in my purse for numbers I called frequently. But I didn't call Gary that often, and his office number and his unlisted home number were in the larger address book that I kept in a desk drawer at school.

I got out the telephone directory and looked up his university.

The campus operator connected me to his office.

To my relief, he answered his phone. But he sounded like his mind was still on whatever he was doing.

"Gary, hi, it's Lizzie Stuart."

"Lizzie? Well, my goodness. How are you?"

"I'm in New Orleans."

"Are you? Well, that's great!" I could almost hear him mentally reshuffling the plans he had made for the weekend. "I'm afraid we're headed out of town tomorrow, but we'd love to see you. You've got to let Maureen and me take you to dinner tonight. Where are you staying? I'll call her and—"

"Gary, thank you, that's really sweet of you. And you know I'd love to see the two of you. But the truth is, I'm here because I'm looking for someone and I'm hoping I can pick your brain about how to get started."

"Well, pick away. Who are you looking for?"

"A blues singer. Probably a former blues singer. She was around in the late '60s. That's when she would have moved here to New Orleans from Chicago."

"I don't know if I can be much help, Lizzie. You know my taste in music is more rockabilly than Billie Holiday."

"I know. But I was hoping you might be able to think of a contact. Someone who would know something about blues in New Orleans."

"Let me think." I pictured him pushing his glasses up on his nose. "Someone who. . . . Well, yes, I may have your man."

"You know someone?"

"A fellow named Brad McGuire. His wife works with Maureen. He plays in a band, so if he doesn't have the information you need, he should be able to hook you up with someone who does."

"Bless you, Gary. I owe you one."

"What kind of research is this? Something for your new institute?"

"I wish. I'll tell you about it at the next conference."

"I'll be looking forward to hearing about it. Let me put you on hold while I call Maureen. I've only met Brad's wife a couple of times at parties, so better let Maureen handle it"

I picked up a guide to New Orleans and flipped through it while I waited.

Gary came back on. "You're all set. Brad's wife is going to call him right now. But she says he might be rehearsing because he and his band have a gig tonight. She says if you get his voice mail, it might be easier to just go by and try to catch him between sets. Here's his info."

I wrote down McGuire's telephone number and the name of the club where the band would be playing.

"Thanks, Gary. Give Maureen a hug for me. I'll buy you both dinner at the next conference."

"We'll take you to dinner. Like I said, we want to hear what this is about."

"The whole story," I said, mentally crossing my fingers as I told that fib. I would tell him and Maureen an abbreviated version. "Have a good trip."

I decided to give it fifteen minutes to be sure that McGuire's wife had gotten through to him before I called. As she had said I might, I got his voice mail. I left a message saying that if I didn't hear from him, I would drop by the club and try to speak with him in person. Then I got out the phone book and found the number for the club, Casey's Blue Dreams.

The guy who answered said the band would start playing at nine.

I didn't ask if McGuire would talk to me if I showed up before he played. I decided to just try it and see. Or maybe he would get back to me before that. If he didn't, what would I do until time to leave for the club? I hated not having a better plan.

I didn't want to get Quinn out of another meeting. I called his office phone and left him a voice mail with my hotel and room number. Then I picked up the New Orleans guidebook again. After fifteen minutes of reading the things to do and see in glorious New Orleans, I knew I was too antsy to sit there waiting for McGuire to call. He had both my hotel number and my cell phone number in the message I'd left.

I decided to walk over to Canal Street. I had stayed at the Marriott near the casino when I was here a few years ago for a criminal justice conference. As I recalled, there was a mall with Saks and some other shops down the street from the hotel. I should be able to pick up a couple more tops and enough underwear to get me through the next few days.

CHAPTER · 35

Canal Street has wide sidewalks, but I slowed and stepped aside for a line of preschoolers who were being herded along by three young women in their twenties. Each child was holding on to the turquoise tee shirt of the child in front of him or her. They looked like a tiny little chain gang, but according to their tee shirts, they were a day camp group.

I glanced up at the sky, where storm clouds seemed to be gathering again, and stopped dawdling.

When I stepped inside the mall, the air-conditioning felt like heaven after the muggy air outside. I stopped to get my bearings, and then I set off.

I planned to be in and out in less than half an hour.

That would have happened if I hadn't ended up loitering and window-shopping as I always do in malls. After making a circuit of the stores, I went back to Saks Fifth Avenue, where a summer sale was under way, and bought a blue sheath dress that would work for evening, a print sundress, a navy blue skirt and matching tunic-style blouse, and a couple of tee shirts. I swooped through the lingerie department and scooped up some panties and a couple of bras.

Then I sat down on a bench on the second level of the mall to enjoy the air-conditioning a bit more before I ventured back out. The store across the way had a line of personal-size American flags unfurled in its window, dangling over a display of patriotic red, white, and blue handbags.

Up above, on the third level and to the left, a sign indicated the location of the cafés at Canal Place. Two people, a couple sitting at a table eating, were visible from where I sat.

I watched the geometric, black Plexiglas elevator shafts moving up and down. Three elevator cubes, surrounded by lights, gliding past each other.

A flash of yellow on the food-court level caught my eye. A boy in a canary yellow tee shirt had another boy in a headlock by the railing.

My glance came back to the closest elevator as it moved upward.

A man looked out at me.

I stood up, trying to see him as he passed out of sight in the elevator that paused on the third level and then moved on to the fourth floor.

He was white, in his late thirties, with dark wavy hair.

A couple walked past, pushing a stroller. The baby inside was crying. Sounds were all around me. Coming from above and below. People talking and laughing. Music in the background. The sounds echoed.

I looked up past the rafters at the sky visible through the panes of the glass roof. People stood by the balcony railings on the upper levels, looking down at what was going on below.

To my left, obscured by a plant in a huge pot, a woman's voice emerged from the other sounds. "I was just shocked . . . seven or eight years ago, he had. . . ." Her voice faded back into the indistinguishable conversations.

I glanced upward again. I couldn't see anyone watching me. But the sky up above had turned purple.

I got up and went over to the elevator. It was time I left.

I made it as far as the doors leading back out onto Canal Street. I saw a flash of lightning; rain began to pour. People moved into the shelter of the mall entrance to wait out the thundershower. I went back inside.

I couldn't leave yet, and it might be better for me to stay anyway. If that had been Nico, I didn't want to lead him back to my hotel if he didn't already know where I was staying. And I didn't want to scurry off as if he had frightened me.

If it had been he.

It could have been a perfectly innocent stranger. I could be paranoid because of what Quinn had said about New Orleans' bowels, its criminal underbelly.

Organized crime had been associated with that underbelly for a long time. One infamous episode of violence in response to the alleged presence of the "mafia" had occurred back in 1891. Eleven of the Italian immigrants who had been accused of the murder of the police chief were taken out of jail and lynched by vigilantes. Undoubtedly Nico knew that side of this city a whole lot better than I did.

I took a deep breath and shook my head. I was assuming he was a mobster because his father had been one. Heaven help me if people automatically assumed I had followed in my mother's footsteps. Wasn't I the one who had told Tess that being a gangster wasn't hereditary?

But then again, Nico had done nothing to make me assume his integrity.

Either he was here and following me, or I was paranoid. Either way, I couldn't go out in the storm, so I might as well go have a cup of tea.

In the third-level food court, I found a coffee kiosk and bought tea and an apple walnut muffin. I sat down at a small table with pink plastic chairs. Someone had left a newspaper on the table across from me. I went over and picked it up and returned to my own table. The story the woman on the shuttle bus had been reading was on page three: "Woman Found Dead in Motel Room."

"She woke up this morning with a rash and fever," a woman said to her companion as they walked past. "He rushed her right to the hospital."

"What do they think it is?" the other woman asked.

"A spider bite."

I put the newspaper down without reading the story.

Quinn had spooked me, that was all. That was the reason I was imagining Naomi Duncan brutally dead, the unidentified woman found in a hotel room.

It was still drizzling when I stepped out of the mall. Three people in odd rain slickers that looked like blue plastic bags walked past. I counted to twenty, waiting for lightning or a rumble of thunder.

I couldn't stand there all day. A little rain wasn't going to hurt me. I waited another couples of minutes and then set off.

As I walked, the sun came out, encouraging me to wander a bit. I made two or three turns down side streets, looking around me and remembering again how much I liked the architecture in New Orleans. The balconies and the grillwork and the shutters on all the windows were what I thought of when I thought of this city.

Before I could stray too far off course, I turned and went back the way I had come. I came out across from Jackson Square.

A line of surreys waited for passengers. The mule drawing the fringed surrey at the front of the line sported a straw hat with plastic flowers.

In the Square, in front of the St. Louis Cathedral, a unicyclist spun a ball on a stick. He wore a red, white, and blue top hat. Nearby, a tap dancer competed for the attention and the coins of the small crowd of tourists.

There seemed to be fewer fortune-tellers then I remembered from my last visit. But the artists were still there, displaying their work on the black iron fence. Art to suit every taste from portraits to caricatures; as I passed, one of them was explaining to a potential customer how she did portraits of pets from photographs.

Too bad I didn't have a photo of George. Not that Quinn would have been inclined to hang it on his wall. But I did have a fun moment imagining the look on his face if I brought him back a street artist's portrait of his dog.

Assuming I didn't "disappear into the bowels of New Orleans."

CHAPTER · 36

I turned up the air-conditioning, stripped down to my panties, and climbed into bed. My gaze fell on the painting of the woman and her suitor. I'd forgotten to throw a towel over it, and I didn't feel like getting up. I rolled over in the other direction.

When I woke up, someone was screaming. I shot up in the bed.

It took me a moment to realize the scream had been followed by laughter and the sounds were coming from the courtyard.

I had slept for less than an hour. It was going on six o'clock. I got up and went into the bathroom and washed my face.

Then I turned on the television to get the local news. The motel murder story followed spots on an ethics investigation and a burglary at a convenience store. Standing outside the motel where an unidentified woman had been discovered dead in one of the rooms, the reporter reminded viewers two other murders had occurred nearby in recent months. The police, he said, had not released details of what appeared to be a particularly brutal murder, but they were pursuing leads about the woman's identity. And, of course, the identity of her killer.

"Back to you, Jane."

Perky Jane turned to the weatherman. I grabbed the remote and started channel surfing, but apparently the other local stations had already covered the motel murder. I couldn't find another report.

If Naomi had come to New Orleans looking for Josephine, it was unlikely that she had checked into a cheap motel in a bad part of town. She owned a beauty shop. She lived in a nice house. She could afford to stay in a decent hotel.

The motel-room victim had been black and in her late forties or early fifties. That description must fit at least a few thousand women in New Orleans.

I took a shower and walked across the courtyard to the restaurant. I declined the headwaiter's attempt to seat me all by my lonesome at a table in the middle of the room. He escorted me to the corner table that I indicated and handed me a menu with a flourish.

The Internet reviews had been right. The menu was innovative with unusual combinations that sounded delectable. I ordered a chicken and artichoke hearts entrée and then struggled to finish the rich caramel bread pudding that I hadn't been able to resist.

Back in my room, I deposited my credit cards and driver's license and Quinn's ring in the closet wall safe.

I had been to Bourbon Street in the past, but always with other people. I would have to be out after dark, but I wanted to get there and back before the nightly revels got too wild.

Bourbon Street at night overwhelms the senses. Color and motion everywhere. Music—hard rock, honky-tonk, blues, Dixieland, jazz—pouring from open doorways and windows. Tourists draped in Mardi Gras beads and wearing silly hats and risqué tee shirts. Bar patrons guzzling whatever it was that fueled their fun from "go-cups" as they ambled—or staggered—along the street.

Casey's Blue Dreams had its doors and windows open, but that didn't mean you could walk right on in. A young man and woman in matching black jeans and shirts stood at the door, eyeing those who sought to enter. I passed muster and was motioned inside. The place was jammed already, even though the band hadn't started to play. I eased my way up to the L-shaped bar and ordered a club soda with a twist of lime. When the bartender set it down, I noticed the names and dates that were printed on metal studs and embedded in the bar.

I turned with my side against the bar to hold my place. There were tables to the right and left of the bandstand. Instruments from banjos to trumpets hung from the ceiling. Couples out on the floor danced to a Cajun beat.

I asked the bartender if Brad McGuire was there. I had to say the name twice to be heard over the noise.

He nodded. "The band's getting ready to go on."

"Any chance I could talk to him before that? He's expecting me to drop by."

The bartender looked me over. Then he signaled to a waitress. She leaned toward him and he said something that I missed. She went off toward the back.

When she returned, she and the bartender had a discussion I couldn't hear over the noise. He turned to me and nodded his head toward the waitress. I assumed that meant for me to follow her.

The guys in the band were not rehearsing or getting dressed. They sat around a portable television, watching a ball game. They were all over thirty and dressed in jeans and tee shirts. The woman with them was wearing tight jeans and a low-cut yellow blouse and cowboy boots. She was eating an apple while she flipped through a magazine.

The balding man who was leaning against a table on which Styrofoam take-out containers were scattered came forward and held out his hand. "You're Lizzie?"

"Thanks for giving me a few minutes. I know you're getting ready to go on."

"I got your message, but you didn't mention who you're looking for."

"I'm looking for a woman named Josephine Gilbert. JoJo Gilbert." I took out the photograph Tad Duncan had given me of his mother and Becca and Josephine. "She's the one on the right."

"This was taken a while ago," he said.

"Yes, she would have come here from Chicago in the late 1960s. I know she was a singer with a blues band."

"Lots of those. This one I've never heard of."

"Oh."

"Hey, but I'm not an expert on the old days. I know a man you ought to talk to. If she was any good at all and she sang here in New Orleans, he would be able to tell you."

"Where do I find him?"

"Same place people have been finding him for the last twenty years. You ask for T-Bone. The bar is called the Jook Joint."

He told me how to get there and we said our good-byes. As the door to the room closed behind me, I heard him say, "Game's over, guys. We got to go play some music."

I made my way through the bar, weaving around the couples who were headed back to their tables from the dance floor. At the street door, I stepped aside to let two men enter. A Rebel yell went up behind me.

I swung around in time to see Brad McGuire, who had seemed quiet and low-key, spring onto the stage. He threw back his head and gave another ear-splitting yell. The crowd responded with hoots and hollers. He picked up a guitar that was already plugged in and did two riffs of a blues song.

The female member of the band rocked back on her booted heels as she turned toward him. She was beating a tambourine. The rest of the band joined in. A moment later, they were singing about going down to Bourbon Street, as the crowd clapped along.

I eased on out the door. I needed to see a man named T-Bone.

The street was jammed by now. I dodged the green plastic snout of the alligator cap that one guy was wearing. Then I had to dodge again to avoid two couples who had stopped to listen to the come-on from the barker in the doorway of a club featuring topless dancers. I did another sidestep around a group of white-haired women staring in wonder—or was it amusement?—at the items featured in the window of one of the tackier souvenir emporiums.

The Jook Joint, when I found it, was a dark and smoky bar. Couples shuffled their feet on the rough planks of the tiny dance floor as the black man sitting at a piano sang, "I've been lovin' you."

He sang it like it came straight from his soul. I wanted one of the CDs I saw a woman holding. I wanted to dance to that song with Quinn.

I hoped the man at the piano was T-Bone, the man I had come to see.

I stopped a passing waitress and asked. She gave me a look that said, *I have now exceeded my limit for stupid questions.* What she said out loud was, "That's him. What can I get you?"

I didn't think she would appreciate an order of a club soda. "Wine, please. Chardonnay."

That answer didn't impress her either. "House okay?"

"Yes, thank you."

When she returned with my wine, I edged up and found a place as close to the piano as I could get. After almost forty minutes, T-Bone pushed back his piano stool and announced he was taking a break. Before I could get to him, a white kid was in front of me, telling T-Bone how much he loved the blues and admired T-Bone.

I planted myself as close as I could get to them, so they would both see me waiting.

The kid would have kept on talking, but T-Bone nodded his grizzled head at me. "Got a lady waiting to tell me how much she liked me too," he said with a sly wink.

The kid took the hint and yielded his spot beside T- Bone's piano.

"You know why they call me T-Bone?" he said to me.

I shook my head.

"Because I'm good to the bone."

That declaration had probably worked well forty years ago when he was a young man in his prime. Now he delivered it like a tag line rather than a pass. He chuckled. I smiled. We moved on.

"So what you want to talk to me about, honey?"

"I was told you might be able to help me. I'm looking for a woman. She was a blues singer. She might still be." I took out the photograph I'd gotten from Tad and showed it to him. "She's the one on the right."

"Need my glasses for this one," he said. He held it up toward the light. "This girl have a name?"

"Josephine Gilbert. Her friends called her JoJo."

"JoJo," he said, squinting at the photo. "Seems to me I remember a girl named JoJo."

"She would have come here from Chicago."

"Yeah. Yeah. Chicago. Chitown." He tapped his finger against the photo. "I used to tease her about that every time I saw her. JoJo from Chitown."

I let out the breath I had been holding. "Do you know where she is? Where I can find her?"

"Been years since I seen her. She used to be out in Jackson Square."

"What was she doing there?"

"Reading people's cards. Did that after she came back."

"I'm sorry. Came back from where?"

"From drying out. Tried to kill herself."

"Do you know why?"

"Her fancy man dumped her. Let her go for a friend of hers. She swallowed some pills and some liquor and tried to make him sorry." T-Bone shook his head. "That's the way it is with some of them. Don't know you just put the hurt right in your music. Sing it on out of your soul."

"Do you have any idea where she might be now? Where I might start looking for her?"

"Like I said, Jackson Square. Ask them card readers and fortune-tellers. If she was singing again, I'd know about it. So she must be either dead or doing something else."

I reached into my purse for my wallet. "Could I buy one of your CDs? Actually . . . make that two. I have a friend I'd like to send one."

He smiled. "Only got one friend?"

"Only have about thirty dollars in my wallet."

He reached for the CDs. "I'll save you a couple more for the next time you drop by."

"Thank you, I'll try to come back before I leave town."

I left the bar and started back to my hotel. What I noticed as soon as I turned off Bourbon Street was that the noise level went down. There were fewer people and more shadows. It was almost eleven o'clock, and I walked fast.

CHAPTER · 37

I'd missed Quinn's call last night. When I got back to the hotel, I had a message from him saying that not only was he playing phone tag with me, he had been doing the same with Wade. He said he'd call me today after he and Wade had talked.

Meanwhile, I didn't have any particular destination in mind for breakfast. I walked out through the courtyard past the swimming pool. It was too early for swimmers, but several people were sitting outside having their morning coffee while they read the newspaper. I had seen the morning news on TV. Nothing new on the unidentified woman in the motel room.

I had dreamed about her last night. She'd had Naomi's face. After that, I had spent the rest of the night tossing and turning.

I crossed the hotel parking lot and entered the Morning Cuppa Café through its back entrance. The front of the café faced out toward the French Market, where I could've sat with the tourists having breakfast at the Café Du Monde. I was happy with the Morning Cuppa menu posted on a chalkboard over the counter.

I ordered orange juice and an egg-whites-only omelet with a side of ham, then sat down to wait for my number to be called.

After I'd eaten, I walked over to Jackson Square. I started working my way down the line of tarot card readers. I had spoken to three who said they had never heard of Josephine Gilbert when it occurred to me that this was like walking into a service station and asking for directions. I always tried to buy something before doing that.

At the next table, I smiled and asked if I could get a reading. The woman, who wore a gyspy-like outfit and had wild gray hair, gestured for me to sit.

She handed me a deck of cards. "Shuffle the cards, please."

I began to shuffle. "I'm looking for someone. Josephine Gilbert. JoJo. I understand she used to read cards here in Jackson Square."

"Why are you looking for her?" she said, watching my hands.

"I'm hoping she can give me some information about someone else I need to find."

"Ten cards now. Face down."

I chose ten cards and put them on the table. "Do you know JoJo Gilbert?"

She held up her hand for silence. "After we have finished the reading."

"All right."

She spread the cards out and began to turn them over. "Your signifier card. The substance of your question. The Knight of Wands. Change is in the air."

"True," I said.

She studied the cards. "You see this one. Temperance. The need for moderation in your life. Self-restraint. But in this reading, also a sign that you should be open to compromise. You have a tendency to be set in your ways."

"Stubborn?"

"Or determined. But you must learn when to yield." She pointed to another card. "The King of Swords. This is a man of good sense and intelligence who can give you sound advice if you will listen."

"I do when he's right."

She nodded. "And sometimes there is conflict between you."

"Yes."

She gazed at the cards. "This one," she said. "The Tower."

"It looks scary," I said, glancing at the tower being struck by lightning.

"Change again," she said. "Dramatic change and upheaval."

"Doesn't sound good," I said, concentrating on the bright sunshine and the beautiful morning.

"Choose one more card," she said. "A clarifier."

I reached out and pulled another card from the deck on the table. I turned it over, face up.

"The Ten of Swords," she said.

I stared down at the prone body with those ten swords protruding from its back.

"Death?" I said.

She shook her head. "More change. The end of a cycle. A loss or perhaps an illness."

I cleared my throat. "I thought card readers only gave positive readings."

"I tell you what I see," she said. "But . . . see this card . . . the Seven of Wands. Your reading shows you have strength. You will need it."

"Thank you for the reading." I took out my wallet. "About JoJo Gilbert."

"Yes. Josephine," she said. "We all know her here."

"The others said they didn't—"

"They hadn't read your cards. They didn't know your purpose." She glanced again at the cards spread out on the table. "She might not want to see you."

"I only want to ask her a few questions about someone we both know."

The woman stared down at the cards as if she were really seeing something there. Then she said, "Madame Josephine. But she may be of little use to you."

I picked up on her tone. "Why?"

"She is afraid."

"Of what?"

"Of the darkness that she sees. We were all glad when she left the Square."

"Where did she go?"

"Inside. She came into money and moved inside. She bought a house."

"Could you give me her address?"

She nodded and reached for the pad in the box beside her. "Don't let her serve you tea."

"Why?"

"She'll read the leaves. That is why she lives in fear. She saw into her own future."

"And are you saying that if she reads my leaves . . . that there's something I should fear?"

"There is always something to fear. Josephine knows that. She has not been able to escape the darkness."

I had a feeling I wasn't going to enjoy meeting JoJo Gilbert.

CHAPTER · 38

I checked my map for the address. Josephine lived near the Garden District, and I decided to take the St. Charles streetcar. I found the stop and waited, and when the streetcar came, I watched the passengers in front of me to make sure I knew how to put my money in the slot.

The driver was wearing black leather gloves with his fingers exposed. I assumed the gloves protected his hands from wear and tear. The fact that he had his pants pushed up to reveal his bare calves was most likely because the streetcar didn't have air-conditioning.

I took a seat behind a young couple with two children. The little boy in a red and black tee shirt clutched a green soda bottle. As the car started off, his little sister put her fingers in her ears. She was not happy with the chugging of the car on the tracks.

I didn't really like the vibrations that came through the bench seats. But it was a more interesting and cheaper way to see a bit of New Orleans than from the backseat of a taxi.

JoJo's house was in a neighborhood of antique galleries, family homes, portrait studios, and restaurants. It was pale lavender with a pocket-sized fenced yard. A discreet sign on the gate announced, "Madame Josephine, Psychic." Stone animals lay scattered about the yard.

I went up the walk and onto the porch. A sign on the door said, "Please enter."

The foyer, furnished with chairs, seemed to be Madame Josephine's waiting room. It was empty, but I could hear voices coming from behind the closed door to the right. I picked up a magazine and sat down to wait.

The magazine was about spiritualism. I wondered if Madame Josephine could do a séance. Maybe I could get in touch with Hester Rose and ask if she had any after-life-inspired knowledge about how to find her daughter.

Eventually, the inner door opened. A round, high-yellow man in a tan suit backed out of the room. He bowed, bobbing twice from his waist, toward whomever he was leaving. When he turned and saw me, he drew himself up. "Good day to you," he said and darted toward the front door.

For a moment, I felt like Alice after her encounter with the Rabbit. Then I heard the jangle of bracelets. A woman dressed in a flowing African gown with a turban covering her hair stood in the doorway. A choker made of black and brown beads circled her neck, biting a bit into the flesh that was running to fat. But her broad, smooth-skinned face was still attractive.

Nothing about this woman's commanding presence suggested fear.

"Madame Josephine?" I said, rising to my feet.

"Come inside." Her voice was musical and deep, with a hint of the islands. "I have what you have come for."

"What do you think I've come for?"

"A look into the future."

She stood aside for me to enter her inner sanctum. The shades were lowered over the windows. Light came from dozens of white votive candles that sat on shelves around the room. The walls and ceiling were painted midnight blue. On the ceiling, stars and a crescent moon seemed to gleam in the light from the candles.

"Sit," she said, indicating a chair opposite hers at the round table.

I sat down. "You are Madame Josephine?"

"I am." She sat down in her chair and reached for a teapot. She poured the brown liquid into a handleless china cup and placed it in front of me. "Drink and I will read your leaves."

"Thank you, but I really didn't come for a reading. I—"

"You want to know your future. That is why you have come to me. To find out what lies ahead. I will tell you."

The scent of all those candles was making me light-headed. "I really would rather not do a reading. I—"

"You are troubled. You need to know what path to take."

"Yes, that's why I've come to you. I'm hoping you can provide me with that information. Are you Josephine Gilbert? JoJo from Chicago?"

She went still. "Who are you?"

"My name is Lizzie Stuart. I believe you knew my mother, Becca, when you lived in Chicago and—"

"No!" She bumped the table as she shot to her feet. The tea sloshed from the cup. "I don't know anyone named Becca. You have the wrong person."

I opened my purse and took out the photo Tad had given me. "This photo," I said. "It's of you and Naomi Duncan and Becca, my mother."

She reached out, her hand feeling in the air until she touched the photo. Then she snatched it from my hand. Her bracelets jangled as she ripped it in half and tossed the pieces on the table. "I am not who you are looking for. Leave now."

"You're blind," I said. "You're blind. How were you going to read my—"

"I don't need the sight of my eyes to see into the future. I don't know these people you are asking about." Her voice was calm again. "Go. Now."

"Naomi Duncan was coming here to New Orleans to see you. She has a son. He's worried about her, and I promised—"

"Get out," she said. Her bracelets jangled again as she pointed toward the door.

The candles seemed to flare. The spicy scent filled my nostrils. "You said I had come to you because I need to know what path to take. You're right. I need to know—"

"You need to know nothing that I can tell you. Go away and leave me be."

Her blind gaze burned into mine. Her expression said that she would not be moved by any plea I might make.

Maybe she was afraid. If she was, it was not of me.

I left her there.

Outside, the sun beat down, burning my skin, but feeling almost pleasant after that room filled with candles.

I walked back to the streetcar stop. The ride back downtown seemed to take longer than it had coming. Maybe that was because I spent most of it staring at the two halves of the torn photo. If Naomi had been to see her already, would Josephine have been as startled as she was when I mentioned Becca's name? If Naomi hadn't come to New Orleans to see Josephine, then whom had she come to see?

I got off at the Bourbon Astor Hotel. A gift center next door advertised "low, low prices." Blues played from a loudspeaker; it was a male lament about a "hard-hearted woman." The sign in the boutique window a few doors down promised "a free ride in a police car if you shoplift."

All right. Now what? What now that I'd struck out with Madame Josephine?

I was a block away from my hotel when it came to me. I needed to talk to T-Bone again.

Would he be there at the Jook Joint during the day, or would I have to wait until this evening to find him? Maybe I could get someone at the bar to give me his telephone number.

CHAPTER · 39

Bourbon Street by daylight looked almost tame. The street cleaners were out washing away the smell of stale beer and liquor. A young couple who had stopped to buy hot dogs from a vendor's cart even had two small children in tow. Presumably they intended to cover their children's eyes and walk fast if anyone ignored the fact that it was daylight and flashed too much skin.

The Jook Joint's daylight business was slower than the night before. As I had feared, T-Bone was not at his piano.

The bartender shook his head when I asked for him. "He had a funeral to go to today. An old buddy of his died." He swiped the bar with his cloth. "It should be starting in about half an hour. If you hurry you can get a good spot."

"A good spot?"

"For the procession. It's starting around Poydras and St. Charles."

"Around— Oh, you mean this is going to be a jazz funeral?"

"You got it. T-Bone is marching with some other musicians."

"Do you think I'll be able to find him?"

The bartender smiled. "You'll see him. If you want to talk to him, just go to the cemetery." He handed me a flyer. "T's going to be saying a few words over the dearly departed."

By the time I met up with the procession, a crowd had gathered on both sides of the street. I heard the music—brass and drums playing "When the Saints Go Marching In." Then I saw the coffin. It was flower-bedecked on an open carriage pulled by two white horses. The carriage was followed by men waving open umbrellas and dressed in bright orange jackets. A crowd trailed behind them, waving handkerchiefs in the air. People were literally dancing in the street. It was chaos and color, more festive than sorrowful.

I scanned the procession as more musicians marched by until I saw T-Bone. He was wearing a dark suit and a bowler hat. He had a portable keyboard slung over his shoulder.

The passing musicians swung into "I'll Fly Away." By then the procession stretched back at least half a mile.

I watched T-Bone pass out of sight. I would have to try to catch up with him at the cemetery.

* * *

I have an abiding fear of being buried alive. It goes back to my earliest childhood exposure to Edgar Allan Poe. Learning that real-life nineteenth century graves were sometimes equipped with a bell system so the unfortunate victim of a premature burial could signal to those above had done nothing to ease my fears.

Given my morbid fascination with burial rites and graveyards, I find the cemeteries in New Orleans well worth visiting. On my last trip here, during that chilly November, I had ventured out for a tour of Saint Louis Cemetery Number One. As we walked among the tombs and mausoleums, the guide explained the above-ground burial system. Because of the lack of drainage in the city, coffins and corpses had sometimes gone floating in the early days. The burial system had been devised to deal with that macabre problem.

The tour had also provided a footnote on what we social scientists call the "social location of stigma." In New Orleans, as in other cities, some neighborhoods—particularly the poor, black ones—get labeled as "bad." That means if you happen to live in one of these "bad" neighborhoods, some people lucky enough not to live where you do think you're dangerous. That day on the tour, as we crossed the street to the cemetery, our guide warned us not to venture down the street and around the corner into the Iberville Housing Project. A member of our group, a woman from Germany, assured us that she had almost made that mistake the day before and had only been saved by the fact that a passing male citizen had run after her and brought her back, warning her that she would be risking life and limb.

She might have been, but I knew one could go there and come out alive. I had gone in the day before the tour with a colleague who was doing research on teenage girls growing up in the projects. The family we had gone to see had a grandfather who had been sitting outside reading his newspaper and a mother who worked two jobs. No one had mentioned them to the German tourist. My attempt to tell her about my trip there had gone no further than "I went with a friend to visit someone in Iberville, and I—" before she gave me an alarmed look and moved away.

It would certainly have been more convenient today if the burial for T-Bone's friend had been in Cemetery Number One. The flyer that the bartender had given me said the interment was to be at Masonic Cemetery. I would have to take a taxi.

I didn't want to arrive before the mourners, so I ducked into a café for a cup of tea. That would give everyone in the funeral procession time to finish their parade through the French Quarter and drive to the cemetery. As it was, my taxi caught up with the black limos and brought up the rear.

Architecturally, the Masonic Cemetery was a marvelous example of a "city of the dead." The cemetery itself was surrounded by a cast-iron picket fence. The monuments and statues, tombstones and vaults proclaimed the ties of the dead to a family or an association. I paused to examine the Gothic-style Perfect Union Lodge tomb with the exterior staircase. I remembered seeing it in a guidebook. At night, ghostly figures were said to climb up and down those steps.

I joined the mourners who had gathered at the grave site of T-Bone's friend. The group that had come out to the cemetery was much smaller than the procession through the Quarter. It seemed to be mainly the musicians who had marched and played. I stood on the edge of the crowd beside one of the four women there and listened to a trumpet rendition of "St. Louis Blues."

Then T-Bone took off his hat and stepped up to the front of the group to speak. He told a funny story about traveling with "Skeeter" on a band tour through the Midwest and the night his friend had almost been killed by a beautiful woman's jealous lover.

He was followed by several other musicians, each with his own remembrance. Then the musicians joined together to play "I'll Fly Away" one last time.

I caught up with T-Bone as he started back toward his funeral-home limo.

"I know you," he said, giving me a nod. "Come to see Skeeter laid to rest, did you?"

"Actually, I came to see you. I know this is a bad time, but I wonder if you could spare me just a few minutes."

He glanced at the remaining cars. "How'd you get out here? You got a car?"

"I took a cab."

"You sure 'nough did want to speak to old T-Bone." He gestured toward the limo. "Come on, you can ride back with me and Riley." He indicated his friend, who was talking to some other men.

"If you're sure it wouldn't be an imposition, I would appreciate that."

"Let's sit down in the car. My legs ain't what they used to be. And you can tell me what you need while Riley's finishing his gabbing."

We got in the car. The interior was only slightly less plush than the limo Wade Garner had sent for me in Chicago. Mourners needed creature comforts.

"Last night I was asking you about JoJo Gilbert," I reminded T-Bone.

"Did you find her?" he said.

"Yes, but she claimed I had the wrong woman."

"Sounds like she didn't like the questions you was asking."

"She didn't like who I was asking about."

"You want to tell me about that?"

"If you wouldn't mind," I said. "And then if you could tell me anything else about JoJo—"

"We'll see after I hear your story."

"Did you know that she's blind now?"

He frowned. "I didn't know that. That's too bad. I've always been scared myself of ending up blind."

"Me too," I said.

"So tell me what you wanted to tell me."

I glanced at his friend Riley, who was walking toward the car.

T-Bone said, "Don't mind Riley. We'll just tell him to turn off his hearing aid."

And T-Bone did exactly that. "I need to have a private conversation with this young lady," he added.

Riley nodded and smiled. He switched off his hearing aid. As the limo driver guided the car out of the cemetery, Riley took a novel with a garish pulp-fiction cover out of his pocket and started reading.

T-Bone motioned for me to go on.

I took out the photograph of Naomi, JoJo, and Becca. "Remember I showed you this last night?"

T-Bone looked at the two halves. "Who tore it like this?"

"Madame Josephine when she was telling me that I had the wrong woman and that she couldn't tell me where to find my mother or Naomi Duncan."

"Why'd you give it to her if she couldn't see it?" he said.

"I didn't realize until I held it out to her that she was blind."

"So you were asking her about the other women in this picture?"

"Yes. The one in the middle is my mother. The other woman, on the left, is Mama Lovejoy's daughter. Both my mother and JoJo Gilbert worked at the Shack, Mama Lovejoy's place in Chicago."

T-Bone nodded. "JoJo used to talk about Mama Lovejoy's. About how she got her start singing there when she wasn't waiting tables." He stared hard at the photograph. "You say this one in the middle is your mama?"

"Yes. Have you seen her before?"

"Light's better here than it was last night in the bar." He reached into his jacket pocket and pulled out an eyeglass case. "Let me put these on before I swear to it."

I waited, biting my lip to keep from hurrying him.

"This is the one. This is her."

"Who?"

"The one who stole JoJo's man away."

I sagged back against the seat. What else had I been expecting? With Becca, there had to be a man involved.

"Tell me about it please," I said.

"If we're talking about your mama—"

"That's all right. We've never met."

"You've never met your mama?"

"She left when I was five days old. My grandparents raised me."

T-Bone studied my face. Across from us, Riley went on reading his book.

T-Bone said, "I don't know all the details. I was out on the road traveling and heard most of it after it was done."

"Whatever you can tell me," I said. "Whatever you know or have heard."

"Well, what I heard was that your mama—did you say her name was Becca? She was calling herself something else back then."

"Yes, she used stage names."

"Well, when she came here, JoJo helped her get hooked up, first as a waitress, then singing in a club. Your mama, she was real good. But JoJo wasn't the kind of woman to be jealous. She had her own thing going on with the band she was singing with. Even had people talking about recording. And she had this man that had her flying high. In lo-o-o-ve. Every time I saw her then, she was smiling, dancing around, singing."

"But then Becca came between JoJo and the man she was in love with?"

"What I heard when I got back was that she took him right on away. And instead of getting JoJo her recording contract, he put your mama on the radio."

"The radio?"

"He owned a black radio station. She was on nighttime. Became real well-known. Simone in the Evening. Simone from midnight till dawn." He smiled. "Still remember that. She had that kind of voice."

"*Had?* What happened to her?"

"She was on the radio, and JoJo's man was smoothing the way for her. Then she jumped ship on him and went to another station." T-Bone shook his head. "I lost regular track of her after that. Think she married this rich man. Maybe another one after him."

"And you don't know what happened after that? If she's still here in New Orleans?"

"Oh, she's here, all right. Got one of them hoity-toity restaurants for people who come to see and be seen. She opened up for business about six or seven months ago."

I sucked in my breath. Sucked it in so hard that I started to cough and choke. T-Bone pounded me on the back.

Riley looked up from his book. "Is she okay?"

I wiped at my watering eyes, and T-Bone handed me his handkerchief.

"Guess I should have eased into that," he said.

CHAPTER · 40

T-Bone and Riley dropped me off at my hotel. I promised to call if I needed anything. T-Bone looked like he was still feeling bad about how he had broken the news about Becca.

Simone. Her name was Simone now. T-Bone had said her restaurant was called the White Orchid.

I opened the door of my room, walked in, and flopped down on the bed. After lying there with my face buried in the covers long enough to slow both my heartbeat and my thoughts, I got up and washed my face.

It was not yet five o'clock. Too early to go to Simone's restaurant for dinner. Did she have a supper show? Did she sing the way she had in Nick Mancini's club with an orchid in her hair?

I got out my cell phone. I had some calls to make.

First, I called Kyle Sheppard in Chicago. The phone rang in his hospital room. A woman picked up. She said that she was Sheppard's "friend" and that he was out of the room having X-rays. I told her that my name was Lizzie Stuart, and she said that he had told her about me. I asked her to tell him that I had called and that I would check back later. It was good to know that Sheppard had a female "friend." I had been worried that he was all alone.

I needed to talk to Quinn, to tell him that I had found—or almost found—Becca. He didn't answer his cell phone. I tried his office and got his voice mail. He didn't answer his home phone either.

I punched in the number for the university police department. The officer who answered informed me that the chief had gone to the president's office for a meeting. I asked for Sergeant Burke, Quinn's right-hand man. He wasn't there either.

I asked if anything was wrong. The officer cleared his throat. "I really can't talk about it, Professor Stuart. We got breaks in two of the cases we've been working on. But I can't talk about it."

"All right. Can you tell me if anyone has been injured?"

"No injuries, ma'am. But the situation's kind of awkward. I'm sure the chief will get back to you as soon as he has a minute. I'll tell him you called."

And I had to be content with that.

Whatever the awkward situation was, it sounded like Quinn had enough on his plate without having me call him from New Orleans to announce that I was about to confront my mother.

Confront? I paused over that choice of word. But it was hardly likely to be a pleasant meeting, was it? From what I had learned about her so far, Becca—or rather Simone—didn't seem the type to welcome her adult daughter with open arms.

She might even take Madame Josephine's line and tell me that I had the wrong person.

I got out the telephone directory. Since it was Saturday night, I'd better call the White Orchid and make a reservation.

A man with a French accent informed me that I could be accommodated if I wished to dine early. Early for him was eight o'clock. I said that would be acceptable.

I hung up the phone and flopped back on the bed with my arm over my eyes. I was too tired to get up and close the wooden slat blinds that covered the upper half of the door.

I woke up and it was twilight in the room, and at first I didn't know what was wrong. Then I heard the knocking again. Someone was at the door.

I stumbled up, tugging at my blouse. I crept over and peered out through the slats. "Yes, what is it?"

A blond male head turned, and a bright blue gaze met mine. "I'm looking for Shannon."

"Sorry, wrong room."

"Are you sure? She told me this room."

"She must have been confused."

A grin flashed. "You want to come out and join the party?"

"No, thanks. I'm ancient."

"I like older women." His head turned toward someone calling out to him. "Gotta go," he said to me. "Come on out if you change your mind." He yelled to his companion, "Save me one of those!" and dashed off.

I closed the wooden slats over the door. It was time to get dressed and go meet my mother.

The wig was an impulse. I saw the display of wigs in assorted colors and styles in the shop window, and it occurred to me that if I really did look like Becca, a disguise might be in order. I wanted to control the situation. I wanted to decide when I would approach her. I couldn't do that if she and everyone else saw the resemblance as soon as I came through the door. A wig wasn't much of a disguise, but it was better than walking in fully exposed.

I had twenty minutes to spare. I tried on several and settled on the one that was the most "not Lizzie." I hardly recognized myself in the mirror. The color was taffy brown. The style was sleek and shoulder length with bangs.

The clerk nodded her head. "Cool. But, like, not with that dress."

She went over to the rack of brash colored garments and came back with a Technicolor dress that would come to about mid-thigh. "This will work," she said.

"I don't think so."

"Umm. Okay. If you want to go more conservative. . . ."

On her second trip to the rack, she found a black silk dress with a shredded skirt. It had the virtue of at least providing adequate coverage.

"Go on. Try it on," she said.

I held it up, looking at it with the wig. "Not at all me," I said and went to try it on.

I persuaded the clerk to let me leave the dress I had come in wearing and pick it up tomorrow. I walked out wearing wig, shredded black dress, and my own black sandals with two-inch heels, which she had pronounced "okay" with my outfit.

If the calls of "hey, baby" and other less savory comments I received from males during the three-block walk to the restaurant was any barometer, the wig at least stirred male hormones. Somehow, I didn't think it would appeal to Quinn. He might like the dress, though.

Of course, the problem was that I might now be too conspicuous.

The maitre d' guarding the entrance to the White Orchid checked my name against his list and signaled for the hostess to show me to my table. He had not reacted to the "Stuart." Perhaps he didn't know Simone's real name. Or perhaps there were so many Stuarts in the world that he didn't make the connection.

He had only spared a glance at my face and my outfit, and it seemed he had not been impressed. The hostess led me to a table for two in the vicinity of the kitchen doors. But that worked; I wanted to be out of sight.

A waiter came over and removed the extra setting and asked if I'd like a drink. I ordered a vodka martini. I didn't think the wig and shredded dress went with club soda.

When my waiter returned, he recited the evening's specials. I ordered pecan-crusted salmon with sweet potato mousse.

Nibbling on the several types of baby lettuce in my salad, I listened to the ebb and flow of conversation. T-Bone had said that this was a place where people came to see and be seen. I could believe that. The White Orchid seemed to have a higher than average number of well-groomed, attractive diners. Some of the faces looked familiar, as if I had seen them smiling from the pages of glossy magazines.

My waiter came with my entrée and asked if he could get me anything else.

I brushed back the strand of my wig that was getting into my mouth. "I wonder if it would be possible for me to speak to Simone."

He shook his head. "I'm sorry, but Ms. Deverill isn't here tonight."

"She's not?" Deflated, I sat back in my chair. All that fuss with the wig and the dress, and she wasn't even here. "When will she be in?"

"If she's back from Monte Carlo, she should be in tomorrow for Sunday brunch."

"Thank you. I'll come back tomorrow."

The rest of the meal tasted like cardboard. I passed on dessert and paid my check.

I didn't feel like walking back to the hotel in my get-up. I signaled to the taxi driver who was dropping off a camera-ready twosome.

According to the anchorwoman on the eleven o'clock news, the case of the woman who had been found murdered in the Rampart Street motel room had taken an unexpected twist. A source close to the investigation had revealed that the victim, first thought to be a woman, was actually a transgender male who was undergoing a sex change.

Well, at least, now I knew the victim hadn't been Naomi. Of course, I still had no idea where to find her.

I got out my pad and wrote "Becca" in the center of it. I should have asked T-Bone more about when she was on the radio as "Simone in the Evening."

If she had been on the radio, obviously she hadn't been too concerned about being found. Or maybe she had counted on no one looking for her in New Orleans or recognizing her voice on the radio if they did.

She seemed to be a chameleon, taking on new identities with almost as much regularity as she took on new men.

One or two rich husbands, T-Bone had said. That explained how she could afford to open an upscale restaurant.

The phone on the nightstand rang, and I jumped.

"Hello?"

"Are you okay?" Quinn said.

"I should be asking you that question. What's going on? The officer I spoke to said you'd had breaks in two cases but it was an awkward situation."

"Awkward in only one of them. We made an arrest in the rape case."

"Who was it?"

"A kid from the same intro psych class. One hundred and fifty students in that class, and he sees her and starts stalking her. He finds out that she walks by the field house on the evenings she works at the campus grill. He waits for her."

"How did you find him?"

"I didn't. DeGrassi, the investigator on the case, did a really good job of getting our victim to think through anything odd that had happened lately."

"Something had?"

"Someone left flowers on her desk in her psych class just before end of semester. She always got there early so she could have a certain seat, and someone had gotten there before she did and left flowers. There were only about twenty or thirty other students in the auditorium when she arrived."

"And he was one of them?"

"And she remembered seeing him other places."

"So his idea of courtship was rape?"

"He said he tried to speak to her, to tell her that he had left the flowers, but she was busy flirting with another guy. A football player."

I withheld comment. "So what's awkward about finding a rapist?"

"I think Officer Van Patton was probably referring to the vandalism case. I need to speak to him about discussing official business with civilians."

"He was talking to your girlfriend, Chief Quinn. Stop stalling and tell me what's awkward."

"The Vice President of Academic Affairs."

"What about him? He's usually quite pleasant."

"Not when his kid has been busted for vandalism."

"What?"

"The kids we caught weren't the kids anyone was expecting us to catch. Our graffiti artists turned out to be the thirteen-year-old son of the Vice President of Academic Affairs and two of his schoolmates—who happen to be sons of professors in political science and history, respectively."

"Oops!"

"That's what they said."

"But why on earth would kids like that have been vandalizing campus property and tagging cars with gang graffiti."

"Why do you think? Because they thought it would be a good joke."

"You mean get everyone excited about the possibility of black gangbangers invading campus, while they—"

"Sat back and laughed about the stupid campus cops they had running around in circles."

"I guess your guys fooled them."

"Well, the truth is, we had some help. The Gallagher PD has a paid informant who's been helping them with a drug investigation. He did some business with a kid who mentioned a rumor he'd heard. Then we used high-tech surveillance to catch them in the act."

"And how has the president taken this particular bust?"

"Not well. He doesn't like being embarrassed."

"But he likes you."

"Not today. Especially when I wouldn't agree to just let the whole thing go away."

"I would think, Quinn, that he would be more upset with his vice president and those two professors. These are their kids."

"You would think so, Lizabeth. But, as he said, kids will be kids. And even good parents can't control their kids' pranks."

"When the 'good parents' are white and middle-class?"

He laughed. "I knew you wouldn't like his position. So how are things going there?"

"I've found Becca."

"You've what?"

"At least, I think I have. I haven't actually spoken to her yet."

I told him about T-Bone and what he had said about Simone. "I went there—to her restaurant—tonight. She wasn't there. But the waiter said she should be in tomorrow for Sunday brunch—if she's back from Monte Carlo."

"Monte Carlo?"

"Sounds like fun, doesn't it? Want to hop over for a weekend?"

"How about on our honeymoon? Although, I thought you might prefer Paris."

"Quinn—"

"You asked. But getting back to the matter at hand. Wait until tomorrow evening to go back to the restaurant."

"Why?"

"Because I've got a plane out tomorrow afternoon. I'll be there in time for dinner."

"You're coming here? But what about what's happening there?"

"The rape investigation is over. I've filed my report with the president about the vandalism. He said he wanted to think it over. I said I had something to do elsewhere."

"Then he knows you're leaving town?"

"I told him I had a family matter I needed to take care of."

I blinked hard, trying not to respond to *family* by bursting into tears. "I thought you were going to call Wade and ask him to find a local PI who could help me with anything that I—"

"I did. Then I called him back this afternoon and told him I was on my way down to keep you out of trouble myself."

"I have actually managed to avoid getting into trouble. But it will be nice to see you."

"Will it?"

"Yes."

"Then I'd better go finish up my paperwork and get packed."

"What are you going to do with George?"

"Sergeant Burke's going to keep him."

"Give him a hug for me."

"The sergeant? Really, Lizabeth!"

"You're in a very good mood for someone who just had an argument with his boss."

"Maybe because I'm picturing having a romantic dinner with you in one of those fancy New Orleans restaurants."

"Becca—"

"Her restaurant wasn't what I had in mind. First, you meet her, and then we get on with our lives."

"Quinn, it isn't that simple. Some of the things she may have done—"

"Have nothing to do with you. Or us."

"She's my mother."

He was silent for a moment. Then he said, "I've never told you about my father."

"Told me about him? You've told me bits and pieces. That he was from old Midwest stock. That he graduated from West Point and then charted out his military career—"

"Did I tell you about the time he beat up my mother?"

"The time he—? Your father?"

"He wasn't a chronic wife beater. That was the only time he ever raised his hands to her. But that once was one time too many. They both knew that if she stayed, it might happen again."

I was shocked into silence. He had never talked about his parents' marriage. His mother had remarried after their divorce. His father had never remarried and had died years ago. Quinn didn't talk about him much at all.

"Things were that bad between them?" I finally said.

"They were mismatched. She could never be what he wanted her to be. He had a wife who was inappropriate for a man in his position. And one night, after a party where she was an utter failure at fitting in with the other officers' wives, they came home and he exploded. He'd had more to drink than he usually did. He was yelling. She was cringing from all that rage. That made him even angrier, and he began to beat her. He was hitting her with his fists, and I ran out and pulled at his arms, trying to make him stop. He turned around and sent me flying, and that was when she began to fight back. She picked up a lamp and broke it over his head. That brought him to his senses."

"And then what?"

"He stumbled out of the house, bleeding. He was gone all night. When he came back the next day, she had our suitcases—hers and mine—waiting by the door."

"What did he say?"

"He nodded, told her that she was right. That it would be better for both of them if she left. He said that what he had done made him sick to his stomach. And then he said he would not allow her to take his son. That I was staying with him."

"And she left you there?"

"He promised her that he would never hit me again. On his word of honor.

She looked from me to him, and then she took me in her arms and whispered that I belonged in my father's world. She was Indian, but I was white."

I have never met Quinn's mother. It wasn't my place to judge what she had done. Maybe she had been right and he had belonged in his father's world. Quinn was close to her now. He was close to his Comanche stepfather and to his half-sister from their marriage. I tried to remind myself of all that before I opened my mouth and said something I would regret.

"Quinn, I don't know what to say."

"You don't have to say anything. I'm telling you this to make a point."

"What point?"

"Lizabeth, my father once beat up my mother. Do you think I might snap someday and start knocking you around?"

"No, of course I don't think that. I know you would never—"

"I'm my father's son, Lizabeth."

"That doesn't . . . you aren't . . . Quinn, why didn't you ever tell me how your parents' marriage ended? When I was telling you about Becca and—"

"Yes, that would have been a good time to mention it."

"Then why didn't you?"

"Because I was ashamed. And because I'd had a hard enough time getting past your defenses without giving you a good reason to back away from me and decide not to risk it."

"But you know that I trust you now. You do know that, Quinn?"

"Yes. But the problem, Lizabeth, is that you don't believe I trust you."

"That you trust me? I know that—"

"See you tomorrow, Professor." He hung up.

He was making a habit of doing that. We would have to have a long conversation about that.

His father had beat his mother? Not quite in the same category as a mother who might have killed her married lover and left an innocent man to take the blame. But another bit of information about Quinn that was worth pondering. It explained why he was always so careful not to touch me when he was angry.

I settled back against the pillows, thinking about that. Could he really be afraid of what he might do if he let himself get out of control?

Strange that I hadn't sensed it, when I had spent my whole life living with that same fear about myself.

CHAPTER · 41

When I woke up in the morning, I knew I couldn't wait until evening when Quinn arrived to go back to the White Orchid. I needed to see Becca alone, just the two of us.

This time I dispensed with the wig. No more games. I dressed in my navy blue skirt with the white and navy tunic-style blouse I had bought while at Saks in the mall. I looked like Sunday morning, not Saturday night.

But I didn't have a reservation for Sunday brunch. When I admitted that, I was told I would have a minimum of a thirty-minute wait. This maitre d' was different than the one the night before. This one was black and his accent was British. He was just as haughty. Maybe that was a requirement to be a maitre d' at the White Orchid.

When he sent a couple of glances in my direction, I turned away to look out at the street. Was he wondering who I reminded him of?

I took a seat on the sofa, as a couple who had been waiting was called in.

A Jaguar pulled up outside. A parking valet rushed over to open the passenger door. The female passenger smiled at him as she swung her long legs in high heels out of the car and rose to her feet.

Her leg swing reminded me of Chicago and Nico.

My conversation with Quinn last night had also reminded me of Nico. I had spent some time wondering if he might be in New Orleans. Then I had thought some more about the assumptions I was making about him. If I assumed "like father, like son," then I would have to assume that Quinn was like his father, who had ended his career as a two-star general but who also had been a wife beater.

How much of the good or bad in our makeup could we attribute to our parents? How much was nature and how much was nurture? I had always preferred to lean toward nurture, but it was easier to do that with other people than with myself.

Maybe Nick Mancini's son had been better off being raised by his mother and her cousin Sonny. Or maybe that's what I wanted to believe because of the role my mother might have played in leaving him without a father.

Well, I should have some answers soon enough. I got up and went to look at the aquarium by the door. I was still staring at the tropical fish swimming back and forth when a woman spoke behind me.

"Ms. Stuart, your table's ready."

"Thank you." I straightened my blouse and followed her into the dining room.

The hostess smiled as she handed me my menu. "You look familiar. Have you been with us before?"

I shook my head. "Would it be possible for me to speak to Simone?"

Her gaze sharpened. "That's who . . . you look like Simone. Are you related?"

"I've never met her. An old acquaintance of hers asked me to look her up and say hello."

"She hasn't arrived yet. We expect her shortly."

"Would you mind letting me know when she does come in?"

The hostess smiled. "You won't miss her."

With that she left me to peruse the menu. There was a buffet complete with a chef making omelets and waffles and another at a carving board with turkey and roast beef. I decided to avoid the temptation of all those calories. I ordered the short stack of blueberry pancakes with Canadian bacon.

The White Orchid was quieter on Sunday morning. Quieter in the sense that the people sitting at the tables seemed to be more concerned with their food and their dining companions than with who sat at the next table.

I was halfway through my meal when an odd silence fell over the room. I looked up and saw everyone else looking toward the open stairs leading up to the second floor. A woman had stopped in the curve of the spiral staircase.

She resembled a lioness. A mane of wavy, coppery brown hair swept back from her forehead and fell to her shoulders. Brows arched over intense golden brown eyes in a tawny brown face. Her simple golden gown skimmed over her full-figured but well-toned body. A large golden pendant dangled in her décolletage. A wide, gold-buckled belt matched the hoop earrings in her ears and the cuff bracelet on her wrist.

If this was Becca, God knows I didn't look like her. Beginning with the breasts that she had and I didn't. Becca would be fifty-eight on her next birthday. This woman looked to be in her forties.

"Hello," she said in a low voice that carried through the room. "Good morning. I'm Simone. Thank you for joining me for brunch."

The people at the tables around me began to applaud. She raised her arm in acknowledgment, and the cuff bracelet glinted in the light. "I've been away, and I'm very glad to be home. So if you don't mind, I'm going to indulge myself."

More applause, and somewhere outside my line of vision, someone began to play a piano. She—Simone—slid into a song that was not what I expected.

It was sultry and bluesy. If she really was Becca, and had been involved in Nick Mancini's murder, it was downright dangerous.

You should have died on Monday,
Never should have lived past Sunday.
You did me wrong,
And now you got to pay.
You did me wrong.
Tell me, daddy,
Why I should let you live another day?

She sang it flirtatiously, as a sexy come-on. Men laughed and clapped. The women smiled. They all applauded.

I applauded too. Whatever else was true of this woman, if this was Becca, Sonny Germano had been right. She had crowd appeal. Had she opened this restaurant as an act of self-indulgence, as a place where she could showcase her talents?

She came down the stairs and began to mingle, making her way around the dining room, stopping at tables to chat. My table, near the unlit fireplace, was in her path of movement.

In less than five minutes, I was going to meet my mother. My knees were knocking together under the table. My heart was beating so hard, I could barely breathe.

If this really was Becca . . . I had only T-Bone's word that Becca had become Simone. Maybe he was confused.

This woman, Simone, looked vaguely like that young girl in the photo. But the girl in the photo had not been polished and sophisticated.

This woman was utterly confident. Beautiful.

What if she wasn't Becca? What if I was about to make a fool of myself?

What if. . . .

She was two tables away. I tried to go on eating, but my hand was shaking like I had palsy. The fork clattered against the plate as I put it down.

I clasped my hands together in my lap.

She was at the next table. I braced myself. . . .

Then in a flurry of movement, a narrow-featured, dark-skinned woman in a beige Sunday dress and high heels strode across the room, clutching her black purse in both hands and making a beeline for Simone. She stopped behind her and cleared her throat. "I need to speak to you."

"Naomi?" I was on my feet without realizing I had stood.

Whether it was because she heard me blurt out her name or because I attracted her attention by rising, Naomi glanced in my direction. But my presence was of little interest to her.

"I need to talk to you," she said again to the person we had both come to find.

Simone regarded the woman in front of her as if she couldn't quite place her. "I'm sorry, have we met before?"

"I'm Naomi. Naomi Duncan." Naomi glanced around and lowered her voice. "You know who I am."

"Oh, yes, of course. It's been a long time." Simone smiled at the couple with whom she had been talking. "Enjoy your meal, and please come visit me again." She turned back to Naomi, who was waiting. "Perhaps we should go upstairs to my office." Her gaze met mine with no sign of recognition. "Are you with Naomi?"

"Yes," I said.

Naomi's mouth puckered, but she didn't open it to deny my claim.

As we crossed the dining room, Simone exchanged words here and there with her customers. She looked serene and unruffled, and no one seemed to notice how tense Naomi and I were as we followed in her wake.

As Simone led the way up the stairs, I whispered to Naomi, "Tad is worried about you. Have you called him?"

She nodded, but her attention was fixed on Simone.

On the second floor, an antique sideboard held a huge vase of white orchids. A mirror above the sideboard reflected the flowers and offered a glimpse of the room into which Simone led us.

It was a pleasant room, sunny, spacious. Gershwin's *Rhapsody in Blue* drifted from the stereo system in the bookcase. The bookcase was adjacent to an antique desk and file cabinet in cherry wood. An Oriental rug separated the work area from the seating provided by a white sofa and matching armchairs. Pillows in ethnic brown and tan prints were scattered on the sofa. More orchids were on a side table beside decanters and glasses. The French doors leading out onto the balcony stood open.

Simone closed the hall door behind us and said to Naomi, "This is unexpected. How long has it been?" She looked at me. "Introductions seem to be in order. I'm Simone Deverill."

My tongue was stuck to the roof of my mouth. Before I could find my voice, Naomi said, "I've come here because I've got something I need to get off my mind." She looked at me. "You may as well hear this too. You may as well hear what she says."

"Hear what I say about what?" Simone smiled slightly.

Naomi's mouth tightened. There was the sheen of sweat on her upper lip. She said, "About Robert—"

"Robert?"

"Robert Montgomery," Naomi said. "You know which Robert I'm talking about. He just died."

"I'm sorry to hear that."

"I want you to tell me the truth about what happened. Robert didn't kill that man. I want you to tell me who did."

"I'm sure there were a number of people who wanted Nick Mancini dead." The statement was matter-of-fact, indifferent.

"You were one of them," Naomi said. "Did you kill him? You told me you didn't when it happened, but I want to know the truth. Did you do it?"

Simone laughed. "If I had killed him, do you expect me to give you a confession all these years later?"

"I need to know. Robert didn't do it. I helped you get out of town, and an innocent man went to prison."

"He confessed," Simone said.

"He confessed because he thought you did it, and he didn't want the police to get their hands on you."

"That was gallant of him," Simone said. "Robert was a sweet boy, and I'm sorry he's dead. But if you'll excuse me, I have a business to—"

"I came all the way from Chicago to talk to you about this."

"I suggest you go back to Chicago," Simone said. "It was all a long time ago. Whatever happened—"

"You didn't watch Robert die, Becca."

My heartbeat caught and then went on. I had verbal confirmation that this woman, Simone, was Becca.

Simone said to Naomi, "I really have had enough of this discussion. I would like you to leave now."

"You knew he didn't do it," Naomi said. "You knew it, and you let him spend all those years in prison."

Simone strolled away from us and around to the other side of her desk. "You did hear me ask you to leave, didn't you?"

"I have a son," Naomi said. "I'm so ashamed, I can't even look him in the eye."

"That's too bad," Simone said. "But that has nothing to do with me."

"Nothing to do with you?" Naomi took a step toward the desk. "You—"

"I asked you to leave." Simone opened a desk drawer. When her hand came up, she was holding a gun.

"No!" I cried out. "What are you doing?"

Simone lowered her hand, but she still held the gun. She smiled at Naomi. "It has been such fun reminiscing, but I have other matters to attend to. I would like you to leave. And take whoever this is with you."

"I'm Lizzie," I said. "Lizabeth Theodora Stuart. I'm your daughter."

She hesitated for half a second, but there was no visible change of expression on her flawless face. Then she smiled, and her gaze moved from my face to my feet and back up again. "Are you sure? I don't see a resemblance."

I felt a hand grab my elbow. Naomi said, "Come with me. Now."

She pulled me along with her toward the door. When we were on the other side, she let go of her grip on my arm.

"Now you've seen her. If you know what's good for you, you'll let it go at that." She sighed, a world of weariness in the sound. "I'm going home. You go home too." That sheen of sweat was still on her upper lip. She looked bruised about the eyes.

"I can't let it go at that," I said. "She's my mother."

Naomi shook her head. "Believe me. You don't want any more to do with her."

"She's my mother," I said again, like a broken record. "I need to find out—"

"You won't like what you find. You don't want anything to do with her. She'll bring you down as low as she is."

Naomi went down the stairs, moving like an old woman, body stiff and head bent. I watched her walk out past the maitre d', and then I went back to Simone's office.

She was sitting behind her desk at her computer, the gun nowhere in sight. "You're back," she said.

"I realize you'd rather I wasn't here. But I am, and we need to talk."

She turned her attention back to the computer screen. "We have nothing to talk about."

"I have a message for you," I said. "Robert Montgomery said to tell you that he'll see you in hell."

"We all go there sooner or later."

"Who was my father?"

"I don't think I can recall."

"I'm your daughter. Doesn't that mean anything to you?"

She leaned back in her chair. A lazy smile curled her lips. "No, it doesn't. If you want a mother, I suggest you take out an ad."

My face burned as if I had been slapped. "Maybe you should take out an ad for a heart."

"I had that organ surgically removed long ago, sweetheart. I haven't missed it." She gestured toward the door. "Mommy's busy. Run along now, Lizabeth."

"Before I go, I want to know who my father was."

"Didn't your grandmother tell you? Your daddy was the devil."

I stared at her. The words I wanted to scream at her were stuck in my throat. She waved her hand. "Run along now. Go play."

I did run then. I ran down the stairs and out the door of the White Orchid. By the time I got out on the sidewalk, I was crying.

I walked back to the hotel. Undoubtedly, passersby thought I was rather pathetic.

CHAPTER · 42

I spent the next few hours curled up in the armchair beneath that dreadful painting of the woman with the menacing suitor. I went over and over in my head all the things I should have said to Becca. Eventually, my stomach growled, and I realized I was hungry. Besides, I couldn't sit there all day feeling sorry for myself and greet Quinn drenched in tears. That thought got me up and moving.

I decided a walk would help. I strolled in the direction of Canal Street.

I had gone with some friends to the casino the last time I was in New Orleans. It seemed as good a place as any to be anonymous and to find a meal. I entered to the ding of coins and the erratic music of the slot machines. Smoke filled the air. Stars sparkled in the hemisphere above the floor. I stood there getting my bearings, and then I headed toward the buffet that stayed open 24/7.

Whenever I walk into a casino, I think of that old "Twilight Zone" episode with the puritanical man who put one coin into a slot machine and found himself unable to break away. The only thing in a casino that I know how to play is a slot machine. One time in Las Vegas, while attending a conference, I had played for ten minutes and hit triple seven. With my grandmother's own puritanical voice in my ear, I had gathered up the clattering coins into my bucket and marched over to the window to cash them in.

But I could see the lure. Winning over $300 in ten minutes had certainly made me want to try for more. It was only Hester Rose's lectures about "the wages of sin" that had gotten me off that stool.

Right now, my stomach kept me moving past the alluring signs that promised big payoffs. Five minutes later, I was sitting at a table, working my way through more food than I needed. Being rejected by one's long-lost mother seemed an appropriate occasion for both roast beef and chocolate cheesecake.

I generally don't like the word *bitch* when used to describe human females. But I was inclined to make an exception in Simone's case.

She was apparently unmoved by Robert Montgomery's imprisonment or his death. She dismissed both Naomi Duncan and her plea for the truth. She had taken Josephine Gilbert's lover and used him to get where she wanted to go. She would not tell me who my father was. In short, Simone—my mother, Becca—was a bitch.

Should I tell all this to Quinn and match my bitch of a mother against his wife-beater father?

Back out on the main floor of the casino, I wandered around. I stopped at a quarter slot machine at the end of a row. I had read that the end machines in casinos paid off more often than the others because the management wanted visitors to see others winning and be drawn into the play.

I sat down on the stool and fished out my wallet. I would play twenty dollars and then I would get up and leave.

A waitress paused beside me, tray in hand. "Would you like a drink, hon?"

"No, thank you. I'm only going to be here a few minutes."

I fed the twenty-dollar bill into the machine and debated playing one quarter at a time or going for two or three. I decided to alternate my strategy and play more quarters when I was winning.

I was pulling the handle when a hand brushed the nape of my neck. Startled, I jumped away. My path was blocked by a male body.

I stared into Nico's smothering eyes. They were bloodshot.

"Good to see you again, Professor." He needed a shave and, from the stale scent of him, a shower.

"You look like something the cat drug in," I said. "What are you doing here?"

"I saw you crossing the floor back there. I'm staying at this hotel."

"Of course," I said. "Where else would you stay but in a hotel with a casino? Gangsters are big spenders, aren't they?"

"Who says I'm a gangster?"

"What do you want?"

"To say hello. Quite a coincidence that we both decided to take a trip down to New Orleans."

"Is that what this is? A coincidence?"

"What did she tell you?" he said.

"Who?"

"Simone. Becca. Your mother."

"How did you know that Simone is Becca?"

"Private investigator. Surprised you didn't get your own down here, too."

"I was going to, but it turned out I didn't need one."

He nodded. "But I bet I know something you don't."

"What do you know?"

"What did Madame Josephine tell you?" he said.

"Did you follow me there?"

"I've been following you everywhere. Everywhere Lizzie goes, Nico has been sure to follow."

"Are you drunk?"

"I drank myself sober. What did Madame Josephine tell you?"

"Why should I tell you anything when you won't share your information? And just why do you think we are suddenly collaborating on this?"

"It was worth a try." He reached into my change bucket and plucked out a quarter. "I'll take this for luck."

"What do you know that I don't, Nico?"

He turned back toward me. "One of my old man's former associates lives in Sarasota, Florida. I flew over last night to visit with him. He said my old man forgot the secret."

"What secret?"

"The secret to dying of old age in your own bed is to know who hates your guts."

"Robert Montgomery confessed to your father's murder."

"The conversation wasn't about who killed him."

"What was it about then?"

"Lies, treachery, and deceit." He smiled and saluted. "See you later, Lizzie."

He walked away. I considered going after him and demanding that he tell me what he had hinted at. What had he found out? Why did he look even worse than I did?

I picked up the bucket and dumped the remaining quarters into my purse. Quinn's flight would be arriving soon. I needed to get back to the hotel.

CHAPTER · 43

"What's the matter with your head, woman?" Quinn stood there scowling. "What you want to open that door for?"

I burst out laughing. "Your Cajun accent isn't quite as bad as your Southern."

"The point is that you're supposed to ask who it is before you fling open the door." He paused, assessing my attire. "Especially when you're wearing a skimpy little robe and nothing else."

"I did peep out through the slats first. And if you'd like to come on in, I might be persuaded to lose the skimpy little robe."

"Might you?" He stepped inside and dropped his bag. "Might you indeed?" He closed the door and locked it.

When he turned around and saw my robe had fallen to the floor, his eyes glistened. "I didn't get a chance to persuade."

"Sorry. I've really missed you."

"I've missed you too." He drew me into his arms. "And I'm very happy to see you."

He was. We spent the next hour making up for the time we had been apart.

I sat up in bed and propped a pillow behind me. Quinn was lying there with his hands behind his head and his eyes closed. He looked so comfortable, I hated to disturb him.

"So tell me about Becca," he said, opening his eyes. He reached over and ran his fingers down my arm. "What was she like?"

"How did you know I went back there?"

He smiled. "Patience when you have something you want to do—"

"I would have waited for you, but I really did need to see her alone."

"So she was back from Monte Carlo and you were able to talk to her?"

"Naomi Duncan was there too."

I told him about Naomi's request to speak to Becca and what Naomi had said when we were upstairs in Becca's office. When I got to the part about Becca and the gun, he said, "Bloody hell!" and sat up.

I said, "I don't think she ever intended to use it. It was a bit of drama intended to scare Naomi into going away."

"Pulling a gun on her must have accomplished that."

"It did. After Naomi left, I went back to talk to Becca . . . although I suppose I should call her Simone."

"I assume you told her who you are?"

"And she said that if I wanted a mother, try an ad."

"I'm sorry. I'm so sorry, Lizabeth."

"The really irritating part was that she wouldn't tell me anything about my father." I cleared my throat. "She said he was the devil."

"Was that her personal evaluation of his character?"

"I think she was throwing back the phrase Hester Rose had used to describe him."

"So what now?" Quinn took my hand in his. "Ready to go home?"

"I don't know what else to do. I'm sorry I got you down here for nothing."

"Don't worry about it. You've already made it worth the trip."

"Thank you. Did I tell you that Nico Mancini's here in New Orleans?"

"No, you didn't mention that."

"Well, he is, and he hired a private investigator. And I'm not sure what he intends to do . . . I mean now that he knows where to find Becca."

"Whatever Nico intends to do, your mother sounds like she's more than capable of taking care of herself."

"Yes, but I feel as if I should . . . as if I shouldn't leave before I know how it's going to end."

"How what's going to end?"

"Nico and Becca. Maybe I need to be here. I still don't know if she was involved in Nick Mancini's murder. And Nico said he had found out something. Something about his father's enemies and lies and deceit. Something that one of his father's former associates who lives down here, or at least in Sarasota, told him."

"When did he tell you all this?"

"This afternoon. I went to the casino to have lunch, and—"

"Let me get this straight. You—Lizzie Stuart—went to a casino for lunch?"

"I've been in casinos before, Quinn. I went for a walk, and it was a convenient place to get something to eat."

"Getting back to Nico—"

"He's staying there in the casino hotel, and he saw me sit down at one of the slot machines and came over."

"And he told you that he has a PI on the case and he has some information that you don't."

"And now—after this morning—I have more questions than I had when I started."

Quinn was silent for a moment, then he said, "Before I left this morning, I called the PI that Wade recommended."

"You did?"

"I gave him the information you had given me. That Becca is now Simone Deverill. He's going to find out what he can and get back to us by tomorrow afternoon."

"Thank you."

"You're welcome."

"We have this hotel room until Tuesday morning," I said. "I told the desk clerk that you would be checking in."

"Who did you tell the desk clerk I am?"

"This man I met on a cliff walk in Cornwall. I said you keep turning up."

"It was that incredible first impression that you made on me." He leaned toward me, then stopped. "If we're going to dinner—"

"We don't have to go just yet."

We went to a restaurant that Quinn remembered from the last time he was in New Orleans.

"Impressive," I said, as I admired the monogrammed silver place setting on the glistening white tablecloth. The menu was in French with an English translation. "Definitely not cuisine a la Short Ribs."

"Just as well," Quinn said. "I stopped at Short Ribs for barbecue on my way to the airport."

I shook my head in wonder. "Forgive me if I find it fascinating that a man who can read this menu without benefit of the English translation has an utterly unexplainable addiction to greasy barbecue."

"Must be in the same category with this Ph.D. I know who likes to stop for one of those high-fat, nauseatingly sweet donuts, bring it home and pop it in the microwave to get it hot, and then slather it with butter."

"Low-fat margarine. And I only do that about once a month."

"That's about as often as I go to Short Ribs."

The wine steward came up in his white shirt and black tie. Quinn slipped into French as he inquired about an item on the wine list.

Once, when we were watching a French film with subtitles, Quinn had told me about his first trip to Paris. Only sixteen, he had set out on his great adventure from the military base in Germany where he lived with his father. I had asked if Quinn spoke French. He had said he was rusty, and he certainly didn't get a lot of opportunity to practice in Gallagher, Virginia.

But the wine steward didn't seem to have any problem with Quinn's fluency. He also seemed impressed by Quinn's ultimate choice of a Burgundy.

It was too bad that I didn't like wine more. Simone would undoubtedly have shared Quinn's appreciation of a superior vintage.

But Simone kept a gun in her desk drawer. Unlike my mother, I would not pull my own gun when Quinn and I had a difference of opinion.

"With the rate of inflation, a penny seems a bit low," Quinn said.

"Pardon me?"

"For your thoughts, Lizabeth."

"I was thinking about us."

"So was I."

"You were?"

"I was wondering what you did with the ring."

"Oh." I reached up and touched the neckline of my blue sheath. "It's in the wall safe back at the hotel."

"Still haven't made up your mind, huh?"

"Could we wait and talk about this when we get home?"

"Are you going to know something else about your feelings for me that you don't know now?"

"No."

"So we're still discussing Becca, aren't we?"

"Quinn, aren't you even fazed by any of this? I have a mother who skipped out of town in Chicago two steps ahead of a murder investigation. She comes to New Orleans and assumes a new identity—"

"And apparently does quite well for herself."

"She keeps a gun in her desk drawer."

"That isn't unusual for business owners in cities with high crime rates."

"Quinn, she pulled the gun on a woman who used to be her friend."

"But you're sure she didn't intend to use it."

"Suppose it had gone off?"

"As we established at the firing range, Lizabeth, guns don't just go off. Not in the hands of someone who knows how to handle them."

"You're assuming Becca/Simone does."

He smiled. "She sounds like a woman who would."

"You sound almost as if you admire her."

"No, I don't admire her. I could hate her for hurting you. But I can also appreciate the fact that your mother seems to have made an art form out of being a survivor."

"And you admire survivors?"

"I appreciate their tenacity."

"And I despise the way they hurt people."

"Some of them do," he said. "But you're a survivor, Lizabeth. And you don't hurt people."

I looked away until I could control the rush of tears that came to my eyes. "Thank you." I raised my water glass. "Here's to us, nice survivors."

He grinned. "As toasts go, that one's a little lame. And I should remind you that toasting with water is bad luck."

"Where did you get that one?"

"From that book you have on your nightstand at home."

"That's research on folk culture for the Institute." I put down my glass and leaned toward him. "So tell me, Chief Quinn, how ticked off is the VP of Academic Affairs going to be now that you've busted his son for vandalism? I need to reschedule my meeting with him and the provost and Amos Baylor."

He shrugged. "At the moment, you probably don't want to remind him of our connection."

"Somehow I think he'll remember. I guess I should be glad the Institute is already fully endowed."

"And you're the executive director. There's not much he can do about that."

"I'm sure he could find some way to express his displeasure." I reached my hand across the table. "Quinn, if you're thinking seriously about Wade's offer after this—"

"Let's talk about that when we get home too."

"What do we talk about here and now?"

"I have a message for you from Mr. Womack."

"About the house? How bad is the roof?"

"The roof needs replacing."

I groaned, but he went on with what he was saying.

"The message was about the Nathans."

"What about them?" I said.

"They're gone."

"They can't be gone. They have a lease."

"Ray Nathan said to tell you to take him to court if you want to. He said his wife couldn't stay in your house another night."

"Because of a leaking—"

"Because of Hester Rose's ghost."

I stared at Quinn. "You're joking, right?"

"He said you warned him that your grandmother would be upset about the flowers he dug up, and sure enough, his wife woke up from her nap and there was this little woman standing by the bed. The woman told her to get up and get out of her house."

"She must have been dreaming." I pressed my hand to my mouth as giggles bubbled up.

Quinn shook his head at me. "It isn't funny. Poor Mrs. Nathan was so frightened that she ran out into the rain, wearing nothing but her slip and a robe. She called her husband at work because she was afraid to even go back into the house."

"And now they've moved out?" I leaned my forehead on my hands. "This isn't funny. I've just lost my tenants."

"But the good news is that Mr. Womack has a nephew who's interested. The nephew says that if you'll reduce the rent to half what you were charging the

Nathans, he'll help his uncle with the roof and any other repairs the house needs for free."

"He's not afraid of Hester Rose's ghost?"

"He didn't chop down her rose bushes."

That did it. I burst into laughter. "Are you telling me the Nathans really believed—" I pressed my hand to my mouth, aware that I was being too merry in this elegant restaurant. "If Hester Rose is running around in ghostly form, I wish she'd come and tell me what to do about her daughter."

"She might suggest going home and forgetting about her."

I sighed. "Would you like to dance with me, Chief Quinn?"

"There isn't any music."

"I know a place we can go after dinner."

T-Bone was at his piano at the Jook Joint. He smiled when I walked up. I made my request, and he broke into a grin.

I went back to Quinn. He drew me into his arms.

"I have been loving you," he said, echoing T-Bone's lyrics. His lips brushed my ear. "It started the day I met you."

"That's a coincidence. That was when it happened to me too."

For that moment, there in his arms, I felt content.

I woke up to the sounds of someone throwing up. It took me a moment to realize it was coming from the bathroom and Quinn wasn't in the bed beside me. I fumbled for the lamp and shoved back the covers.

"Quinn?" I knocked on the bathroom door. "Are you all right?"

More gagging and coughing. Then a hoarse "Just something I ate. Go back to bed."

I stood there staring at the door. I knew him well enough by now to know that he would not appreciate it if I came barging in to hold his head. "Okay. Holler if you need me."

No response. Only more gagging.

Of course, I couldn't go back to sleep knowing that he was in there sick. I reached for the remote control and turned on the television. I thought Quinn would appreciate it if I was focused on the late show rather than the sounds he was making in the bathroom.

In a marvelous bit of synchronicity, the movie was Faye Dunaway in *Mommie Dearest*. I had come in on the scene where Dunaway, as a frenzied Joan Crawford, hacks down the tree in the garden, as her frightened children and her house-keeper look on.

I wondered if Becca/Simone ever lost her chilly exterior and flew into a rage. Somehow I couldn't imagine her getting that exerted.

"Feeling better?" I said when Quinn finally came out of the bathroom.

"Yeah." He started to get into bed and then went over to the closet and pulled out his suitcase.

"What are you looking for?"

"Pajamas. I think I threw a pair in here."

"You're putting on pajamas? You *must* be sick." I watched as he tugged on the pants. "You can turn the air conditioner off if you like."

"No, I'm okay now."

"I forgot to pack stomach remedies, but I have some aspirin if that would help."

"I'm okay."

He sat down on the bed to finish the buttons on the shirt. When he was done, he stretched out and rolled onto his side, facing the wall.

I let him alone. A head cold and he might have liked being pampered. But throwing up and diarrhea fell somewhere else on his scale of masculine pride.

I clicked off the television and lay down again.

Half an hour later, Quinn jackknifed into a sitting position and bolted for the bathroom.

C H A P T E R · 4 4

By morning, Quinn was alternating between trips to the bathroom and shivering under the extra blanket I had found on a shelf in the closet.

I suggested calling a doctor. He told me he was all right and didn't need a "damn doctor."

At a little after nine, I did barge into the bathroom. He was on the floor with his head hanging over the commode.

"Go away and let me die in peace," he said, scowling as much as he was able.

"I'm going to call a doctor," I said.

I went back into the bedroom and picked up the phone.

The desk clerk gave me several names. The doctor I called listened to my description of Quinn's symptoms and diagnosed a stomach virus.

"Are you sure it's not food poisoning?" I said.

"We haven't had any other reports. And it doesn't sound severe enough—"

"Not severe enough? He's been throwing up all night. He has diarrhea. He's on the floor in the bathroom."

The doctor chuckled. "No offense to your friend's condition. What I meant was that food poisoning generally displays with symptoms that are severe enough to merit a trip to the emergency room."

"Well, I still think it could be food poisoning. It was probably that lunch he had at Short Ribs before he flew down here."

"It might have been that fancy French restaurant last night," Quinn said from the doorway. Holding his stomach, he staggered back to the bed and flopped down beside me. "Tell the damn doctor to get over here."

"He's coming," I said.

"On my way," the doctor said on the other end, chuckling again.

The doctor arrived about half an hour later. Quinn did not appreciate being required to roll over and pull down his pajama bottoms for a shot in his rear end. He made me look away.

The doctor assured us that the "cocktail"—the mixture of drugs in his hypodermic—would have Quinn back on his feet by tomorrow. He said it like a man who had a great deal of experience with visitors who'd had too much of the New Orleans nightlife.

Quinn moaned as he rolled onto his back and told me to get a credit card out of his wallet.

The hotel room "house call" cost $300. I spared a moment to hope that Quinn's insurance carrier would reimburse. I should have thought of calling first to check. But it was an emergency. Even if his insurance wouldn't pay, he couldn't have spent the rest of the day on the bathroom floor.

Instead, according to the doctor, he would spend it sleeping off the shot. The doctor left me with instructions about making sure the patient didn't become dehydrated. He told me to buy over-the-counter medication to supplement the injection. And, of course, call if we needed him.

At his prices, I was hoping we wouldn't.

I spent the rest of the morning watching Quinn sleep, now and then checking his forehead to see if he had a fever. When the maid came to the door, I explained the situation and she said to call when he was awake and she would come back to change the bed. She handed me fresh towels.

I needed to go out to get bottled water and the diarrhea medicine for Quinn.

I had taken a shower earlier. I substituted a less wrinkled pair of shorts for the pair I was wearing and ran my fingers through my hair. Then I wrote a note telling Quinn where I had gone and left it on the nightstand beside him.

I had my hand on the doorknob when the telephone rang. I tripped over a chair, trying to answer before the noise woke Quinn up.

"Hello," I said.

"Professor Stuart? Is that you?"

I straightened from my hunch and looked at Quinn. He hadn't moved. I said in my normal tone, "Mr. Sheppard? I'm so glad to hear from you. How are you feeling?"

"Still got a few aches and pains, but I checked myself out of that hospital before I could catch something."

"Are you sure that was a good idea?"

"Take more than a bump on my hard skull to keep me flat on my back. Anyway, I had some unfinished business I'd been thinking about." He paused and then said with satisfaction in his voice, "Remember Wesley Deavers, the guy who was supposed to have come back with the car to pick up your mama and TJ and Reuben on the night of the drive-by? I've located him."

"You did? You've found him? Where? I thought he had disappeared, that the police couldn't find him."

"Friend of mine on the force did some checking for me. They knew where he had probably gone even back then. But no one was particularly interested in pursuing the matter. Reuben James and TJ had been Blackstone Rangers. Gang members." He placed the phrase in verbal italics. "Then they joined up with the Panthers. By then the FBI was calling the Panthers a terrorist group."

"So when two Panthers were shot down on the street—"

"As far as the Chicago PD was concerned, someone had performed a public service."

"But your friend was able to give you a lead?"

"And I found Wesley in Detroit. A good family man, retired from Ford Motors with a disability pension. Got four children and grandkids. His wife died last year, and now he's living with one of his sons and minding his grandkids while the son and his wife are at work. Had himself a pretty decent life, he says."

"Did he tell you what happened that night?"

"He wasn't there when it went down. Becca came out of the house and told him they were going to be in there a while longer. She smiled at him real pretty and asked him to make a run over to Mama Lovejoy's and get them some fried fish dinners. Said Reuben and TJ were going to be hungry when they came out."

"So Wesley was at Mama Lovejoy's when the drive-by happened?"

"The Shack was only a couple of streets over. He thought he'd be back in plenty of time. He figured that if Becca had come out there and asked him to go, then Reuben would want him to do it."

"It didn't occur to him to ask Reuben?"

"He didn't want to interrupt the meeting," Sheppard said. "Wesley was younger than the rest of them and glad to be included. And when Becca told him Reuben would appreciate what she was asking him to do—"

"He went off to get her fried fish."

"And this is the kicker. The reason he said he was so long that they ended up standing out there on the street . . . Naomi Duncan."

"Naomi?"

"The regular cook at the Shack was out sick. Naomi was working in the kitchen that night. When Wesley came in, she told him to come on back there and keep her company while she fried the fish. She was flirting with him . . . flirting so hard, she let the fish burn."

"She let—"

"Then she had to fry up another batch. Before the fish was ready, somebody comes running in off the street with the news about the drive-by. And Wesley just walked on out of there and kept going."

"So because Becca asked Wesley to go for fish and Naomi burned the fish, Reuben James died that night."

"Well, whoever shot him—or ordered a hit—was responsible for him dying. If I had to bet on who might have ordered a hit, my money would be on Nick Mancini."

"Did Wesley say anything else? Anything about Mancini?"

"That was all he knew." Sheppard paused and then added, "The man cried.

He said he's been living with that all these years. That if he hadn't gone, that if he had got back sooner. . . . He said he felt sorry for Naomi, so he was trying to be nice to her."

"Why did he feel sorry for her?"

"Because JoJo and Becca got the men. Because he thought Naomi had been sweet on Reuben, and once Reuben saw Becca, Naomi didn't have a chance."

"But Naomi married TJ."

"Yeah. That's an odd one, ain't it?" He coughed. "Wade said your man's down there with you in New Orleans. You all right?"

"Yes, I'm fine. I followed Naomi to Wilmington, and the trail led me here. And yesterday, I met Becca."

"You don't sound as if it worked out too well."

"She isn't interested in having a daughter. But, at least, I've solved the mystery of what happened to my mother." Before he could offer sympathy, I said, "Thank you so much for finding Wesley, Mr. Sheppard. I wanted some answers, and you've helped me find them."

"We got some answers. But we still don't know who killed Nick Mancini. If Robert Montgomery didn't do it, then who did?"

"Maybe it was whoever the bartender said Mancini was worried about. Whoever it was that he thought was watching his house and following him."

"My buddy on the PD suggested that it might have been the feds."

"The FBI? But the FBI wouldn't have killed him."

Sheppard said, "At least, not with pruning shears."

I laughed, and Quinn turned over and moaned. "Mr. Sheppard, could I call you back if anything occurs to me? We're supposed to have another PI working on this down here, but we haven't heard from him yet—"

"Wade says he's on the job. So he'll probably be in touch. But call me if you think of anything else you want me to check up this way."

"Thank you. You've been wonderful."

"Just earning my paycheck," he said and rang off.

I tucked the sheet around Quinn again and picked up my shoulder bag. I still needed to go out and get bottled water and medicine.

I opened the door and stood there blinking at the bright sunlight. I felt like a bear coming out of hibernation. Quinn and I had been inside with the blinds closed. The day had gone on without us. The sidewalks outside were bustling with Monday afternoon activity.

I decided to cut through the courtyard. That way I could stop in the Morning Cuppa Café and order lunch, then pick it up on my way back.

It took me longer than I had expected to find the pharmacy. I was sure I knew which corner it was on, but I ended up making a circuit around several blocks before I found it. I got the diarrhea medicine and several bottles of water.

My order was ready and sitting on the counter when I got back to the café.

All told, my excursion had taken a little over an hour. Quinn was still asleep when I tiptoed back in. In fact, he was sleeping so soundly, I decided it was safe to turn on the television and get the midday news while I ate.

The piece of pineapple I had speared bounced from the desk to the floor. I grabbed the remote and turned up the volume. A female reporter stood in front of the blackened remains of a house.

". . . the woman in the house died in the fire. The man, described only as a white male in his mid to late thirties, was struck by a car driven by the person who fled this house. He is reported to be in critical condition at a local hospital. No names have been released, pending notification of family members. Back to you, Mark."

"Lacey, the woman in the house . . . we understand that this was the home of a psychic who called herself Madame Josephine."

"That's right, Mark."

"Can we assume she was the woman who died in the fire?"

"The police are not confirming that yet, Mark. As I said, the body was badly burned."

"What about the man hit by the car of the person fleeing? Do we know the hit-and-run victim's relationship to Madame Josephine? Was he a neighbor?"

"The police have told us that he was not a neighbor. They've found a rental car that they believe he was driving parked on the street near the house."

"Do they have any idea why he was there?"

"Nothing on that, Mark. A neighbor did report to the police that he had observed the car pulling up as he was looking out the window just before going to bed last night."

"And all of this happened around midnight?"

"That's right, Mark. About that time, neighbors heard a car speeding away and then saw the flames coming from the house. Knowing that Madame Josephine was blind, several of them rushed over to the house, but they were unable to enter the interior room that served as the office where she saw her clients. That was where the body—presumably Madame Josephine—was found."

"And it is confirmed that the neighbor who saw the person fleeing from the house believed that person was a man?"

"That's correct, Mark. But the description is a bit sketchy. The neighbor says he had only a glimpse of someone, possibly black, running toward a car that he describes as a light-colored, late model sedan. He thought the person was male because this person was wearing pants and a cap. But he admits he couldn't be sure."

"Thanks, Lacey. We know you'll keep us updated on this developing story."

I sat there with my heart thumping in my chest. I looked over at Quinn, who lay there fast asleep. I couldn't wake him up. It would do no good to wake him. He was too sick to help me deal with this.

Who was the man who had been hit by the car?

A white male in his mid to late thirties. A white male who would have reason to be at Madame Josephine's house. A thought sent me to my feet. The PI that Quinn had said was investigating Becca's transformation to Simone would have had reason to talk to Josephine Gilbert. But why would he have had her house under surveillance?

Or maybe it had been Nico. He had asked about Madame Josephine, wanted to know what she had told me. Suppose he had been watching her house?

I could call the police and ask if they had identified the man . . . but then they would want to know who I was and why I was interested.

I could try calling hospitals. "The hit-and-run victim last night—was he brought there? Could you tell me who he is and if he's going to be all right?"

Quinn had Wade's number programmed in his cell phone. I could call Wade and ask him the name of the PI. In fact, by the time I put through the call, the PI might be calling us. Both Quinn and Sheppard had said he was on the case, that he should be getting back to us this afternoon with anything he had found.

Unless he was fighting for his life in a hospital intensive care unit.

As I waited for Wade to answer his phone, I tried not to imagine Becca fleeing Josephine Gilbert's burning house with her hair under a cap.

I left a voice mail message for Wade, telling him that I needed the contact information for the PI here in New Orleans and asking him to call as soon as possible. He would wonder why I was calling him when I could have asked Quinn, especially since he knew Quinn had been on his way here. But I couldn't get into all that in a phone message.

Three hours later I was still waiting for Wade or his PI to call. Quinn was still asleep. I had tried taking a nap too. Then I had tried reading.

But all the bits and pieces of information, the lies and half-truths about Reuben and Mancini and Becca and TJ and Naomi and Josephine kept tumbling around in my head.

I got out my pad and tried brainstorming using that idea-mapping exercise where you write a word or topic in a circle and branch out. I started with Becca. What I thought of was names. Reuben. TJ. Wesley. Montgomery. Mancini.

And Sonny Germano. I had almost forgotten him. Those were the men.

What about the women? Mama Lovejoy. Naomi. JoJo.

Mama Lovejoy was long dead, and JoJo had probably burned to death in her house. Reuben had died in the drive-by, and Mancini had been stabbed in his office. TJ was gone, and now so was Montgomery. Wesley was a grandfather living in Detroit.

That left Naomi, Becca, and Sonny.

The only three remaining from the old days in Chicago.

No, that wasn't true. Angela, Nick Mancini's widow was still very much alive. And Nico, his son, who had been a child in 1969 and was an adult now.

Then there was the possibility that the FBI had been involved.

The FBI and Mancini. The FBI and the Black Panthers. And COINTELPRO, the FBI's counterintelligence operation for gathering information and engaging in activities intended to bring down individuals and organizations the Bureau had labeled "subversive" and/or "criminal."

Informants. Quinn had mentioned an informant that the Gallagher police had on its payroll. An informant who had given the Gallagher PD the tip that they then passed on to Quinn about his graffiti vandals.

The FBI had used informants. Their informants had infiltrated the Black Panthers. Informants in the Mafia had given up their former comrades.

Mancini had thought he was being watched. Sheppard's police contact thought it had probably been the feds. I had considered this possibility once and then let the idea slip away. What if Becca had stayed with Mancini after Reuben was murdered because she wanted revenge? What if she had stayed because she was trying to bring him down?

The night Mancini died, he and Becca had quarreled. He said he knew she was up to something. What if he suspected she was betraying him? Maybe later that evening he had caught her in his office going through his files. Maybe she had panicked and killed him. Then Montgomery found the body and knew she had been in Mancini's office. He confessed to save her.

But if Becca had been working as an FBI informant, would she have needed Naomi's help to get out of Chicago? According to recent revelations about the agency, some FBI handlers had shielded their informants who committed crimes, including murder. But maybe Becca had been unwilling to put her fate in the hands of the feds.

If she did kill Mancini . . . she had denied it when Naomi confronted her at the White Orchid. But, of course, she would. As she herself had asked, why would she confess now?

For that matter, why would Naomi confront her now, after all these years? She claimed it was because she had watched Montgomery die. But Naomi was the x factor here, the puzzle. Naomi was the reason Wesley hadn't come back on the night of the drive-by. Then years later, Naomi had divorced her first husband and married TJ, even though Wesley suspected she had been in love with Reuben.

Had she been trying to make up to TJ for what had happened that night when she had kept Wesley away? And what about Montgomery? Why would she take him in? Why would she go out of her way to meet him in prison and then bring him into her home?

I drew more circles around Naomi's name. Then I put down my pad and turned the television back on to distract myself until Wade or his PI called.

A weather service message was scrolling across the bottom of the screen. A storm was on the way.

CHAPTER · 45

I got out the telephone directory. When the casino hotel operator came on, I asked for Nico Mancini's room.

"Please hold while I connect you."

The phone rang two times. Three. Then a male voice said, "Hello?" He sounded as if he had been asleep.

"Nico?"

"Yes? Who is this?"

"Is this Nico?"

"Who's calling?"

"You first," I said. "Who is this?"

"Detective Daniels of the New Orleans PD. Are you trying to reach Nicholas Mancini?"

"Yes. Is he there?"

"Mr. Mancini has been involved in an accident. If you'll tell me who you are. . . ."

I eased the receiver back into its cradle.

I hadn't said anything about Josephine Gilbert. I hadn't said anything to indicate why I was calling. Unless they had managed to trace the call, they might assume that I was one of Nico's girlfriends who didn't want to chat with the police.

Had Nico been in contact with Sonny? Had he told Sonny that I was in New Orleans? If the police found out about me and that I had gone to see Josephine, they would have some questions.

They would ask me what I knew about Becca and Josephine.

All I knew was that JoJo had once been Becca's friend and Becca had stolen her lover. But when I spoke to her, instead of telling me what Becca had done to her, Josephine had denied knowing her.

That house. How had she been able to afford it? The fortune-teller in Jackson Square had said Josephine had come into some money. Maybe Becca had been the source of that money. Maybe JoJo knew something that Becca was willing to pay her to keep quiet about.

But now people were asking questions. I was here, and Nico was here, and we were both asking questions. Maybe Becca/Simone had wanted to make sure Josephine wasn't tempted to tell what she knew. Maybe Simone had been behind the wheel of the car that struck down her murdered lover's son.

I got out the telephone directory again. The phone at the White Orchid rang. Just as a recorded message was coming on, someone picked up.

"Hello, the White Orchid. Simone speaking."

I hung up.

I tucked my cell phone into my shoulder bag. I put Quinn's cell phone and a bottle of water on the nightstand beside him. Then I scribbled a note explaining that I had to run an errand but would be back soon.

I walked through the hotel office to ask about getting a taxi. As the bell captain was saying it would take about ten minutes, one pulled up with an arriving guest. The guest got out and I got in. The White Orchid wasn't that far, but I wanted to get there as quickly as possible.

If Simone had been involved in an arson homicide and a hit-and-run, why would she be at her restaurant? Could she be that cold-blooded? Or maybe she was there because she thought someone might be looking for her at home. Someone like Sonny, who might have her home address by now.

Quinn would say this was one of my less sensible ideas, dropping by to discuss my suspicions with a woman who might have committed murder. But the one fact that I kept coming back to was that she was my mother. I needed to know. I needed to know if she could kill.

CHAPTER · 46

I stood beside the taxi, looking at the "Closed" sign on the door of the White Orchid. Sweat trickled down my back. The sky was purple, and the air pressed down so close, it was hard to breathe. In spite of the heat, I was shivering.

This side street was too quiet for an afternoon in rowdy New Orleans. Where were the tourists? Had everyone retreated inside because of the humidity and the approaching storm?

There was a light on in Simone's office. Up on the second floor behind the French doors, a light was on.

"I think someone's here," I said to the driver. "But could you wait just a minute?"

I pressed the buzzer beside the black wrought-iron door and flinched at a flash of lightning.

The cab driver was on the radio to his dispatcher. I wanted to get back into his taxi and return to the hotel.

I started as the door was flung open. Simone stood there, her hair in a pony-tail, wearing tangerine slacks and a matching top. The linked silver chain around her neck matched the bracelet on her wrist. She had black sandals on her slender feet. She looked too young to be my mother.

"This is unexpected," she said. "I thought I'd gotten rid of you."

"We need to talk."

"I think we've covered everything."

"Not quite. Shall we go inside?"

She tilted her head, and her lips curled into a smile. "I suppose it would be rude of me to say no." She stepped back and held the door open.

"It's all right," I called out to the taxi driver. "Thanks for waiting."

He pulled away, and Simone said, "You really should have kept him. It looks like rain."

She sounded amused. I turned around to look at her.

The telephone at the maitre d' desk rang. She said, "Close the door, will you? This may be the call I'm expecting."

I closed the door and stood there in the twilight foyer. She plucked up the receiver.

"Hello? . . . No, I'm sorry. We're closed on Mondays. . . . Yes, please do that."
She hung up. "A hungry tourist. Let's go upstairs."

The second-floor landing was also in shadows. The white orchids glowed in their vase, reflected eerily in the mirror above the sideboard.

As we stepped through the door of Simone's office, lightning lit up the sky outside. A moment later a clap of thunder echoed.

"Lemonade?" she said, indicating the pitcher on a tray on her desk.

"I'm not thirsty."

"It's safe. I'm your wicked mother, not your stepmother."

"Mothers have been known to poison their offspring," I said.

"Not after all the trouble I went through birthing you." She dropped ice cubes into two glasses and filled them from the pitcher. "That was not a pleasant experience. I was in labor for nineteen hours while your grandmother prayed over me. That was when I realized that if I lived, I would have to leave. I'd had my fill of being prayed over."

"Thank you," I said when she handed me one of the glasses. I took a tentative sip. It was tart and cold with a hint of cherries.

"Hester Rose wanted me to be as prim and proper as she was," Simone said. Her glance took in my navy skirt and white blouse. "She seems to have accomplished that with you."

Score one for Mom. She was elegant; I was dowdy.

"I'm not here to discuss my taste in clothes," I said.

She settled on the arm of the sofa, her expression inquisitive. "What are you here to discuss? I'm open to any subject except 'Mommy, where did I come from?'"

"Don't you think I have the right to know that?"

"If you've gone all these years without knowing, why would you want to know now?"

Thunder crackled as a flash of lightning lit up the room. Then it was gone and we were left in the cozy light of the lamp on her desk.

She was watching me, as if interested in what I would say.

"Because there is a man who has asked me to marry him. Because I would like to be the mother of his children."

"Then you had better get started. It may be fashionable these days to have children in your forties, but from what I've seen, running around after them takes energy." She tilted her head, inquisitive, amused. "Are you sure you want to have children?"

"Would you rather not be a grandmother?"

She shrugged. "I don't expect to volunteer for baby-sitting."

It was an odd conversation. Almost surreal. After throwing me out of her office yesterday, now she seemed amused by the situation.

"Tell me about this man you think you want to marry." She motioned toward the sofa. "I've done it twice, and you really should give it some thought."

I sat down on her white sofa with the throw pillows in shades of brown and tan. "Did you marry Josephine Gilbert's lover?"

"He was my first husband. But he was never really her lover. She only wanted him to be." She set her glass on a coaster on the coffee table. "He found what I did in bed more interesting than what she did."

"And so you took him?"

"I accepted what he was offering. It would have been a shame to let a perfectly good man go to waste."

Lightning flashed once again, and the sky opened. Beyond the French doors, rain poured from the purple sky. If he woke up, Quinn would be worried about me. He knows how much I hate storms.

"Were you there last night?" I said.

"Was I where last night?" Becca/Simone said.

"At Josephine's house when it was set on fire?"

"Josephine?" She stood up. A jerky, startled movement. "Is she all right?"

"Are you saying that you don't know what happened? How could you not have heard it on the news?"

"I haven't been listening to the news," she said. "I spent the night here on the sofa."

"Why?"

"Because I didn't want to go home. Is Josephine all right?"

"If she was the woman they found in the house, then she's dead."

"Dead? JoJo?" Simone walked away from me, over to the French doors. I couldn't see her face, but her shoulders were hunched. After a moment, she said, "Do they know who did it?"

"All they have is a vague description of someone wearing a cap and driving a light-colored car. This person also hit a man while fleeing the scene."

Simone drew the drapes over the French doors and walked over to the wall switch. The chandelier came on, warming the room and shutting out the storm. "Who was this man? One of her neighbors?"

"No. Actually, I think the man was Nick Mancini Jr. When I called his hotel, the police were in his room."

She turned then. "I didn't realize the two of you knew each other."

"But you did know that he was here in New Orleans?"

"Josephine told me."

"When?"

"When he first arrived and came to see her. His visit upset her."

"Why?"

"Because he was asking questions about me and about his father's death."

"Questions she didn't want to answer?"

Simone walked back toward me. "And didn't have to answer . . . as I told her last night."

I watched her pick up her glass from the coffee table. "So you did see her last night?" I said.

"She called and asked me to come over. What time was the fire reported?"

"Around midnight."

"I went there after closing last night, at around 10:30. I was there for about half an hour. I was back here in my office by 11:30."

"Where you spent the night?"

"Yes."

"Any witnesses?"

"I was alone. Getting back to Nick Mancini's son. . . . How do the two of you know each other?"

"We met in Chicago when he gave me a lift from the airport."

A hint of a smile formed around her lips. "I have the feeling there's a story there."

"There is. But it isn't relevant to the matter at hand. Nico and I met because I was looking for you. He followed me here to New Orleans. He's hired an investigator to check into your past."

She sat down beside me on the sofa and crossed her legs. "That should make interesting reading."

"The police are probably going to question you about Josephine's death."

She shrugged. "If they should arrive before I leave, I'll be happy to talk to them. I have nothing to hide."

"You're going somewhere?"

"Out of town."

I took a swallow of my lemonade. "Then JoJo wasn't blackmailing you?"

"Now, why would you think that?"

"Where did she get the money to buy her house?"

"I gave her the house."

"That was generous of you."

"The house was a freebie. Someone gave it to me; I gave it to her." She picked up her glass and drained it. "I owed her that much." She stood up. "A refill?"

I shook my head and said, "I suppose I should have asked if this lemonade is nonalcoholic."

"This isn't your grandma's kitchen table, baby girl."

"She was raped, you know."

Her hand paused over the pitcher. "Who was raped?"

"Hester Rose."

Simone picked up the pitcher and refilled her glass. "I don't recall that she ever told me that story when she was lecturing me on sex and sin."

"She didn't tell me either. I found out when I was doing research on the lynching that happened in Gallagher."

"She left there when she was a child."

"She left when she was twelve years old, on the day of the lynching. She was hiding in the woods, watching. One of the men in the mob found her there."

"And he raped her?"

I nodded. "And she left town that night on the freight train that brought her to Kentucky."

"And now you expect me to forgive her? You provide me with this revealing insight into her traumatized psyche, and I now understand why she was a prudish, sanctimonious old witch and forgive all?"

"She was your mother."

"The lowdown about that is that she never wanted to be." Simone took a long sip from her glass. "I was the best she could do."

"The best—"

"I had a brother. She was in her thirties when she got pregnant. He was stillborn. That just about broke poor Walter Lee's heart. But a few months later, she became pregnant again . . . with me. She was terrified during the whole pregnancy because she thought I would be born dead too. I expect sometimes she wished I had been."

"What about Walter Lee?" I said. "He loved you."

"I suppose he did. But when we talked, we might as well have been speaking two different languages. He spent so much time on those trains, Hester Rose and I had way too much of each other's company." She lifted her glass to me. "And now that I've given you my version of our family history, I'll call you a taxi." She set her glass down with a click and walked toward the telephone on her desk.

The thunder crackled. I flinched. "I don't think it's safe to talk on the telephone right now. And we haven't finished our conversation."

"Haven't we?" Her tone taunted me.

"I'm sorry you had a less than ideal childhood, but that doesn't give you the right to play games with my life. If you don't want to be my mother, that's fine, but I want to know who my father was."

"Why? So you can go give him a hard time too?"

"He's still alive? My father is—"

"That was a hypothetical question," she said.

I put my glass down and stood up. "Is he alive?"

"I have no idea. I haven't seen the man—or 'that devil,' as your grandmother preferred to call him—in over forty years."

"Since before I was born." I swallowed. "I want his name."

"He's not the kind of man who would welcome the discovery that you're his daughter."

"Then meeting you will have been good practice. Now, give me his name, damn you."

Her lilting laughter mocked me. "What do you intend to do if I don't?" She shook back her hair. "You were better off without me, and you're better off not knowing—"

"Do you think that's your decision?" I said, and something tore lose inside me. "I've spent my whole life putting up with shit because of you. I grew up living with the whispers, with the boys who teased me and tried to do more because I was your daughter. Becca, the town slut! I grew up afraid of who I was and what I was." I moved toward her, wanting to shake her. "I don't give a damn whether you think I'm better off not knowing. I want to know who my father was, you bitch!"

Something—some emotion—kindled in her golden eyes. "If you believe in retribution, then your father was a sin for which I paid dearly. Even bitches—"

The door to her office exploded inward. We both swung toward it.

CHAPTER · 47

Sonny Germano stood there. Water dripped from him onto the floor. His short-sleeved shirt and his khaki pants clung to him, bunched over his protruding belly. His feet were bare in soggy sandals. His straggly mustache drooped over his lip. His thinning hair was plastered to his skull. His bald spot glistened in the light.

He would have been a comic figure if not for the rage in his eyes.

Simone said, "Sonny? Another face from my past."

"You bitch," he said.

We seemed to have a consensus.

But Sonny had his own list of accusations. "I tried to help you back then with Nick," he said. "I put you together with the feds so you could get away from Nick. And this is what you do to me?"

This was about Nick Mancini. These two—Sonny and Becca—had been working together?

"What do you think I've done to you?" Simone said.

"He knows," Sonny said. "Nico knows someone was ratting out his father. He called me last night. He asked if I knew who had set Nick up with the feds."

"And you said you had no idea," she said. "So I don't understand what your problem is."

"He knows it had to have been someone close to Nick. Someone who had access."

"Tell him it was me," Simone said.

"I told him that," Sonny said. "And he asked me how I knew. He asked if I knew it back then, when it was happening."

She smiled. "Sounds like you screwed up that conversation."

Sonny's face contorted. "The way he spoke to me—"

"How did you expect him to speak to you when he thinks you sold his father out so that you could get control of the club? That *is* why you did it, isn't it, Sonny? Because you wanted what Nick had. Everything Nick had."

His fists clenched. "Was it you in that car? Did you run Nico down?"

"Now, why would I want to kill Nick Mancini's son?"

"Did you do it? Tell me that. Did you do it?"

"What would you do about it if I said yes?" Simone laughed. "Sonny, you're still a stupid little man who imagines he's—"

He was across the room and at her before she saw what was coming.

He had his hands at her throat. She pried at them.

But he was strong. Stronger because of his fury.

She was trying to claw at his face. To twist free. But he had her on her back, across her desk, her legs pinned.

"Stop! Let her go!" I grabbed at his arms, at his wrists. I yanked at his collar.

He sent me reeling with a backhand. My head struck the edge of the desk, and I saw stars.

I staggered to my feet. Simone was making gurgling sounds. Her hands had fallen to her side.

I ran around the desk and pulled open the drawer. The gun was there. "Let her go! Do you hear me? Let her go."

He didn't look at me. Didn't let up on the pressure he was applying to Simone's throat. Her eyes were rolling back. I was watching him strangle my mother to death.

Aim for the torso, Quinn said in my head. *Always aim for the torso.*

I fired. Sonny screamed and fell back, away from Simone.

I put the gun down on the desk.

I ran around and knelt on the Oriental carpet beside him, where he lay writhing in pain. "Call 911!" I yelled at Simone.

She laughed. A hoarse, broken sound. "You shot him in the damn butt."

"I was afraid I'd kill him if I shot him anywhere else. And his butt was right there. There's a lot of blood. I might have hit an artery."

Sonny was alternating between prayers and curses.

Simone stood there with her hands at her throat.

"Simone, call the paramedics!" I said. "Don't move, Sonny," I said to the man on the floor.

Pressure, should I apply pressure? I tried to remember my Red Cross first-aid course. There was so much blood.

Sonny had slumped back. I checked his pulse. It was rapid.

"Sonny, can you hear me?"

He groaned and cursed.

"Simone, damn it, call for help!" I said.

She started to reach out for the telephone. She had it in her hand. Then she stopped.

I twisted around to see what had caught her attention.

My heart went into overdrive.

CHAPTER · 48

I kept my voice calm as I turned to Simone. "That call you were going to make, Simone. The paramedics. We need the paramedics for Sonny."

"Not just yet." She replaced the telephone receiver. She was looking at Naomi. "Hello, Nay, I thought you'd gone. JoJo said you'd gone back to Chicago."

Naomi took a step into the room. A soggy baseball cap drooped over her face. Her tan shirt and beige slacks were soaked and clinging to her body. The glittering, disconnected expression in her eyes chilled me.

Her voice was hoarse when she spoke, tired. "I couldn't go back," she said. She glanced at me, there on the floor beside Sonny, without a great deal of interest. "I couldn't face my Tad and look him in the eye. You know it's been eating at me, Becca. It's been eating at me so."

"What has?" Simone said.

"The things I've done. The bad things I've done."

I heard Simone's breath hiss out. "Was it you last night, Naomi? Last night when JoJo was—?"

"It was an accident, Becca. You know I wouldn't have hurt JoJo. But she had candles all over the place. A blind woman shouldn't have candles." Naomi waved her hands. "She had set up some kind of altar with these big chunky candles. And when we were talking. . . ." She rubbed her hand over her glistening face. "I was trying to explain to her, but she was afraid. I don't know why she was afraid of me."

She took off the cap and stuffed it into the tote bag on her shoulder. Her hair stuck out in damp spikes, but she looked more like the woman I had seen in her house in Chicago. "I tried to explain it to her, Becca. But JoJo was backing away from me, and she fell onto her altar. And she was screaming . . . and she started to run because she was on fire. . . ." Naomi wrapped her arms around herself. "And I ran out the door and got in my car."

"You hit someone," I said.

She frowned. "Some white man. He scared me, grabbing at me like that. He was saying something about you and his daddy, and I shoved him away and ran to the car. But he jumped in front of me. . . ." She twisted her hands together. "I didn't mean to hit him, Becca." She was looking at me when she spoke. Speaking to me as Becca.

On the floor, Sonny made a sound. His eyes were open again. His lips were moving. I leaned down to hear what he was trying to say.

"Her . . . the one," he whispered. "She's the one . . . the one . . . saw run out . . . the alley." Sonny grimaced and his hand fell from my arm. He was trying to keep his head up enough to watch Naomi.

She was saying, "I thought if I played it smart, I could find out."

"Find out what?" I said. I could feel Sonny's blood soaking through the tail end of his shirt that I had pressed against his wound.

"If he really had Reuben killed."

"Do you mean Nick Mancini?"

Naomi nodded, her gaze fixed on me. "You said he did it, Becca. But I thought it could have been one of the gangs. I thought if I mentioned Reuben, then I could see how he'd react and I'd know."

"Why did you want to know?" I said. "Why was it so important to you?"

"Because if he didn't have him killed, then it wasn't me. It wasn't because I sent him that note."

The real Becca said, "You sent Nick a note about Reuben and me?"

Naomi nodded, shifting her glance to Becca. "You sat there at my mama's table, talking about how much you loved Reuben, and how soon as JoJo got back to town and helped you get those pictures, you were going to be rid of that gangster. Talking about how you and Reuben were going to be together. And then you looked at me and laughed and asked when I was going to get me a man." Her chin came up as she challenged Becca. "Do you remember that? Do you remember what you said? You said, 'But maybe you're like your mama, Nay. Maybe you rather get yourself a pretty woman.'"

Her voice thick from the choking and from whatever emotion she was feeling, Becca said, "And that was why you sent Nick the note? Because I teased you about Mama Lovejoy?"

"You teased me about being like her," Naomi said. "I wanted to spite you. I thought if that gangster knew about Reuben, he would make you stay away. I didn't know he would have Reuben killed." She shook her head. "I swear to God, Becca, I didn't know he would kill him. I didn't know he'd send someone to drive by there and shoot him dead on the street while I was talking to Wesley."

Becca said, "While you were talking to Wesley?"

"Mama had me working in the kitchen that night when Wesley came in." She smiled slightly. "You know how good-looking Wesley was, and I thought. . . ." She frowned. "I wanted to prove to you that I could get a man too. And we were talking, and I let the fish burn 'cause I wasn't paying attention, and then I had to fry another batch. And before I could get that done, someone come running in and said there'd been a shooting. That Reuben and TJ had been shot. And Wesley went running out. I never saw him again after that."

Becca said, "So the reason Wesley didn't come back to pick us up was because you kept him—"

"It was your fault too. TJ said it was your fault that Reuben wasn't paying attention that night. TJ said you were climbing all over Reuben and that's why he didn't go back inside like TJ wanted him to."

Becca said, "And so that's why what you did doesn't matter?"

"I know I shouldn't have done that, Becca. I know I shouldn't have sent that gangster the note."

"What happened when you went to see him?" I said.

"He grabbed me and started asking me questions about you, Becca. He said he knew you were up to something. I was afraid he was going to make me tell him about how you were talking to the FBI."

"So you stabbed him," I said.

"He was hurting me, he wouldn't let me go. And I reached for something to hit him with . . . I thought I must not have really killed him when you told me about Robert confessing." She sighed. "But then I met someone who knew Robert, and I knew I had to go in the prison and see him. And I heard his lawyer talking about his case, and I knew he didn't do it. He confessed because of you."

"But *you* killed Nick," Becca said.

"I thought you did it," Naomi said. Her eyes were wide as she stared at Becca. "That's why I came down here, to hear you say you did it. That you went back in there and killed him after I left. Did you, Becca?"

Becca shook her head. "You killed him, Naomi."

"Don't lie, please, Becca," Naomi said. "I got a son. I got to be his mama."

"You have two sons," I said.

Her gaze moved from Becca down to me. "Percy was my punishment, him being like he is, like Mama. But I tried to do right. I tried to make up for Reuben dying. I married TJ when he got out of prison, and I tried to be a good wife. And I took in Robert. I took in Robert, and I watched him die after you ran off and left him to go to prison for what you—"

"For what *you* had done," Becca said. "You killed Nick Mancini."

Naomi frowned and seemed puzzled. Then her eyes flashed with anger. "You wanted him dead, but you couldn't do it. First, you had that big plan of yours about how you and JoJo were going to set him up with a drag queen and get pictures and blackmail him. Then you talked about how you and him"—she nodded at Sonny—"how you were helping the FBI get information on him. And I knew you were doing that 'cause you didn't have the nerve to right out kill him." She wiped at her mouth with the back of her hand. "I did it for you. I was trying to explain that to JoJo."

"And I have to do this for Reuben," Becca said. "I should have killed Nick. I can kill you."

I looked around. The gun was in her hand and pointed at Naomi.

C H A P T E R · 4 9

"No!" I screamed out the word so loud, it echoed in my head.

But the sound of that shot was louder. Naomi staggered.

Becca fired again. And then again.

Naomi fell to the floor.

I heard the gun clatter against the wood of the desk.

Becca said, "I have to leave now. But feel free to make yourself at home until the police arrive." She picked up an overnight case from the floor beside her desk and took her purse from another drawer.

I was still kneeling on the floor, pressing Sonny's crumpled shirttail to the wound in his posterior. Becca looked down at me as she passed.

"I had to kill her," she said. "You know that song? That was the way I felt about Reuben James. I loved him with all my heart and soul. That night when I was kneeling beside his body, this mangy dog started howling, and I. . . ." She smiled and brushed back her hair. "But it's over now. So long, baby girl."

She was almost at the door when she turned around. She came back to her desk. I watched her pick up the gun and open her overnight case.

"Why are you taking that?"

"Just making it simple for the gendarmes. Your fingerprints are on this. Tell them that I shot Sonny." She flicked him a glance. "He won't dispute it. Will you, Sonny?"

He groaned and cursed her.

"Then it'll be a question of which one of you they think they can believe," she told him.

She strode across her office to the door. This time, she didn't turn around. The rumble of thunder drowned out her footsteps going down the stairs.

I grabbed the side of her desk with my bloody hand and pulled myself up. My knees felt weak.

I dialed 911. The operator verified the address and told me to stay on the line. She said help was on the way.

I hung up. I needed to call Quinn.

His cell phone rang. He didn't answer. I hoped he wasn't in the bathroom throwing up again. Not after what he'd paid that doctor for that shot.

I waited for his voice mail.

"Quinn, it's me. I'm at the White Orchid. The police are on the way. Naomi Duncan is dead, and Sonny Germano has been shot. And I think I'm going to need a lawyer."

I clicked off.

On the floor, Sonny tried to turn onto his other side. He grunted and his eyes rolled back in his head.

I knelt down on the carpet beside him and felt for the pulse in his throat above the gold chain. He was still breathing.

I looked over at Naomi crumpled in the doorway. Her eyes were wide open, blank. Becca had stepped over her body when she left.

CHAPTER · 50

The paramedics wanted to take me to the hospital too. The one who examined the bump on my forehead and shone his light in my eyes said he thought I had a mild concussion. The uniformed officer who was questioning me said I wasn't going anywhere until the guys from homicide arrived.

It was during their discussion that I wished I had called Miss Alice back in Gallagher and gotten the name of her nephew, the New Orleans police detective.

Well, when the guys from homicide arrived, I could always ask if they knew who he might be. They would be certain to appreciate my question since, at the moment, I was refusing to say anything except that my name was Lizzie Stuart and I wanted a lawyer before I made a statement.

Sonny, bless him, had passed out when the paramedics started working on him. So all I had to do was keep my mouth shut. Keep saying I wanted a lawyer before I made a statement. If it took Quinn time to arrive with one, then I could at least give Becca a head start. I owed her that. We had that much kinship between us.

The police had ordered me downstairs to the dining room, out of the way of the crime scene technicians. The medical examiner hadn't arrived yet. Naomi's body was still upstairs on the floor in Becca's office.

What would Tad say when they told him that his mother was dead?

Had Percy, her other son, suspected all along that something was seriously wrong with his mother? Was that why he had been so concerned about Robert Montgomery in her house? Because it was making her worse?

That would explain the visit he and Earl had made to Sheppard's office, if they had gone there not just to get back at Sheppard, but to see if he had anything in his files about Naomi.

A man stopped in front of me. He was black, beefy, and tough looking with rolled-up shirt sleeves and a loosened tie. "Ms. Stuart? I'm Detective Bodine. Could you tell me what happened here?"

I shook my head and regretted the movement. I focused on his face. "I'm a criminal justice professor, Detective Bodine. I know better than to make a statement without having an attorney present."

He gave me a look that bordered on irritation. "Then if you will come with us to the station, we'll arrange for an attorney."

I stood up and almost fell down. He caught my arm.

I heard someone say, "The paramedic wanted to take her to the hospital. He thought she might have a concussion."

Bodine cursed. "Then why didn't you send her with them? We don't need a damn suspect dying in custody."

"I'm not going to die. It's just a bump on the head."

He said, "I want a doctor on record saying that. Come on."

The door was standing open. The rain had stopped, but the air still felt saturated. "If we're going to the hospital first, should I call Quinn and tell him to meet me there?"

"Is Quinn your attorney?" Bodine said.

"My cop. He wants to marry me. He used to be a homicide detective."

Bodine stopped and looked at me. "You're going to be a royal pain in the butt, aren't you?"

I winced, thinking of Sonny. But Bodine seemed not to have been thinking of that. "I'm sorry," I said. "I'm not enjoying this much, either."

At the hospital, the doctor in the emergency room poked and prodded me. He concluded that I would indeed live but I might have a headache and some dizziness for a few days. He was writing that down on his chart when we heard raised voices outside.

"Quinn," I said by way of explanation. "He's here." I held onto the examining table as I slid to the floor.

By the time I'd made it out to the corridor, Quinn and Bodine were standing toe-to-toe. Neither of them looked happy.

"Did you find an attorney?" I said to Quinn.

He reached out to touch the bandage on my forehead. I hoped I looked better than he did. "She's going to meet us at the station. Are you all right?"

"Fine. Just a little headache."

Quinn looked at Bodine. "I apologize," he said. "I know you're only doing your job."

Bodine stared back at him, then nodded. "As one cop to another."

"As one cop to another, could I please speak to Professor Stuart alone?"

Bodine shook his head. "I'd like to be accommodating. But unless you have a law degree as well as a badge, and you happen to be your girlfriend's lawyer, speaking to her alone—"

"It's all right," I said. "I'm all right, Quinn. I just wanted an attorney before I made a statement."

Bodine must have picked up on the silent message that I was trying to send to Quinn: *Don't say Becca's name.* He said, "By the way, we've been trying to locate the owner of the White Orchid, Simone Deverill. Did you happen to see her there tonight?"

Quinn said, "Detective Bodine, if we are following procedure, Professor Stuart's request for an attorney means you don't get to ask any more questions until her attorney arrives."

Bodine's smile was a bit thinner this time. "Then let's get on over to the station and see if your attorney is there, Ms. Stuart."

"I'll be right behind you," Quinn said.

We waited for almost an hour before the attorney arrived. Bodine left me sitting in one of the interview rooms. Quinn was outside in the lobby.

My attorney shook hands and told me that her name was Karen Monroe. She was blonde, blue-eyed, and looked as if she played tennis. She looked almost as young as my optometrist, Dr. Bauer.

I hoped she wasn't going to be the bearer of bad news too.

She seemed to know what she was doing. She told Bodine she wanted to speak to her client alone, and he went away without giving her any fuss.

"All right," she said. "Tell me what happened."

"Someone else is involved," I said.

"Who?"

"My mother. Becca—Simone Deverill."

"The owner of the White Orchid?"

I made the mistake of nodding. It hurt. "Yes."

"How is she involved?" Monroe had her pad and pen out now.

"I shot Sonny Germano because he was trying to choke her to death. She shot Naomi Duncan because Naomi confessed to a murder—two murders—that happened in Chicago in 1969. She committed one and caused the other."

Monroe stared at me without speaking. Then she got up and went to the door. "Hey, can I get a cup of coffee in here? We're going to be here for a while." She turned back to me. She looked invigorated. "You want coffee too?"

"No. Just some water, please."

When we had our beverages, Monroe settled down with her pad and pen again. "Okay. Start at the beginning."

"Today? Or Chicago in 1969?"

"However you have to tell it so I understand it."

I told her. It seemed to take a long time, but maybe that was because of my headache. When I finished, she said, "You're going to have to tell them that your mother shot Naomi Duncan."

"Yes, I know."

"If Sonny Germano pulls through okay, we should be all right on that one. He was engaged in a violent attack on your mother. You shot him to save her." She smiled. "A well-aimed, clearly not lethally intended bullet in his derriere."

"Will I have to stay here in jail tonight?"

"Bodine's going to be pissed with you for holding back about Simone

Deverill. But it's not up to him." She went to the door. "Tell Detective Bodine we're ready to talk."

Bodine came in. He took the chair across from me.

Monroe sat down again with her pad. "Go ahead," she said. "Tell him what you told me."

"All of it?" I said.

"From the top," she said.

I pressed my fingers to my eyes and closed them. I was so tired that I would have given a lot to be able to put my head down on that grungy looking table and sleep.

I heard Monroe say, "She didn't kill Naomi Duncan, Bodine."

"I'm waiting to hear her tell me who did."

"Go ahead, Lizzie," Monroe said. "If we're going to get you out of here, you have to tell him what happened."

I dropped my hands and opened my eyes and sat back in my chair. "Could I make one request? Would you please let Quinn come in?"

"Sorry," Bodine said. "That's not procedure."

"When's the last time you worried about procedure?" Monroe said.

"Since I got my ass in a sling the last time I didn't," he said. "What happened at the White Orchid, Ms. Stuart?"

I looked at Monroe. She nodded, and I said, "I shot Sonny Germano because he was attacking my mother, Becca—Simone Deverill. She shot Naomi Duncan." I reached for my cup and took a long swallow of water. "Are you going to record this. I would rather not have to go through it again."

"If you're ready to make a statement for the record," Bodine said.

"I am."

I told him what happened. The truth. That I had shot Sonny. That Becca had shot Naomi. And why.

Monroe had been right. Bodine was not happy that I had delayed his search for Becca.

"I ought to lock you up for something," he said. "Obstructing justice. There are probably some other charges I could find to lock you up for."

"Don't bother," Monroe said.

He looked at her. "As a matter of fact, we got a statement from Germano about five minutes ago. According to him, he was shot by accident. He says the gun went off while he and your client were having a conversation."

Monroe nodded. "I guess he didn't want to admit he was trying to choke Simone Deverill to death when he got plugged. What did he say about Naomi Duncan?"

"He says your client was playing Florence Nightingale, trying to render first aid to that hole he accidentally got in his butt when it happened. He says her mother, who he described in colorful language, shot Duncan down in cold blood."

I cleared my throat. "I've told you what happened, why she—"

"And we still got ourselves a dead woman," Bodine said.

After a moment, I said, "Is Nico—Nick Mancini—going to be all right?"

"They don't know yet." He stood up. "That should do it for now."

I looked at him, not sure what he meant.

He said, "It pays to have your own high-priced attorney and a boyfriend who's a cop."

I found my tongue. "What happens if you don't?"

He smiled. "You don't want to know."

Quinn got to his feet as we came out of the interrogation room.

Bodine said, "Interview over, Chief Quinn. I'm releasing Professor Stuart into your custody. But I want her to stay in town another few days. I may need her for something."

Quinn opened his mouth.

I said quickly, "I don't mind staying, Detective Bodine. Will you let me know if you have any news about my mother?"

"You'll be the first to hear."

Monroe dropped us off back at the hotel. Bodine seemed to have been right about her fees. She drove a Mercedes sedan.

She waved good-bye and said to call if we needed her.

As we passed the hotel office, I reminded Quinn that we were due to check out in the morning. He told me to go on to the room; he would take care of it.

I unlocked the door. The maid had been in. The bed was freshly made. There was even a mint on each pillow. I dropped the mints on the nightstand, pulled back the covers, kicked off my shoes, and climbed in.

At some point, Quinn woke me up enough to take off my clothes. Then he got in beside me, and I curled up against him and went back to sleep.

CHAPTER · 51

The story about Naomi Duncan's presence when Josephine Gilbert had gone up in flames was on the morning news. The twist guaranteed to enthrall viewers was the information that Becca—Simone Deverill—had killed Naomi. The reporter, live on location at the White Orchid, said it was "a bizarre story" of three women who had known each other in Chicago in the 1960s, "a story of love and murder and betrayal."

Somehow in this version of events, Sonny Germano and I just happened to be visiting Simone at the White Orchid when Naomi arrived. We had witnessed the argument between the two women that had led to Naomi's death. Sonny had been caught in the cross fire when Simone shot her former-friend-turned-enemy.

There was no mention that I was Simone's daughter.

The fact that Nico had been hit by Naomi as she fled the fire was, it seemed, a matter of his having been in the wrong place at the wrong time.

"Fortunately," the reporter said, "Mr. Mancini has shown improvement. His doctors say his prognosis is good for a full recovery."

"That is good news, Megan," the morning anchor said. "Fascinating story, and one that has caught the patrons of the White Orchid by surprise. Certainly no one could have suspected that the restaurant's popular and beautiful owner, Simone Deverill, a former radio personality and twice-married socialite, had a past that would lead to murder."

I clicked off the television and looked at Quinn, who sat in the chair at the desk. "How did that happen?" I asked. "How did Sonny and I become mere witnesses?"

"I guess Bodine decided to go with the sanitized version. Keep it simple."

"Of course, Quinn, it might be a conspiracy of silence. Orders from the feds. Maybe the FBI still has secrets about what the Bureau did in Chicago and other places during the '60s that the government would rather not have come out." A thought occurred to me as I was imagining this web of deception. "Do you think they were hoping that with Becca as an informant they might get two for the price of one—a mobster and maybe a few more Black Panthers?"

Quinn rubbed at the back of his neck. He still looked tired. "I'd like to know who proposed that alliance between Becca and Sonny. Did she walk up to him and say, 'Would you like to help me bring down your cousin's husband?'"

"However it happened, Sonny obviously spent more time talking to her than he led me to believe that day over lunch. And obviously, she thought he was an idiot. She stood there taunting him about the possibility that she might have been the one who ran Nico down and assumed he wouldn't do anything about it."

"So Sonny Germano and Rodney Dangerfield have the same problem. They 'don't get no respect.'"

"And even worse, now Nico knows that Sonny betrayed his father."

"I guess Nick Sr. didn't show Sonny a lot of respect either."

"Do you think Angela Mancini knew what Sonny did?"

"I think her son probably wonders if she knew." Quinn stood up and stretched. "But whatever happened then or last night, Lizabeth, you are out of it now."

I leaned back against the pillow. "You're forgetting, Quinn. They still haven't found Becca."

Three days later, they were no closer to finding her. She had disappeared without a trace. Bodine looked more than a little put out when he called us down to the station to tell us that. He looked us over like he was wondering if somehow we had managed to help Becca make her getaway.

I wanted to tell him that I was as surprised as he was that Becca—Simone—had walked out of her office and disappeared. I wanted to know how she'd done it too.

Quinn had called off Wade's local PI because I was worried he would find something and then we would have information that the police should have.

But I did want to know where Becca had gone.

However, I sensed Bodine wasn't in the mood to share speculations.

We had reached a lull in the conversation. He was sitting there with his fingers steepled under his chin, staring at me.

I glanced over at Quinn.

He said, "I assume Professor Stuart is free to leave New Orleans now, Detective Bodine."

Bodine stared at me a moment longer. Then he shrugged. "Why not? We know where to find her if we need her."

"Good-bye," I said as we left.

"You have a good trip home," he said. "Be sure to come back and visit us."

Quinn and I went back to the hotel to pack our bags. We were on standby for a flight to Greensboro. It looked like we would be able to make it.

With the efficiency of a veteran traveler, Quinn was packed and ready to go in less than ten minutes. He watched me fold a blouse and then asked if I was almost ready. When I nodded, he went over to the phone to call for a taxi.

I dumped the rest of my clothes into my suitcase. The ring Quinn had given me was still in the wall safe. I slipped into the closet and knelt to work the combination.

"Our taxi is on the way," he said, a warning in his voice that I needed to get a move on.

When he turned, I held the ring out to him.

We had not talked about the future while we were waiting to hear about Becca. I had told him what happened, including a detailed account of my conversation with her. And then we had moved into a kind of limbo. We had played at being tourists. We had gone out to eat. We had walked around the French Quarter. Yesterday, we'd even taken a sight-seeing tour to one of the antebellum plantations.

And last night I had called Tad at his cousin's house in Wilmington. He cried when I said I was sorry. I cried when he said he missed his mother.

And Quinn took the phone from my hands and held me in his arms.

He had been there for me every moment. But we hadn't talked about our relationship. We needed to do that now.

He looked down at the ring in my hand. "Are you giving it back?"

"Yes. But there's something I need to say to you."

"What?"

"That I'm Hester Rose and Walter Lee's granddaughter. And I'm Becca's daughter. And my unknown father . . . I'm his daughter too. And I'm Lizabeth Theodora Stuart. And as you should have realized by now, that can be quite a package. But if you want me . . . if you are sure that you want me and that you trust who I am . . . then I'm all yours."

"Lizabeth, I'm an Irish-Scot-Comanche cop with warring ancestors and mismatched parents and my own recent battle scars, including a kid that I shot and a marriage that ended badly. If you can live with all that . . . if you can trust me . . . then believe me, I can handle who you are."

"Yes."

"Yes what?"

"Yes, I can live with all that. Yes, I trust you."

"I trust you too. So I'll ask again. Will you marry me, Lizabeth?"

"Yes, I will."

He touched my cheek with a hand that was not quite steady. "I want it all, Lizzie. Children too."

"Children too. Except there's something else. I wanted to say I would marry you first so that you would know that I trust you to love me and that now I trust myself. But there could be a complication."

"What kind of complication?"

"The eye exam I had. There may be a problem." I told him what the optometrist had said.

"Give me the ring and hold out your hand, Lizabeth."

I did.

He slipped the ring onto my finger. "Now we're going home and you're going to have that test that you should have had before you went chasing after Becca."

"Okay," I said.

He drew me into his arms. "It's going to be all right, Lizzie. Whatever happens, we're going to be all right."

I leaned my forehead against his shoulder, letting go of the knot in my stomach. "And you might even learn to like my coffee."

CHAPTER · 52

I perched on the edge of the chair opposite her desk as Dr. Bauer looked down at the results of the test I had taken. The test, designed to detect deterioration of peripheral vision, had consisted of sitting in a darkened room in front of a machine and clicking whenever I saw a flash of light on the screen.

She looked up and grinned. "Good news, teach. You passed. It seems you just have yourself two pupils that don't match."

"All in my genes?" I said, making a joke that sounded a little breathless even to my own ears.

"Or something," she said. "But nothing we have to worry about. We'll keep an eye out for any changes, but right now you're fine."

I drove to Quinn's office and told him the news. He let out a whoop and grabbed me up and swung me around. When he lowered me to my feet, he was smiling, that slow smile that started in his eyes and worked its way down to his mouth.

He was smiling like a man who loved me. I smiled back.

Maybe Becca had loved Reuben James with all her heart and soul.

I couldn't put myself in her place, couldn't understand who she had been while growing up in Drucilla and who she'd become when she ran away to find another life.

I couldn't pretend that because she'd loved Reuben, she'd had the right to kill Naomi. But wherever she was, wherever my mother was, I hoped she was okay.

EPILOGUE

The postcard arrived without fanfare a couple of months later.

It was one of those generic color photos of gorgeous bodies on a beach. One sun-bronzed beauty had the words *Rio de Janeiro* stamped on her bikini-clad bottom.

I took a deep breath and turned the postcard over.

The message on the other side was written in dashing script: *On my way elsewhere. Good luck if you're still planning to wed. Advise keep list of divorce lawyers handy in case your prince turns into a frog.*

It was signed "B."

Quinn groaned when I showed it to him. He mumbled something that sounded liked "meddling mother-in-law on the lam."

I didn't ask him to repeat what he'd said.

Author's Note

For those readers who are wondering what in this book is fiction and what is true, the general description of the civil rights movement, the Black Panthers, and the FBI counterintelligence program, COINTELPRO, reflect the scholarly research on the era and recent revelations. The newspaper articles that are unrelated to the fictional story depicted here reflect the true media coverage of the events occurring during this era. I have inserted fictional persons, such as Reuben James, into this story of the 1960s. In the same manner, I have inserted fictional businesses such as the Club Floridian and the White Orchid into the real-world geographies of Chicago, Wilmington, and New Orleans.

Readers who would like more information on the 1960s, including the real people and events, and about the cities that provide the settings for this book should consult my Web site at www.frankieybailey.com for resources.

The following questions are intended to enhance reading group discussions of Frankie Y. Bailey's *You Should Have Died on Monday*. Additional resources can be found on the author's Web site, www.frankieybailey.com

Discussion Questions

1. Lizzie goes from Gallagher to Chicago and then on to Wilmington and finally to pre-Katrina New Orleans. Are the settings important to this story?

2. What did you think about the FBI's COINTELPRO program? Were the tactics used an appropriate response to perceived domestic threats?

3. Early in the book, Quinn tells Lizzie that she is sometimes "too damn nice." Do you think this is true? Does she become less nice?

4. Do you think Quinn was dishonest when he failed to tell Lizzie about his father earlier in their relationship?

5. Lizzie has been reading books about relationships since she and Quinn became romantically involved. Do you think she has learned anything useful? Do you think this relationship would survive in real life?

6. What did you think of the other characters that Lizzie encountered: Nico Mancini? Sonny Germano? Kyle Sheppard? Robert Montgomery? Tad Duncan? Percy and Earl?

7. Do you agree with Lizzie and Tess that sometimes women allow their romantic relationships with men to affect their friendships with other women?

8. What do you think the friendships of Becca, JoJo, and Naomi might have been like when they were young women?

9. Aside from Lizzie's relationship with her mother, Becca, this book contains a number of other parent-child relationships. How did you feel about the various parent-child relationships you encountered?

10. Reuben James is shot down in the first chapter of this book. By the end of the book, we know why he died. Does the responsibility for his death rest only with the person who shot him?

11. A member of the writing group that the author belongs to described Becca as "evil." What did you think of Becca?

12. What ethical dilemmas do the various characters have to deal with in this book?

13. What are the major themes in this book?

14. Which of the characters—other than Lizzie and Quinn—would you like to know more about? Spend time with? Avoid at all costs?

Also by Frankie Y. Bailey

African-American, thirty-eight, and a crime historian, Lizzie Stuart has spent most of her life in Drucilla, Kentucky. When her grandmother dies, Lizzie decides it is time for a vacation. She joins her best friend, Tess, a travel writer, for a week in Cornwall, England, in the resort town of St. Regis. Lizzie finds her vacation anything but restful when she becomes an eyewitness to murder and the probable next victim.

Crime historian Lizzie Stuart goes to Gallagher, Virginia, as a visiting professor to do research for a book about a 1921 lynching her grandmother witnessed as a 12-year-old child. Lizzie's research is complicated by her own unresolved feelings about her secretive grandmother and by the disturbing presence of John Quinn, the police officer she met in England. When an arrogant but brilliant faculty member is murdered, Lizzie begins to have more than a few sleepless nights.

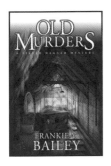

While a bitter battle for the heart of downtown Gallagher, Virginia, is brewing between an out-of-town multimillionaire real estate developer and a local entrepreneur, a local artist turns up missing. At the same time, the story of a 50-year-old murder resurfaces, and someone wants to make sure the truth about the case is buried forever. At the center of it all is criminal justice professor Lizzie Stuart, who has a talent for trouble both professionally and personally.